P9-DGG-977

"*Over the Edge* is the third book in the Melissa Craig series, and . . . it may be the book that puts her over the top . . . Enjoy your trip to the French countryside . . . but stay away from the cliffs."
—Michael Seidman,
Mystery Editor, Walker and Company

*Don't miss these thrilling
Melissa Craig Mysteries
by Betty Rowlands*

FINISHING TOUCH
*Melissa teaches a writing course at the local college
where a slashed portrait—and a murdered secretary
—put her crime-solving skills to the test . . .*

"CONFIRMS MELISSA CRAIG AS A MODERNIZED
(AND YOUNGER) MISS MARPLE."   —*Publishers Weekly*

A LITTLE GENTLE SLEUTHING
*The beauty of the Cotswolds is marred by murder . . .
and Melissa goes roaming in the gloaming
to find a killer!*

"SPLENDIDLY LIVELY . . . GOOD PLOTTING, WELL-
CRAFTED WRITING, AND BELIEVABLE CHARAC-
TERIZATION."   —*Publishing News*

"A DELIGHTFUL SURPRISE . . . A PERFECTLY DE-
FINED IF OFF-BEAT SLEUTH." —Ellen Nehr, *Murder Ad Lib*

MORE MYSTERIES FROM THE
BERKLEY PUBLISHING GROUP ...

Over the Edge

BETTY ROWLANDS

BERKLEY PRIME CRIME, NEW YORK

For Hilary, Michael and Dorothy

All the characters and events portrayed in this
work are fictitious.

This Berkley Prime Crime Book contains the complete text
of the original hardcover edition.
It has been completely reset in a typeface
designed for easy reading, and was printed from new film.

OVER THE EDGE

A Berkley Prime Crime Book / published by arrangement with
Walker and Company

PRINTING HISTORY
Walker Publishing Company, Inc. edition published 1993
Berkley Prime Crime edition / August 1994

ISBN: 0-425-14329-5

Berkley Prime Crime Books are published
by The Berkley Publishing Group,
200 Madison Avenue, New York, NY 10016.
The name BERKLEY PRIME CRIME and the BERKLEY PRIME CRIME
design are trademarks belonging to Berkley Publishing
Corporation.

PRINTED IN THE UNITED STATES OF AMERICA

10 9 8 7 6 5 4 3 2 1

One

WHEN THE TWO ENGLISHWOMEN AR-
rived at the house called Les Châtaigniers, the gates were unfastened by a man in blue working clothes who informed
them, with a vague gesture, that Monsieur Bonard was
awaiting them on the terrace. They thanked him and, being in
no hurry, paused for a few moments to admire in silence the
rambling, ancient edifice of sun-baked brick, with its atten-
dant huddle of outbuildings, before allowing their eyes to
move away across the gravelled courtyard to the gardens,
lush and flower-splashed like a Monet canvas, and thence on-
wards and upwards to the majestic backdrop of the Cévennes
mountains.

Melissa brought them back to earth by remarking that it
would make an ideal setting for a glitzy murder plot and Iris
responded rather tartly that she hoped Melissa wasn't having
one of her premonitions.

"And don't let Philippe hear you say that," she added,
chewing her bottom lip.

"Why not? Is he superstitious?"

"Not that I know of."

"Then what's the problem?"

"Just don't think he'd like it, that's all."

It crossed Melissa's mind that Iris had become progres-
sively more jumpy from the moment they landed in France
and throughout their journey southwards. For weeks she had
been full of enthusiasm for the trip; now that it was a reality
she seemed as nervous as a kitten.

Melissa tucked a hand under her friend's arm. "Don't worry, I'll be terribly circumspect," she promised. "Come on, it must be this way."

Following the sound of voices, they rounded the angle of the building. About a dozen men and women of various ages were assembled on a paved terrace overlooking a swimming pool, sipping drinks and making conversation in the slightly forced manner of extras on a film set awaiting the entrance of the star. At the same moment, as if their arrival had been his cue, a tall figure moved from the far corner to centre stage.

"Get the Rossano Brazzi look-alike in the Armani suit!" Melissa murmured out of the corner of her mouth.

Iris's grey eyes shone and the tan in her cheeks deepened to a glowing red. "That's Philippe! Handsome, isn't he?" She hurried forward; he came to meet her half-way, took both her hands in his and kissed her on both cheeks before leading her back to where Melissa stood waiting.

"This must be your friend, Madame Craig, of whom you speak so much!" He bowed low over Melissa's hand. "I look forward to this pleasure since a long time."

"I'm delighted to meet you, Monsieur Bonard," said Melissa warmly. "Iris has told me so much about you and your work in the field of education."

He had greeted her in heavily accented English; her reward for replying in the French that she had recently been at pains to brush up was a smile of devastating charm.

"I am most flattered. She has likewise told me of your fame as a writer but not"—Bonard wagged a reproachful finger at Iris—"of your excellent command of our language. Permit me to compliment you on your superb accent."

"Monsieur is very kind."

"Bah! Let us not be so formal. One is among friends, no? You will call me Philippe and permit me to say 'Melissa'?"

"But of course." She was conscious of being the focus of two pairs of expressive eyes. Bonard's, black and brilliant, were full of admiration, while Iris's held a hint of proprietorial pride as she glanced from one friend to the other.

"Splendid!" Their host took each of them by an arm.

"Come and meet my family of students." He clapped his hands to call for attention.

"Mesdames et Messieurs," he announced. "I have the honour to present two very famous ladies. Madame Iris Ash" —he inclined his head in her direction and received a self-conscious smirk in return—"will, as you know, be directing our art course entitled 'Nature's Designs.' Her dear friend, Madame Melissa Craig, the well-known novelist"—here it was Melissa's turn to receive the gracious bow, which she acknowledged with a brisk nod—"is also honouring us with her presence while she carries out research for a new book."

He paused briefly to allow the company to respond with friendly smiles and murmurs of interest. "Now, we will take lunch." He turned to a severe-looking woman presiding over a laden buffet table. "Come, Juliette, will you serve my guests some of your excellent cuisine?"

"Yes, Monsieur." The woman's face was expressionless as, with a minimum of words, and speaking French with a strong local accent, she invited them to make their selection from the various dishes. "There is bread in that basket," she gestured towards the end of the table, "and you have sauces, butter, cheese, wine . . ." There was an indefinable quality in her manner; unsmiling, yet by no means hostile, respectful but not in the least subservient, she had an air of detachment and composure that could have been a mask for almost any emotion.

"Is she the housekeeper?" asked Melissa as she and Iris helped themselves to glasses of chilled rosé and went in search of somewhere to sit.

"Could be. Never seen her before. He's the only one I recognise." Iris nodded towards a man in impeccably cut slacks and a monogrammed shirt, who was explaining to a fat, perspiring woman and her tall, thin husband the nature of the dishes on offer. "Alain Gebrec, Philippe's indispensable assistant."

There was an edge to her voice which made Melissa raise an eyebrow. She glanced at the man; he was of slim build and medium height and she guessed his age to be in the mid-forties, although his fresh colouring and the lock of brown hair falling over his forehead gave him a boyish appearance.

"Don't you like him?" she asked. "He looks pleasant enough."

Iris shrugged, pushing a morsel of *charcuterie* to the edge of her plate with a grimace of disgust. "Told the woman I don't eat meat," she muttered pettishly. "Might as well talk to myself."

"It's only a tiny bit, it must have got in by accident. Tell me what you've got against Alain Gebrec."

Iris made a dismissive gesture with her fork. "Nothing really. Does his job well enough. Philippe thinks the world of him."

"Ah!" Melissa took a mouthful of wine and set down her glass. They had settled into the shade of a canvas umbrella on one of the numerous seats dotted round the edge of the pool. At their back was an expanse of grass with an orchard beyond where pear and apple trees drooped under the weight of ripening fruit. Iris, her irritation forgotten, glanced round with a contented sigh.

"Lovely place, isn't it?"

"It certainly is."

"You made a hit with Philippe, speaking the language so well. Sure way of pleasing him. Do my best, but I know my accent makes him cringe." Iris sighed deeply; it was evident that she regarded the approval of Philippe Bonard as something to be sought after and cherished.

"Is he one of those Frenchmen who make a sacred cow of their mother-tongue?" asked Melissa.

Iris shook her head in mild disapproval. "He has a deep love of and respect for the language, and makes it his mission to encourage others to feel the same," she pronounced. This utterance was, for her, an unusually long and formal one, instantly recognisable as a quotation from the glossy brochure issued by the newly established Centre Cévenol d'Etudes, of which their host was the proprietor.

Melissa's lips twitched. "I suppose he believes it should never be polluted by the intrusion of foreign expressions like 'le dirty week-end' for example?" she murmured.

Iris was not amused. "Don't make fun. Means a lot to him."

"Oh, don't worry, I won't take the mickey to his face, but you'll have to excuse me if I can't take him quite so seriously as he takes himself." Or as you seem to take him, she added mentally.

Iris sniffed and looked offended. A trace of chill in the air was relieved by the approach of a genial-looking man of fifty or so.

"May I introduce myself? Jack Hammond." His smile was directed principally at Iris. "I'm enrolled on your art course, Miss Ash."

Iris squinted up at him, shading her eyes with a thin brown hand. "How d'y'do," she said.

"I've been looking forward to it for weeks. It's such a pleasure to meet you . . . and you too, Mrs. Craig," he added hastily.

"Thank you," said Melissa, as Iris acknowledged the compliment with the briefest of nods.

"May I take your plates? How about some dessert?"

"What a nice man!" said Melissa as he went off on his errand.

Iris, still shading her eyes as she searched the sunlit garden, did not seem to have heard. "Wonder where Philippe's got to. Supposed to be giving a little talk," she muttered.

"He's probably waiting till we've all finished scoffing," said Melissa. "Here comes our waiter," she added as Jack returned with bowls of chilled fruit in white wine. "Thank you so much. Why don't you join us."

"Thank you."

He found an unoccupied chair and pulled it across. Melissa observed him with approval as he settled into it. He obviously spent much time in the open air, for his face, neck and arms were deeply tanned and his light brown hair had a bleached appearance. His eyes were blue and clear, and there was an air of openness about him that appealed to her. Someone you could rely on in a crisis, she thought.

"Nice idea this, inviting all the participants for a get-together before the start of the courses," he commented. "I must say, it's a most beautiful spot. Should be an inspiration, don't you think?"

"Hope so," said Iris.

"Quite a mixture of ages and types, too," he continued, showing no sign of being discouraged by her laconic responses. "I've just been chatting to those two over there." He indicated a young man and woman who had slipped off their shoes and were sitting on the edge of the pool, dabbling their toes in the water. "Proper pair of young hippies they are— living in an old motor caravan on a neighbouring farm."

"Good luck to 'em," Iris observed without looking. "Takes all sorts."

"I wonder why Monsieur Bonard invited us for lunch instead of supper?" said Melissa in an effort to compensate for Iris's lack of interest. "I understand some people aren't arriving until this evening."

"Always keeps Sunday evening free. Likes to plan his lectures for the week." Iris stood up and Jack leapt from his chair and stood aside to let her pass. "Want a word with him. See you later."

They watched her as she headed towards the house, arms swinging, her thin figure held stiffly erect.

"I take it she knows the old boy?" Jack said off-handedly.

"He used to live in a village near Avignon where Iris has a cottage," Melissa explained. "He ran vacation courses from his home for several years, more as a hobby than a business. Setting up on this scale was a lifetime's ambition, so Iris tells me."

"He's got a big investment here." Jack's glance took in the extensive, well-maintained grounds and the complex of carefully renovated buildings that had once been a farm. "Hope he makes a go of it. Ah, there he is!"

Philippe Bonard emerged from the house, advanced to the terrace and clapped his hands.

"Mesdames et Messieurs, may I say once again what a pleasure it is to meet you all. I trust that you will find your course of study here both instructive and rewarding. I also trust that the arrangements we have made for your *logement* prove satisfactory, but if you have any problems, my aide"—he gestured at Alain Gebrec, who had materialised silently at his elbow—"will be pleased to assist you. I speak English"—here a hint of condescension crept into his voice—"for the benefit of those who are here to study subjects other than French. However, it is a rule of the centre that French is spoken at all times whenever possible. And now, Alain, you have a little excursion to propose, no?"

Gebrec cleared his throat and stepped forward.

"I suggest we make a short walk to a belvedere which affords a particularly splendid view," he said.

"How far?" demanded the fat woman.

"Perhaps ten or fifteen minutes. The way is a little steep, but we will walk slowly."

"Bit hot for hiking, isn't it, Eric?" she complained, turning to her husband.

"You're right, Daphne," he agreed and raised a hand to attract Gebrec's attention. "Can't it wait till it's a bit cooler, Monsieur?"

"It is that the light is particularly effective at this time of day," explained Gebrec. "Of course, no one is obliged to undertake the excursion, but I do most sincerely recommend that you do so. The prospect is quite spectacular."

"Come on, Daph, let's make the effort," coaxed Eric. "Might see some wildlife. I'll get my binoculars from the car."

After a short consultation, the rest of the party also made up their minds to make the effort. Gebrec led the way across the garden and through a gate in the metal perimeter fence which enclosed it.

"This gate, it is locked at night for reasons of security, but students at the centre are free to pass through into the forest during the daytime," he informed them. "Please, however, do not attempt the path to the belvedere without a guide, in case of accident."

He set off at a gentle pace and everyone followed in a straggling line. After a few minutes of easy walking along a grassy track among the trees, he clambered through a gap in a stone wall and they found themselves scrambling up a steep, uneven pathway that appeared to have been only recently cut through the undergrowth.

Conversation was sporadic, limited mainly to generalities. This was not entirely due to the heat; most people were still trying to absorb names and remember who was following which course of study. The exceptions were two middle-aged Englishwomen and a handsome young German, all of whom, it emerged, had already spent a week at the centre improving their French. These three walked a little apart from the others.

Melissa, observing them with the eye of a novelist, noted how Rose Kettle kept a shade closer to Dieter Erdle than was absolutely necessary, responding with coy smiles and fluttering eyelashes every time he spoke to her; how she seemed to make a point of stumbling now and then, and how ready he was with a steadying hand beneath her arm. Dora Lavender strode beside them, wielding a golfing umbrella like a walking stick, giving monosyllabic responses when addressed, but otherwise keeping silent and unsmiling, her eyes watchful.

"Do I detect an atmosphere?" whispered Iris in Melissa's ear.

"A distinct whiff of disapproval, I'd say," Melissa whispered back.

"Expect he's after her money."

"What makes you think she's got any?"

"Got to be some attraction."

"Iris, you're being catty!"

The path climbed rapidly, densely shaded at first by mature chestnut trees. Alain Gebrec, delicately picking his way over the rough ground, turned occasionally to exchange a word with those nearest to him. Presently, they came to a wider track leading down the hill to their right.

"Why didn't we come that way?" demanded Daphne. "It looks much easier."

"It is also much longer," Gebrec explained. "It joins the road nearly a kilometre from the house. We can take a short rest, if you wish."

"Oh, might as well get it over with," she grumbled, but Eric had adjusted his binoculars to track a squirrel scurrying along a branch, and the rest of the party craned their necks and pointed as the little creature appeared and disappeared among the foliage.

Melissa glanced back the way they had come. The main part of the house was hidden, but the central portion, a circular tower with a roof shaped like the lid of a honey-pot, was visible above the treetops.

"There must be a superb view from those top windows," she said enviously to Iris, who was standing next to her. "If I lived here, I'd never get any work done for gawking out of them."

"Yes, it's pretty spectacular," Iris agreed. "Windows all round."

"You've been up there?"

Iris coloured. "Philippe showed me round when he was negotiating to buy the place. Wanted my opinion," she added defensively, as if to forestall possible disapproval.

"Shall we continue?" Alain Gebrec was becoming restless. "The light, it changes all the time." Obediently, the party moved off again. A short way further on they came to a clearing where a man was unloading wooden rails from a trailer hitched to a small tractor.

"Isn't that the chap who let us in?" said Melissa.

Iris glanced across. "Looks like it."

"*Hé*, Fernand!" called Gebrec as they passed. The man raised his head, nodded, and returned to his task. "Fernand is a most valuable employee," Gebrec continued, speaking French in accordance with the recently stated rules and raising his voice a little. "He can turn his hand to anything. Isn't that right, Fernand?"

The man stood gazing at the party for a moment with an expression as wooden as the rail he had just lifted from the trailer. Then, without a word, he added it to a growing heap on the ground before reaching for another. Either he had not heard the praise, or cared nothing for it.

"Not exactly a chatterbox, is he?" someone observed.

"Looks a bit of an oddball to me," said someone else.

"He's Juliette's brother," said Dora Lavender. "I understand they belong to one of the oldest families in Roziac." It was the first spontaneous remark she had made since they set off.

"Does he always work on Sundays?" Eric wondered.

"I have the impression that days of the week mean little to him," Dora replied. Her implication was obvious. There were murmurs and curious glances. One of the party asked if Fernand had been in the Resistance.

Gebrec shook his head. "I have no idea. It is possible."

Rose Kettle gave an excited squeak. "Perhaps he thinks we're the Gestapo!" she giggled, earning a look of scorn from her friend, but a chuckle and a squeeze on the arm from Erdle.

"Or spies?" he suggested, with a sly glance in Gebrec's direction.

The Frenchman reddened, nervously flicking the lock of hair from his forehead. He had removed his sunglasses and his pale blue eyes blinked in the strong light.

"Oh, Fernand is a good fellow really," he said hurriedly. "A little suspicious of strangers perhaps—like quite a few of the people round here."

"Never take him for a Frenchman, would you?" Iris commented to Melissa.

"You mean Gebrec? No, he's not exactly typical."

"Didn't seem to appreciate the joke."

"I'm not surprised. That young man should have known better—life wasn't funny for these people during the Occupation." A thought struck Melissa. "You go on—I'll catch up."

She returned to the clearing, where Fernand was stooping over his pile of rails. He straightened up as she approached, his black eyes watchful. He was a wiry man of fifty or so with strong weather-beaten features and sinewy arms as brown as the chestnuts for which the region was famous.

"That must be hard work in this heat," she said with a smile.

His expression did not relax. "Hard enough."

"They tell me you have always lived in Roziac."

"So?"

"I'm a writer—I'm interested in the history of these parts. I've read a lot about the Camisards and their struggles and I thought perhaps . . ."

The word "Camisards" had an extraordinary effect on Fernand. He grabbed Melissa by the arm, a fanatical gleam in his eyes.

"I am with Roland!" he said in a hoarse whisper. "Villars is not to be trusted. Tell the others!" He released her arm and made agitated gestures to where the last of the party were vanishing among the trees. "Tell them! Warn them to go to the secret refuge!"

"The secret refuge?" Melissa was nonplussed. "Where is that?"

Fernand's manner became suddenly hostile. "Who are you? One of Villars' spies?"

"No, of course not," she said uneasily, taking a step backwards. "I . . . I'm with Roland too . . . but I come from Florac."

"Ah! You bring news?"

"Only . . . that the fight goes on," said Melissa, desperately improvising.

The man nodded eagerly. "To the death!" His eyes switched to the path the group had taken. "Hurry! Warn them!"

"Yes . . . yes, immediately." Melissa beat a hasty retreat. As she rejoined the track, she glanced over her shoulder. Fernand was calmly sorting rails as if he had forgotten her existence.

When she caught up with the others, they had come to a halt just short of the point where the path emerged into the open and were standing in a little knot around Gebrec.

"What was all that about?" Iris wanted to know.

"Just some preliminary research. Don't worry, I'll tell you later," she added, as Iris gave a dubious frown.

"Mesdames et Messieurs, please listen carefully," Gebrec was saying. "We are approaching the belvedere. The cliff here is some two hundred metres high with a sheer drop into the river. There is a guard rail, but in places it is broken. Please, under no circumstances go too close to the edge as it may be unstable. Does everyone understand?"

One or two people exchanged doubtful glances and shook their heads.

"Could you say that in English, please?" said Daphne, looking up from the guide-book she was studying.

"It is against the rules, but in the interests of safety . . ." Gebrec repeated the warning in impeccable English.

"And in German, if you please!" The request, accompanied by a bland smile, came from Dieter Erdle. "In the interests of safety, of course!"

There was no answering smile from Gebrec. "I am sorry, I do not speak German," he said stiffly, in French.

"You surprise me. It was my impression that you were . . . multilingual."

For the second time Gebrec's colour rose. "I know only French and English," he declared.

"My mistake." Erdle gave a little bow. "*Entschuldigen Sie bitte* . . . excuse me, please."

"Did you not understand my warning about the guard rail?"

"*Aber natürlich.* I merely thought there might be other German speakers present." With eyebrows raised, he glanced round the group but no one responded. "In that case . . ." He turned back to Gebrec. "Shall we continue with our promenade?"

"That looked like deliberate aggro," whispered Melissa. "I wonder what the game is."

"After the same woman?" suggested Iris.

Melissa shook her head. "More to it than that."

The party moved on. Through the thinning trees they caught glimpses of massive peaks soaring above their heads, stacked one behind the other like shapes on a collage, the lower slopes wooded, the bare, rocky crests baking in the sun. There was no movement in the air; as they emerged into the open, they were met by a searing blast of heat. Sunglasses were adjusted against the glare, hats tipped over eyes. Daphne reeled back into the shade and began fanning herself with her guide-book.

"I've had enough of this—you can keep your *vue panoramique!*" she gasped.

Her husband tenderly mopped her brow with his handkerchief.

"Just rest for a tick and you'll be all right, lovey," he assured her. "Can't miss it after coming all this way, can we?"

Dora Lavender unfurled her umbrella and beckoned to

Rose Kettle. "Come under here," she commanded. "You know you can't stand the direct sun." Her voice was resonant and authoritarian, in total contrast to her friend's high-pitched, excited chatter.

Rose, still keeping close to Dieter Erdle, shook her head. "I'll be all right. I've got my shady hat . . . and my new sunglasses." She adjusted both items as she spoke, beaming archly up at Erdle. "Balenciaga!" she informed him. "The glasses, I mean. Dreadfully expensive, of course, but I couldn't resist them. Do you think they suit me?"

"Most becoming," he assured her. "Now, let us admire this so-magnificent view that fellow keeps talking about."

"There's no need to look so cross, Dora," she said pettishly, over her shoulder.

"You'll have a migraine this evening."

"No I won't." She trotted after Erdle. Dora shrugged and turned away, biting her lip.

"What did I tell you?" Iris hissed in Melissa's ear. "I'll bet she's loaded."

"Never mind them. Just look at that!"

Gebrec had not exaggerated. Far below them, the little river Mauzère boiled and foamed over huge boulders between sheer, apparently unscaleable cliffs. The sun poured into the canyon like a giant searchlight, turning the spray to rainbows and the naked rock to glistening gold against the hard blue of the sky.

Uttering exclamations of admiration and delight, the members of the party split into twos and threes and wandered about, commenting and pointing, occasionally turning to their guide with a question. Cameras were focused, clicked and focused again. Daphne was coaxed into the open, still poring over her guide-book.

"Come on, can't miss this!" urged her husband.

"What's this place called, Eric? I can't find it in here."

Gebrec, standing a few feet away, turned to explain. "The fact is, Madame Lovell, that compared with, say, the Gorges du Tarn, this is really not so well known. Still, I am sure you will agree that it is quite impressive."

"Oh rather, jolly impressive!" agreed Eric with enthusiasm,

adjusting his binoculars. "Look there, Daph! A red kite! What a bit of luck!"

A few heads turned to watch the majestic flight of the bird, lazily circling in the still air.

Melissa and Iris wandered over to what remained of the guard rail, a short distance from the edge of the cliff. From where they stood, they had a clear view in both directions.

"There must have been some mighty powerful volcanic activity to chuck this lot up in the air," commented Melissa. "Look at the strata lines in that rock, they're almost zig-zag!"

Iris nodded. "Awesome, isn't it? Wonderful patterns, though." She craned forward to look down at the tossing, tumbling waters. "Hullo, there's someone down there. Must have abseiled."

"Where?"

Iris pointed. "Lying on that ledge with his arms in the water. Trying to catch a fish by the looks of him. Or having a drink."

"He's not moving," said Melissa, suddenly anxious.

"Damn! Lost him!" Eric stood behind them, gesticulating with his binoculars. "Got a good long look, though! Splendid specimen!"

"I wonder if you'd mind lending me those for a moment?" said Melissa.

"Certainly!" He unhooked the strap and handed them over. "Seen something interesting?"

Trying to conceal her anxiety for fear of causing unnecessary alarm, she fumbled with the focus. "There's something at the foot of the cliff."

Eric leaned on the rail and peered into the canyon. "Good Lord, it's a man! Looks as if he's fallen over." He turned and beckoned to Gebrec. "Monsieur, come here a minute! No, Daphne, you stay away! Someone's been badly hurt."

"*Oh, mon Dieu!*" Gebrec recoiled in horror, clawing at his mouth with shaking fingers. "What shall we do?"

"Is there a way down?" asked Eric. "Someone ought to try and get help to him."

Melissa had at last succeeded in focusing the binoculars. What she saw made her stomach turn over.

"I'm afraid he's beyond help," she said.

Two

ning and thunderclap, there were several moments of silence as the party absorbed the news. Eyes widened, hands flew to mouths; everyone's gaze, at first riveted on Melissa, travelled beyond her to the sagging rail, over the edge of the cliff and into the void. There were horrified gasps, exclamations of "How dreadful!," "My god!" and "Are you sure?" before the spell of immobility broke and everyone rushed to see for themselves.

"Mesdames, Messieurs, have a care, I beg you!" Alain Gebrec, his face grey, flew after them like a distraught sheepdog. "Keep away from the edge or there will be a disaster!"

Rose Kettle, peering downward, appeared to recognise the victim. "It's Wolfgang—Wolfgang Klein!" she screamed and broke into wild sobs. Dora Lavender took her by the hand and tried to lead her away, but she broke free and threw herself at Dieter Erdle, who obligingly took her into his arms and began patting her shoulder, murmuring soothing words in German.

"Rose, stop that ridiculous noise at once. You're making a complete fool of yourself!" Dora snapped. "You shouldn't encourage her," she told Erdle, making another futile attempt to draw her friend away.

"She has had a great shock." Erdle, still embracing Rose's quivering form, returned Dora's glare with a frown of reproof. Melissa, who had hastily stepped clear of the scramble to view the body, thought she detected a gleam of malice and the hint of a smile as he added, "She is a very sensitive lady."

"We're all shocked, but we're not screeching like hysterical schoolgirls." Scowling with fury and frustration, Dora rounded on Gebrec, who was wringing his hands and whimpering. "Don't stand there with your mouth open! We must return to the house at once and report the accident," she scolded him in French.

"Yes, yes, of course." He seemed grateful that someone else was taking charge.

"There's discipline for you," Melissa murmured. "Sticking to the school rules even in a crisis!"

"Tough lady, that," Iris whispered back.

Hardly speaking a word, the party hurried back the way they had come, slipping and stumbling over the uneven ground. Halfway between the top and the clearing where Fernand had left his tractor, they met him hauling a bundle of rails across the track by a rope. He stood aside to let them go by, his face inscrutable. Gebrec stopped and blurted out the news, but the man's expression hardly changed. Glancing over her shoulder, Melissa saw him dump the bundle in some undergrowth before following at a short distance when everyone else had passed.

The ancient *mas* which was now the home of the Centre Cévenol d'Etudes was called Les Châtaigniers after the stately chestnut trees among which it was set. It was built on two floors, with thick walls, small windows and a low-pitched roof covered in tiles shaped like flattened scallop shells. In the centre of the original façade, effectively dividing the house into two separate wings, rose the tower which Melissa had observed from the forest path; below it, an archway led to a gravelled courtyard dotted with huge pottery urns overflowing with geraniums. On the far side, an opening in a stone wall led into the garden through a pergola hung with clematis and trumpet vines.

No expense had been spared in the conversion. In addition to the three lecture rooms and a well-stocked library, an extension at the rear housed a salon, a games room with sliding glass doors on to the terrace and a conservatory which doubled as a second salon when rain or cold drove the students indoors.

Bonard must have been watching from his private quarters in the tower as the party returned and guessed from their demeanour that something was wrong. When they straggled into the courtyard, he came hurrying out to meet them. Alain Gebrec rushed at him and buried his face on the older man's shoulder. Bonard patted his head as if comforting a hurt child, murmuring, "Quietly! Quietly! Tell Philippe what has happened."

Gebrec began babbling incoherently.

"There's been an accident," Dora interposed, eyeing the pair with an expression of mingled contempt and disgust. "Someone—we think it may be young Wolfgang Klein—has fallen on to the rocks below the belvedere. We're afraid he may be dead."

Bonard gasped in horror. "But this is terrible! We must call the *garde champêtre* . . . the *sapeurs pompiers* . . . an ambulance . . . come, Alain!" Leading his shaken assistant by the arm, he hurried indoors, leaving the others standing about in small groups, uncertain what to do.

"Revolting display!" snorted Dora. She strode across to a line of cars parked under an awning of bamboo canes. Opening the boot of a dark red Sierra, she flung in the golfing umbrella, slammed the lid and glanced at her watch. "It's nearly teatime!" she announced to the world at large. "We could all use a cup. Let's go into the garden." She led the way and the others trailed after her.

"Rose, you'd better go and lie down in the salon," continued Dora. "I'll bring your tea in to you."

"I'm all right, really. Dieter is looking after me," simpered Rose. She gazed up at Erdle with a besotted smile on her round face as he installed her on a chaise-longue, adjusted a sunshade over her head and arranged cushions at her back.

Dora flushed and turned away. "I'll go and have a word with Juliette about the tea," she muttered and disappeared into the house.

Iris and Melissa exchanged glances.

"Going to be an explosion before long," whispered Iris.

"What a dreadful thing to happen!" Eric Lovell, mopping his face with a handkerchief, sank beside his perspiring wife on a canopied swinging couch. The others settled down to discuss the situation, first in subdued whispers, then more animatedly, some even making vaguely flippant comments, at which one or two laughed nervously and then looked uneasy, as if they had been caught telling risqué jokes in church.

"That lady and her friend seemed to recognise the . . . whoever it was," said a frizzy-haired girl called Sue.

Everyone glanced in Rose's direction.

"I don't see how they could have . . . not at that distance," said her friend Janey, frowning. She looked round from one to the other. "Anyway, you couldn't see his face, could you?"

"Perhaps it was by his clothes," suggested the bearded young man in torn T-shirt and cut-down jeans whom Jack had described as a hippie. Melissa had learned on the walk that he was called Mervyn and his girlfriend Chrissie.

"They said it was a Wolfgang Klein," said Eric. "There's no one of that name in our group, is there?"

"Must have been in last week's lot," suggested Jack, standing up. "I'll go and ask Mrs. Kettle."

"He seems a nice man. Is he on his own?" enquired Daphne.

"Think so. Here to do art," said Iris.

"Ah, yes! You're our tutor, aren't you?" Chrissie fixed light brown eyes on Iris. She was a wan-faced, earnest-looking girl clad in a shapeless, black-washed-to-grey cotton dress a size too large for her. "I'm so looking forward to having your guidance!" She spoke in a low-pitched vibrato that Melissa suspected had been carefully cultivated. "There's so much here to inspire one, don't you think?"

"Hm, yes, suppose so." Iris fidgeted her feet in her canvas shoes and looked away.

"Thought so," said Jack, returning from his fact-finding errand. "They're both pretty certain it's a young chap from Munich who was here last week to study French. They recognised him by his gingery hair and the brightly patterned shirt he was wearing. It seems his hobby was pot-holing and he was staying on for a few days to poke around in grottoes."

"We keep using the past tense, but are we quite sure he's dead?" said Mervyn. "They should be getting medical help."

"He might not have fallen from the top. He could be just stunned," suggested Sue.

For a moment, the atmosphere lightened. Perhaps there was hope after all.

"I'm afraid not," said Melissa. "I looked at him through the binoculars, and . . . " She put a hand to her mouth, suddenly and uncomfortably aware of what she had eaten for lunch. "The back of his head was bashed in, as if he'd hit it on a projecting piece of rock or something when he fell."

"That's right," said Eric. "I saw it too. It was gruesome."

As if the shock of what he had seen had only just reached him, he covered his face with his hands. Daphne put a plump arm round him and he leaned against her while everyone murmured in sympathy.

"Here we are!" Dora emerged from the house carrying a large tea-pot. "Will one of you gentlemen kindly fetch the tray?" It was a command, not a request; several volunteers leapt to their feet. "I had to do it myself, that's why it took so long," she explained. "Juliette is in a terrible state and poor Fernand is getting a fine old telling-off."

"What about?" asked Eric.

"I'm afraid I couldn't understand very well." Dora made the admission with evident reluctance. "They both seemed very agitated and they were speaking so fast, and using a lot of patois," she explained defensively. "But I did catch some references to the Camisards."

"What are they?"

"I'm not sure. Weren't they crusaders or something?" Dora looked round for enlightenment.

"My friend knows," said Iris. "She's researching a novel about them."

All eyes turned on Melissa. Chrissie's face lit up with admiration.

"Of course, you're a writer!" she breathed. "I think that's thrilling! I do feel"—at this point she invited everyone with a sweep of her glowing eyes to share her sentiments—"that writers have a great deal in common with artists. Don't you agree, Iris? I mean, like us, they go straight to the core of the meaning of life!"

"Melissa goes to the core of the meaning of death!" said Iris drily. "She writes crime novels."

"Oh!" The monosyllable was heavily charged with disappointment and disdain.

"Tell us about the Camisards," said Jack.

"They were victims of religious persecution during the late seventeenth and early eighteenth centuries," Melissa explained. "This has always been a strongly Protestant region and for years there was a kind of guerilla warfare between them and the Catholics, who were of course backed up by the King's troops. It got pretty nasty at times."

"But what would that have to do with Klein's death?" asked Daphne.

"Probably nothing, but Fernand seems to have a bit of a fixation about them." Melissa related her encounter on the way to the belvedere. "This area is riddled with grottoes that made splendid hideouts—incidentally, they were used by the Maquis as well, during the Occupation. There are some famous ones at Trabuc, but there could be any number of others, less well known or even undiscovered."

"And that's what Klein was interested in. Maybe he'd been asking Fernand about them . . ."

". . . and he'd told him where to look . . ."

". . . and now he's getting it in the neck from Juliette . . ."

". . . blaming him for sending Klein to his death . . ."

". . . must be overcome by remorse . . ."

". . . absolutely ghastly . . ."

Speculative remarks bounced around like ping-pong balls amid the rattle of cups and saucers as Dora poured the tea.

"Rose would like hers weak with no sugar." Dieter Erdle approached with an ingratiating smile, which was not returned.

"I'm well aware of how Rose likes her tea, thank you!" Ignoring the outstretched hand, Dora swept past him with a full cup and marched towards the chaise-longue where Rose was still reclining, watching the others with a vague smile and apparently quite recovered.

Everyone except Erdle looked uncomfortable at this open declaration of hostilities, but he merely shrugged, threw a mocking grimace at Dora's back and strolled away in the opposite direction.

"I do not drink tea. I shall take a swim," he announced and vanished into the changing room.

At this point Philippe Bonard reappeared and everyone waited expectantly as he approached. His face was pale and his manner agitated.

"What news?" asked Jack.

Bonard spread his hands in a helpless gesture. "It is terrible, terrible! The matter is in the hands of the *Sécurité Civile*, who are making arrangements to reach the unfortunate victim. We cannot be certain, but we fear it is poor young Wolfgang Klein."

"He was here on a French course last week, wasn't he?"

"Yes, that is so. He has been coming to me for tuition for several years—he was delighted when I moved here and he could combine his studies with his passion for speleology. What a tragedy!"

Bonard seemed about to break down, but controlled himself. Iris went to his side and put a hand on his arm.

"However will they get to him—Klein, I mean?" asked Janey. "That ledge is an awfully long way down and the river's too shallow for a boat."

The question was immediately answered by the clattering roar of a helicopter. Flying low, it passed overhead and disappeared behind the house.

Janey gave a squeal of excitement. "How thrilling! Let's go and watch!"

Iris gave her a sharp look. "Not a sideshow. Someone's been killed," she reproved.

"Quite so," said Bonard.

Janey looked abashed, but it was evident from the restless movements and craning necks that several others shared her curiosity.

"The path to the belvedere has been closed," said Bonard. "It is to be kept clear for use by the rescue teams."

"Perhaps from up there?" suggested Mervyn, glancing up at the central tower.

"Please!" begged Janey. One or two people moved forward expectantly.

Bonard, apparently torn between a sense of propriety and a wish to please his paying clients, hesitated and then gave a resigned shrug. "Oh, very well. This way."

"Not you too!" said Iris severely as Melissa made a move to follow.

"I think I should . . . I might want to use a helicopter rescue some time."

"Suit yourself. I'll wait here." Her features set in stony disapproval, Iris flopped on to a chair.

There was a loud splash as Erdle took to the water. Glancing over her shoulder, Melissa saw Rose being led by her friend towards their car. "I think that round went to Dora," she murmured to herself as she followed the others into the house.

Three

EVEN TO ACCOMMODATE PHILIPPE
Bonard, to whose interest, it appeared to Melissa, she was excessively devoted, Iris would not have accepted his invitation to tutor a week's art course if she had not been assured of a vegetarian diet and a room with enough floor space to practise her yoga. Fortunately, the Auberge de la Fontaine in the village of Roziac, a short distance from Les Châtaigniers, was able to meet all her requirements.

Iris and Melissa were not the only members of the party to be staying there. When they walked into the little salon with their evening apéritif, they found Dora Lavender sitting alone in a corner, reading *Madame Figaro* and sipping a glass of muscat.

"Hullo, Mrs. Lavender," said Melissa. "May we join you?"

"Of course. Do sit down. And please, call me Dora." She put the magazine aside with a smile of welcome. She had changed from the plain skirt and blouse she had worn earlier into a draped print dress that softened the rigid lines of her figure. Her features, too, had relaxed; caught unawares, she had a forlorn, almost wistful expression. "Do you know if they've recovered that poor young man's body yet?" she enquired.

"I believe so," said Melissa, "but we couldn't really see what was going on because of the trees."

"Hard luck!" jeered Iris.

"I suppose you were taking a professional interest," continued Dora. "Do you think there'll be a police investigation?"

Her expression became more animated, as if talk of the tragedy provided a welcome diversion from her thoughts.

"I imagine so. They'll want to know how he came to fall. The path is completely cordoned off and there are people in uniform all over the place." Melissa had been hoping for an opportunity to observe the proceedings on the ground, but had been sternly repelled by a portly gendarme.

"Your friend got over her wobbly?" asked Iris. The twitch of her mouth and the gleam in her eye made it plain that she regarded the whole episode of Rose Kettle's hysterics as something not to be taken too seriously, but Dora's expression darkened.

"Oh, she's all right, I suppose, but she's sulking. I'm really very concerned about her. You see . . ." She broke off, looking from one to the other and then down at her glass. The steel-blue eyes that had challenged Dieter Erdle now looked troubled and uncertain. Melissa felt she could read her thoughts. Should I confide in these two? she seemed to be asking herself. Would they be bored, or embarrassed—or think me disloyal?

Iris, with her usual bluntness, came straight to the point.

"Worried about that German chap, aren't you? Think he's a fortune-hunter?"

"That's exactly it," said Dora eagerly, evidently grateful for the lead. "Rose is so impressionable. Usually she listens to my advice, but this time she seems quite infatuated. He hangs around all the time, fawning over her and paying her silly compliments, and she laps it up—won't hear a word against him. And we're all here for another week . . ." She fiddled with the stem of her glass, her strong features puckered in anxiety.

"You've been friends for a long time, I take it," said Melissa.

"We were at school together. It's quite a bizarre story—you might use it in a plot for one of your novels." Dora gave a wry smile. "She used to get teased a lot because she was so small and skinny, and I looked after her. After leaving school we corresponded for some years, then we both got married;

Rose went to live abroad and Charles and I . . . anyway, I lost touch with her."

There was a pause. Dora took several slow sips from her glass, but she seemed to be swallowing something else besides the wine and when she spoke again her voice was a shade unsteady.

"The next time we met was in a morgue, waiting to identify the bodies of our husbands who'd been killed in the same plane crash. Macabre, wasn't it?" Again, she forced a half smile.

"How ghastly for you!" exclaimed Melissa.

Dora blinked hard. "It was, rather."

Iris, ever practical, put out a hand for her empty glass. "Like a refill?" she offered. "Or maybe something stronger?"

"No, thank you. I must go up to Rose in a minute and try to persuade her to come down to dinner."

"That must have been a devastating experience." Melissa's imagination was already conjuring up images and sensations of grief, shock, confusion and horror. "However did you cope?"

"One of us had to." A shrug and a resigned sigh told it all. "Rose was completely beside herself, so I took charge of everything for both of us."

"Must have seemed like old times," commented Iris.

Melissa winced, afraid that her friend's pragmatism might not go down well in the circumstances, but Dora showed no sign of having taken offence.

"You could say that. And that's more or less how it's been ever since. Her husband left her with more money than she knew what to do with and she hadn't—still hasn't—a clue about how to manage it. Charles left me with a load of debts I couldn't pay." Dora blinked again, dabbing at her eyes with the back of her hand. Melissa had the feeling that to dry them with a handkerchief, openly admitting to tears, would have been a gesture of weakness that she was not prepared to make. "Rose helped me out with a loan, I agreed to handle her affairs—I work in the investment department of a bank— and after a while I sold my flat and moved in with her. We've kept one another company ever since."

"Hmm," said Iris, studying her glass with an abstracted expression.

"I can understand your concern over Dieter Erdle," said Melissa.

Dora stood up. "Oh, I'm sure she'll get over it once we're away from here." She had recovered her composure and there was an underlying firmness in her voice, as if she was stating a fact rather than expressing a hope. "A few good rounds of golf will get him out of her system. We're spending our final week in Antibes; we've got friends who belong to a club there. By the way," she dropped her voice, "you won't let her know I've told you all this?"

Iris was swift to respond. "Not a word!" she promised and Melissa nodded agreement.

"Thank you. And thank you for listening."

As she left, Dora almost collided with the proprietor, clad in chef's hat and apron. He was a small, bird-like man of enormous energy who ran the *auberge* with the aid of his wife and a seemingly endless supply of pretty daughters.

"I come to apologise for the lateness of the evening meal," he said, clasping his hands and bobbing his head in all directions like a starling pecking at a lawn. "It is the excitement, you know. The women talk of nothing else . . . and there are rumours."

"What rumours, Monsieur Gauthier?" asked Iris.

He bent forward, his eyes gleaming as if he had spotted an extra choice worm. "That the death of that poor young man was not an accident!"

The Englishwomen stared at him in disbelief.

"You mean someone pushed him?" said Melissa. "Are you serious?"

"It is all over the village that the victim was in the Bar des Sports a few evenings ago, asking questions about a grotto near here. No one knew anything about it, or at least they pretended not to. People round here don't talk much about such things to strangers. According to Madame Pavy at the *boulangerie*, that crazy Fernand Morlay was in there and got very angry . . . threatened him . . . warned him not to go poking his nose in what did not concern him. So now they are suggesting . . ."

"That Fernand killed him? But that's ridiculous!" declared Melissa. "I know the man has these strange fantasies about the Camisards, but surely . . ."

"Oh, it wasn't the Camisards he was thinking about the other evening, it was the Gestapo! When he is not pretending to be one of Roland's men, he is looking over his shoulder for German spies. He is a little . . ." Monsieur Gauthier tapped his forehead, then looked at his watch and threw up his hands. "*Oh, mon Dieu!* I must see what those women are doing!" Muttering to himself, he scurried out.

"Who was Roland?" asked Iris.

"One of the leaders of the Camisards," replied Melissa. "The King sent a man called Villars to offer an amnesty, but Roland insisted it was a trap. A few stood by him and fought on, but most of the people were so weary of the constant killing that they gave in."

"You reckon Fernand was confusing Villars with the Gestapo?"

Melissa frowned, remembering the wild look in the man's eyes when she mentioned the Camisards. "I suppose it's possible. Maybe he was in the Resistance, as someone suggested this afternoon. Klein was a German; he might have seen him as the enemy—but surely he wouldn't . . ."

"Sounds completely batty to me." Iris turned a stern eye on Melissa. "You keep away from him. No more encounters in the woods!" she commanded.

"Oh, don't worry." Through the open doorway Melissa saw Monsieur Gauthier emerge from the kitchen, immaculate in white jacket and black trousers. He beamed, bowed and gestured towards the dining-room. "Come on, I think dinner's ready at last."

The dining-room was furnished in rustic style with dark, heavy furniture and green curtains patterned with overblown roses that made Iris, whose textile designs enjoyed an international reputation, shudder with distaste. But there were fresh flowers on every table and the food was excellent. Even

Iris, who tended to be suspicious of everything she had not prepared herself, could find no fault with it.

Rose and Dora appeared to have made their peace for the time being, but there was a steadiness in Rose's manner and a lift to her slightly faded but still pretty ash-blonde head that hinted at future battles.

Monsieur Gauthier had given his four English guests a table by the window with a magnificent view of the mountains, their harsh outlines mellowed by the evening light.

"Isn't it beautiful!" sighed Rose. She turned to Melissa. "Dora tells me you're setting a novel in these parts. Is it a romance?"

"No, a thriller—a sort of historical detective story. I'm planning to do some background research while Iris is running her art course."

"How exciting! Isn't it, Dora?" Rose turned to her friend with an eager expression on her mobile face. In the request for endorsement of that simple remark she revealed a glimpse of the vulnerable child turning to the stronger companion for support.

"Very exciting," agreed Dora with an indulgent smile.

"You should talk to Dieter," Rose continued. "He's interested in history."

"Really?" Seeing the shadow that passed over Dora's face, Melissa kept her tone casual, but Rose was determined to pursue the point.

"Yes, really. He's been reading lately about France under the Occupation. Did you know that people from all over Europe came to the Cévennes to hide from the Nazis? Even some Germans—although, of course, some of them were spies trying to infiltrate the Resistance."

"I suppose that explains those so-called jokes the pair of you were making earlier," said Dora with a frown. "I must say, I thought they were in rather poor taste."

The atmosphere was becoming distinctly edgy and Melissa made an effort to restore harmony. "People don't change, do they? The same sort of thing happened during the religious wars that I'm researching."

"You simply must talk to Dieter," insisted Rose. Her face

fell as a thought struck her. "Will our lessons still go ahead, do you think? I mean, the police won't want to close the centre after that terrible accident?"

"Don't be a goose, Rose," said Dora. "Why ever would they do that?"

"I only thought they might say there'd been negligence or something—because the safety fence was broken."

"You mean that path and the belvedere are on Philippe Bonard's property?" asked Melissa. "It was his responsibility to see that it was safe?"

"Yes, but we were all warned that it was dangerous, and anyway the path was quite overgrown until recently," Dora explained. "Fernand spent all last week clearing it and he'd only just begun mending the fence. That's what the rails are for."

"So Mr. Klein knew he shouldn't have gone up there?"

"Oh, yes, but you know what young people are. He was so keen to find this grotto thing, he might not have taken any notice of warnings."

"So you think our class will go ahead as usual?" persisted Rose.

"Of course it will." Dora was beginning to sound impatient, no doubt guessing what lay behind her friend's single-minded questions. "The police may want to speak to everyone, but I'm sure it won't interfere with the running of the school. I do feel sorry for Philippe Bonard, though. The publicity won't be very nice for him."

"He's a friend of yours, isn't he, Iris?" asked Rose.

"Known him for a while." A tinge of red crept into Iris's cheeks and she gave close attention to the cheese and walnut flan that one of the Gauthier girls had just put in front of her.

"He used to live near Avignon, in the same village as Iris," Melissa explained.

Dora raised her eyebrows. "You live in France?"

"November to March," said Iris gruffly. "Can't stand the English winters—too damp."

"Dieter's firm has an office in Avignon. That's why he has to improve his French," said Rose, suddenly animated. "Although it's very good already," she added with a touch of pride.

There was a moment's uneasy silence before Melissa, in response to an exasperated glance from Dora, remarked, "I believe Philippe used to be quite a prominent figure in Avignon. Isn't that right, Iris?"

Iris nodded enthusiastically. "Still is. They wanted him to run for mayor last year, but he had too many business commitments. Been planning this enterprise for years ... great dedication to promoting and protecting the French language ... keen on the arts too ... should have been a teacher ... really gifted."

Even among close friends, Iris was not often as communicative as this. Not for the first time in recent weeks Melissa felt a twinge of uneasiness on her friend's behalf, which gave her common cause with Dora.

"He seems very attached to Alain Gebrec," commented Rose.

The remark brought a sniff of contempt from Iris. "Can't think why!" she said disdainfully.

"I must say, I didn't care for all that public display of emotion this afternoon," said Dora primly. "I consider Philippe was far too soft with him."

"He must have been very shocked—I know I was," said Rose.

"One expects a man to show a little more backbone," asserted Dora. "Don't you agree, Melissa?"

Melissa had her own views on the relationship between Bonard and his assistant, but felt this was hardly the time to express them. She murmured something non-committal and changed the subject to golf, which proved to be Dora's ruling passion and kept them going until dessert.

They were drinking coffee when Monsieur Gauthier came hurrying over to inform them that "a person" wished to speak urgently to all who had been present when—at this point he discreetly lowered his voice—the dreadful discovery had been made.

"Who is this person?" asked Melissa.

Monsieur Gauthier glanced nervously round the room as if

afraid the information would ruin the digestion of his other guests.

"*Un flic,*" he said in a contemptuous whisper. "He awaits you in the salon. One at a time," he added, with bobbing glances round the table.

"Oh dear!" Rose looked dismayed. "I don't think . . ."

"It'll be all right, dear, don't worry." Dora patted her hand.

"You first." Iris nodded to Melissa. "You're used to this sort of thing. And we could all do with a *digestif,*" she informed Monsieur Gauthier.

"But of course!"

Melissa made her way to the salon. As she entered, a uniformed gendarme rose from a chair, stood to attention and gave a little bow. He was a striking figure with flashing dark eyes, aquiline features that suggested a Moorish ancestor, and a luxuriant moustache of rich chocolate brown.

"My apologies for disturbing you, Madame. I am Officier de Police Judiciaire Hassan, at your service."

"Good evening, Officer," said Melissa with a smile. "How can I help you? Please sit down."

He complied with a slight air of surprise, as if unaccustomed to such a friendly reception. He pulled a notebook from his pocket and opened it.

"May I first have your name?"

Melissa spelled it out for him. As he wrote, his solemn expression relaxed into a broad smile, displaying a set of large teeth the colour of clotted cream.

"Is it possible? Are you the famous Mel Craig?" She nodded. "But I am one of your most ardent fans! I read every one of your novels!" Excitement sent his eyes swivelling in their sockets.

"Oh, thank you!" It was a declaration that she had heard many times, but it never failed to give her pleasure.

"I have them all at home," he went on. "Would you . . . could I possibly ask you to . . . ?" Quite overcome, he seemed unable to complete his request.

"Autograph them? With pleasure," she assured him.

For several seconds he sat gazing first at her and then at her name in his notebook. "Mel Craig," he repeated, then cleared his throat and assumed his official expression. "When did you arrive in Roziac, Madame?"

"Yesterday evening."

"And you were with the party who found the body of Monsieur Wolfgang Klein this afternoon?"

"That's right. The proprietor of the study centre invited us all for an informal lunch and then suggested we walk to the belvedere. It was very hot, but it seemed that the afternoon was the best time to go because of the light."

"You study French at Les Châtaigniers?"

"No." Briefly, Melissa explained her presence and he lowered his notebook to gaze at her in wonderment.

"But what an honour for Roziac! When may I hope to have the joy of reading this masterpiece?"

"Not for two years or so, I'm afraid," she said, and his face fell. She pointed to his notebook. "Don't you think we should proceed with the interview, Officer?"

"Ah yes, quite so." He coughed. "Can you tell me exactly what happened at the time the body was discovered?"

"It was my friend, Miss Ash, who actually saw him first."

As accurately as she could, Melissa related everything that the members of the party had done and said from the time they arrived at the belvedere, while Hassan scribbled furiously in his notebook. Having trained her powers of observation and memory over the years in the interests of her writing, she was able to give a detailed account that caused his eyes to widen.

"You are the perfect witness!" he informed her with another massive smile. "Now, one more question. On your way up to the belvedere, did you observe anyone other than the members of your party?"

"There was a man unloading rails from a trailer. I understand he was preparing to mend the barrier ... he is employed by Monsieur Bonard."

"You know his name?"

"Monsieur Gebrec addressed him as Fernand."

"Ah yes!" Hassan nodded and riffled through the pages of his notebook. "Fernand Morlay. I have not yet had time to interrogate the personnel. This man could perhaps be a key witness!" He gazed at Melissa with flaring nostrils, like a hound on the scent. "This is a very peculiar case, Madame," he said, pursing his lips and assuming a mysterious expression.

"In what way, Officer? I understood it to be an unfortunate accident."

"Ah!" He tapped the side of his prominent nose with his pen. "There are some unusual features."

"Oh?"

"But we must of course await the report of the *médecin légiste*—that is to say, the *pathologiste*. Meanwhile, my investigation will continue." With some reluctance, it seemed to Melissa, he got to his feet. "I am most grateful for your help, Madame." He hesitated for a moment before saying, "And I should be most obliged if you would do me the great honour . . . your books . . . could I perhaps be permitted to call here again before you leave Roziac?"

"Yes, of course. Come about this time tomorrow evening, if you like!"

"Oh, thank you, Madame." The admiration in his gaze was almost embarrassing. Then, remembering his official role, he cleared his throat once more and asked her if she would please be so kind as to ask another of the ladies to spare him a few moments. "Although," he added gallantly, "I doubt if they can improve on your so-professional observations."

She found them sitting round a low table on the little terrace, surrounded by containers full of bright flowers. A candle in a glass shade threw a soft light on their faces, reminding Melissa of a painting by Georges de La Tour. The air was fresh and fragrant; somewhere in the deepening dusk, a nightingale sang.

The mountains, all detail by now obscured, made an irregular pattern of dark, brooding shapes. The sky overhead was clear, but clouds had rolled up from the west and were lying low on the horizon, so that in places it was hard to see where the land ended and the sky began. The Porte des Cévennes, two mighty peaks that rise on either side of the Gardon valley like the fortified gateway to an ancient town, had become looming shadows, the space between them lost in impenetrable darkness. Melissa had an impression of being enclosed, trapped in some primeval stone prison with no way out. Despite the mildness of the evening, she shivered.

"You've been a long time," Iris commented.

"Was it very frightening?" asked Rose timidly.

"Not a bit, just a few routine questions. You've nothing to worry about."

"Oh well, better get it over with." Dora got to her feet. "Come on, Rose, we'll go together. He can't eat us."

"But he said 'one at time,'" said Rose hesitantly.

"I don't care what he said. I'm not having you intimidated."

Dora practically marched her friend indoors. Melissa sank into a chair and picked up the glass of brandy that Iris had ordered for her.

"What's this copper like?" asked Iris.

"A Barbary pirate with a grin like a banana split!" said Melissa with a chuckle. "He's quite young—I suspect he may be newly promoted."

"Oh?" Iris looked up from her *crème de cassis*. "Why?"

"He's very keen to make a mystery out of that poor lad's death. Talked about 'interrogating the personnel' and 'unusual features of the case.'"

"What unusual features?"

"He didn't say."

"Maybe he's been listening to the village gossip."

"That's probably it."

It occurred to Melissa that she had said nothing to Officer Hassan about her brief conversation with Fernand Morlay. She hadn't deliberately withheld the information; he simply hadn't asked the right question. Another reason to suppose that he might be a little inexperienced. Her old friend Detective Chief Inspector Kenneth Harris of the Gloucestershire CID would not have made that elementary mistake.

Four

BREAKFAST WAS SERVED ON THE TER-
race. The air was fresh, the sky a limpid, cloudless blue. The
morning light gave the encircling mountains a newly-washed
quality and Melissa fancied that they had stepped back a little, their rocky arms outspread as if pointing towards the distant Porte des Cévennes and saying, "Look, the gate stands
open. You are free to come and go as you please."

She was hungry and tackled the fresh, crisp rolls with
gusto, but Iris fiddled abstractedly with hers, making no attempt to eat and responding morosely to the greeting of little
Brigitte Gauthier, neat and pretty in her black skirt and white
blouse, who came to serve them with coffee.

"Something on your mind?" Melissa had learned during
the three days it had taken them to reach Roziac that Iris
tended to be uncommunicative first thing in the morning. Today, however, she was more than usually preoccupied. "Not
worried about the course, surely? Everyone seemed pretty
keen and looking forward to it. I'm sure they'll find it all
most inspiring!"

Iris managed a half-smile at the mimicry of Chrissie's
husky voice and intense gaze, but she was plainly ill at ease.
"Wish I felt inspired," she muttered, reaching for a dish of
apricot jam. She peered at it suspiciously, jabbing it with the
spoon. "Wonder if this is home-made."

"Don't know, but it tastes all right." Melissa sank her teeth
into her second croissant. "What's up, Iris?"

"Not looking forward to this. Not sure I'll be any good."

"Why ever not?"

"Never really wanted to do it."

"Then why on earth did you?" As if I didn't know, Melissa added mentally.

"Philippe can be very persuasive," Iris mumbled, her nose buried in her coffee cup.

"Oh, Iris! Fancy you falling for a load of Froggie flannel! I thought you had more sense!"

Iris frowned and began picking at the crumbs on the paper tablecloth with restless fingers. "This venture means a lot to him," she said after a pause. "Wanted to help."

"And so you will. Stop worrying and eat your breakfast. Everything'll be fine, you'll see."

"Hope so." Still looking doubtful, Iris swallowed the mangled remains of her roll and drank a second cup of coffee.

Melissa had spoken confidently but, for reasons totally different from Iris's, she too felt uneasy. It wasn't the first time her friend had become overfond of an unsuitable man. And if her own assessment of Philippe Bonard was accurate, he was more unsuitable than most, but with Iris panicking at the prospect of facing a group of strangers who had paid considerable sums to be instructed by her, this was hardly the moment to voice her doubts. Moral support was called for.

"You'll have that lot eating out of your hand in no time!" she declared. "Just dash off one of your brilliant designs as a demo and then send 'em off to do their own thing. Piece of cake, you'll see."

"Thanks." Iris looked marginally less downcast. "What are your plans?"

"I'm going to Le Mas Soubeyran to visit Roland's house."

"Roland?"

"The Camisard leader I was telling you about yesterday. There's a museum there as well. It should be fascinating."

"Really into this Camisard thing, aren't you?"

"Oh, I am!" Melissa felt the familiar surge of enthusiasm that always accompanied the birth of a new and promising idea for a plot. "I've been doing a bit of background reading and I'm sure I can use it as a setting. I wish I could get

Fernand to talk about it rationally. I'll bet he's got loads of stories to tell."

"You promised to stay away from that nutter! May be something in that gossip!"

"Oh, calm down, Iris. I'm sure he's harmless enough. Anyway, we'd better be going. You want to arrive before the students, don't you?"

In the small reception area they met Rose and Dora on their way to take breakfast. The four exchanged greetings and approving comments on the weather, and wished one another a pleasant and profitable morning.

"They seem cheerful," Melissa remarked as she and Iris made their way to the car. "Let's hope Dora has talked some sense into Rose."

"Silly creature! Much too susceptible!" said Iris.

Melissa hid a smile. "How right you are," she murmured.

They had driven down through France together in Melissa's car so that she would be free to travel around on her researches during the day while Iris was busy with her course. The friendship between the two had developed over several years of living in adjoining cottages in the Cotswold countryside and they took a keen interest in one another's work. Iris loyally bought and read every one of Melissa's novels; Melissa had learned to appreciate Iris's natural flair for spotting designs of delicate simplicity in the random juxtapositions of the natural world: a feather from a bird's wing lying beside a mossy stone; a fallen leaf floating on still water; a cloud of seedheads blowing in the wind.

During the short drive from the *auberge* she said little, responding to Melissa's remarks with grunts and monosyllables, but, as they entered the courtyard at Les Châtaigniers, her eyes lit up at the sight of Philippe Bonard, immaculate in a suit of cream linen, silk shirt and cravat. He strode across the yard and shook them cordially by the hand.

"Ah, my dear Iris, you see with what magnificent conditions we greet you!" he exclaimed, spreading his hands and beaming up to heaven as if claiming personal responsibility for the sunshine. "All is most propitious for your enterprise.

Yours also!" He swept a bow towards Melissa as she prepared to help Iris unload her equipment.

"But no, I cannot permit." He clapped his hands and raised his voice. "Morlay! Come here at once!"

After a moment, Fernand emerged from an outhouse. His expression was at first sullen, but when he saw Melissa his face lit up and he hurried towards her, his right hand extended and his black eyes shining with pleasure.

"Bonjour, Madame!" he exclaimed. *"Ça va?"*

As she gave him her hand and returned his greeting, Melissa was aware of disapproval on the faces of the others. Iris's merely registered anxiety, but Bonard's expression was one of disdain. In his book, no doubt, servants did not shake hands with ladies.

"Carry Madame's equipment into the classroom," he commanded.

"Yes, Monsieur." Fernand lifted Iris's easel, portfolio and box of water-colours from the car and the two of them marched off.

"Good luck, Iris," Melissa called after her. "See you this evening."

Iris glanced over her shoulder and waved. "Thanks!"

Bonard turned again to Melissa. "We serve an alfresco lunch at mid-day," he said with a gracious smile and a flash of gold teeth. "Should your day's programme permit, we should be most honoured if you would join us."

"I'd like that very much—thank you," she said, and he turned and followed the others into the house. No one would have guessed, she reflected, that a fatal accident had taken place on his land less than twenty-four hours ago.

Juliette appeared, carrying a large watering-can. She was very like her brother, with the same fine dark eyes, but her skin was pale as if she had spent most of her life indoors. Her grey hair was drawn into an old-fashioned bun; in her striped blouse and plain dark skirt, she had the air of a village schoolmistress. She responded laconically to Melissa's greeting as she began attending to the flowers, carefully removing spent blossoms and drenching the containers with water.

"I wish I could grow geraniums like that," said Melissa. "Do you enjoy gardening?"

The woman did not lift her eyes from her task. "It is part of my duties," she replied.

"This is a beautiful place. Have you always lived here in Roziac?"

"Yes." The monosyllable was accompanied by a sharp sideways glance. It was not encouraging, but Melissa persevered. Juliette would almost certainly be a more reliable source of information than her brother, if only she could be persuaded to talk.

"Then you must know a great deal about the history of the region."

Juliette spent several seconds shaking the last drops of water from the can before replying, with apparent reluctance, "Our history has not always been happy, Madame."

"I know. I have recently been reading about it and today I plan to visit the Musée du Désert."

"You will no doubt learn there all you need to know."

The conversation would probably have ended there if Fernand had not returned. He hurried over to the two women with the same eagerness he had shown a few minutes before.

"Madame! Permit me to present my sister. Juliette, Madame shares our cause!"

"Fernand, kindly refill this for me!" Juliette held out the can. "So you are a Protestant, Madame? Have you visited our Temple in Anduze? It is a very fine building."

Melissa was sure that Juliette had intentionally misinterpreted her brother's remark and was itching to probe more deeply, but before she could think of some diplomatic way of doing so, Alain Gebrec emerged from the house.

If the previous day's tragedy had caused Bonard shock or distress, any such feelings had been concealed behind his courteous welcome. The same could not be said of his assistant, who was pale and heavy-eyed, his expression sombre. He returned Melissa's greeting mechanically and addressed Fernand in a voice stiff with suppressed emotion.

"Today you will continue repairing the barrier."

Fernand responded with a resentful glare. "Impossible!" he

declared shortly. "The path is still closed and in any case I have other work to attend to." Muttering under his breath about "*sales flics*," he deliberately turned on his heel and strode away.

Gebrec's colour rose; his eyes dilated and his nostrils quivered. He took a step forward and opened his mouth as if to call the man back and reprimand him for his insolence, but at that moment the first students arrived and he checked himself, forced a smile and went to greet them. There was no sign of Juliette, who had evidently finished watering the flowers and gone back indoors. Returning to her car, Melissa set off on her morning's expedition.

The tiny hamlet of Le Mas Soubeyran, perched high above the River Gardon, basked contentedly in the morning sun. Melissa found a shady spot to park the Golf and spent a little while strolling among the old stone houses, admiring the magnificent trees and the towering peaks that encircled them.

At that early hour few tourists had arrived, but already there was plenty of activity. A tractor was dragging a hay-tosser round a tiny field; women in bright overalls were opening up the handful of cafés and souvenir shops, wiping tables and chairs and adjusting sunshades, chasing cats from doorways and exchanging greetings with the post-girl as she puttered past on her moped. Every corner was a riot of brilliant flowers; Melissa exclaimed aloud at the sight of a lemon tree laden with ripe fruit and a woman leaning from an upstairs window waved and called a greeting.

In contrast to the heat outside, the air in the museum was cool and refreshing. The time flew as Melissa moved from one room to another, studying the exhibits, poring over old documents and filling pages of her notebook. She emerged a couple of hours later, steeped in history, burning with ideas for her novel and hungry for her lunch.

Back at Les Châtaigniers, a police car was parked alongside the other vehicles in the yard. As Melissa drove in, Officer Hassan emerged from the house. He spotted her immediately and strode towards her, his face almost bisected by his enormous grin.

"Good day, Officer. How are your investigations going?"

The grin faded. "The report of the *médecin légiste* suggests that the death was accidental," he confided in a low voice which Melissa could have sworn held a note of regret. Her suspicions were confirmed a second later as he continued, "But myself, I am not entirely satisfied. I shall pursue my enquiries for a few days further."

"You mean you do not share the view of the *médecin légiste*?"

"Oh, undoubtedly the man died as the result of a fall from the cliff. The injury to the head was almost certainly caused by striking a projection as he fell—there were fragments of rock in the wound. But what caused that fall, Madame?" He tilted back his head, compressed his lips and paused for dramatic effect. "That is what we must establish," he intoned, wagging a forefinger. "That is the purpose of my investigation. This morning, I have been examining more witnesses." He leaned forward again, rolling his eyes towards the house and back. "There are certain persons who seem to find my questions . . . disturbing."

"Are you suggesting there may have been foul play?"

"One must take nothing for granted! Always one probes beneath the surface in these cases." He tapped his nose and Melissa struggled to keep a straight face as she pictured him burrowing for clues like an anteater in search of termites.

"Well, I'm sure you have had considerable experience," she murmured, suspecting that he had nothing of the kind.

He nodded importantly, mouth bunched, cheeks blown out. "You understand these matters better than most, Madame. Well, I have other cases to attend to." He stepped back and saluted. "I shall return in a day or two. And this evening—if I may be permitted to remind you of your promise, Madame?"

"To sign your books? With pleasure!"

"Madame is most kind!" He gave an obsequious little bow, returned to his car and drove away. A few minutes later, a minibus with "Centre Cévenol d'Etudes" painted on its sides rolled through the gateway. Alain Gebrec was at the wheel and beside him, stiff-backed and with her head held confidently erect, sat Iris. The vehicle crunched to a standstill on the gravel and the members of her class began scrambling out, lugging their artists' paraphernalia.

"How did it go?" asked Melissa.

"Brilliant!" said Chrissie with an air of rapture.

"Fantastic!" agreed Mervyn.

There was vigorous head-nodding and exclamations of "Splendid!" "Most inspiring!" and "Fascinating!" from the rest of the group. Jack stepped forward to help Iris alight and carry her easel and box of water-colours. She accepted the praise and attention with a gracious smile; in her flowing dress of printed cotton and her wide straw hat decorated with flowers, she had the air of a priestess of some rustic cult, surrounded by her acolytes.

Alain Gebrec returned from putting the minibus away. "Lunch will be served on the terrace in fifteen minutes," he informed them.

"Just time for a wash and brush-up." Iris led the way indoors, swinging her arms like a child playing at soldiers.

Melissa fell into step beside her. "I told you it would be a doddle, didn't I?"

Iris gave a serene smile, her grey eyes shining. "Seem happy, don't they?"

"Ecstatic! You've got off to a flying start."

"Hope I can keep it up."

"Sure you can."

The buffet lunch was once more laid out on the terrace. The members of Philippe Bonard's class were already gathered round the table, chatting in French—at various levels of competence—under the attentive ear of their pedagogue. Observing him, Melissa found herself admiring his professionalism; like the proprietor of a high-class restaurant, he spoke to every individual in turn, inviting comments, listening to responses, discussing particular difficulties.

Waiting his turn to reach the buffet, Dieter Erdle was talking to Janey, who was listening with her glossy fair head tilted at an engaging angle, while Rose, wearing a cat-like smile that barely concealed her antagonism, hovered at her elbow. Dora Lavender was helping herself to food; when she had taken what she wanted, she picked up an empty plate and without a word pushed it into her friend's hand. Every line of her body registered contemptuous disapproval.

Juliette bustled to and fro, bringing supplies of bread, checking that all was in order. Observing her, Melissa sensed that feelings of anxiety lay beneath the composed correctness of her manner. Once, she caught the woman looking directly at her; for a moment, the guard dropped and the sombre eyes seemed to signal an appeal before someone approached her with a request and she turned away to comply.

Melissa had a shrewd idea what lay behind Juliette's unease. There was no doubt in her mind that Hassan's mysterious nods and nose-tappings were a reference to Fernand; he must have picked up the gossip that Monsieur Gauthier had repeated and his eagerness to find evidence of foul play in the death of Wolfgang Klein was transparent. She remembered how Dora Lavender had reported hearing Juliette scolding her brother after the discovery of the body. So far from a concern that he had carelessly, albeit unwittingly, allowed Klein to embark on a fatal expedition, she must have been fearful that his eccentric fantasies and public hostility towards the young German might rebound on them both.

When lunch was over, people began drifting away to drink their coffee in some shady corner of the gardens. Iris was sitting cross-legged on the grass under a tree, surrounded by her students and entirely at her ease. She glanced across and beckoned, but Melissa, pretending not to notice, returned to the table where Juliette was loading plates and cutlery on to a tray.

"Allow me to help you," she said.

There was a moment's hesitation, as if Juliette was weighing in her mind the propriety of accepting such an offer from a guest of her employer against her own desperate need of a confidante. Then she gravely inclined her head.

"Thank you, Madame."

"Fine. Is there another tray in the kitchen?"

"But yes, on the buffet. I will fetch it for you."

"No need. I'll get it—I know the way."

Ignoring Juliette's protests, Melissa went indoors. Having

some while earlier spotted Fernand trudge across the yard and into the house by a side entrance, she had a shrewd idea of where to find him and was burning with curiosity to hear what—if anything—he might have to say about his interview with Hassan.

She found him seated at a wooden table in the large kitchen with his back to the window, staring down at a plate of food. The shutters were closed against the sun, throwing his face into shadow, but his eyes glittered in the subdued light as he lifted his head and gazed at Melissa in the tense, wary attitude of an animal in the wild.

"Has he gone?" he asked in a hoarse voice.

"Officer Hassan? He went long ago. You are quite safe," she replied.

His shoulders relaxed a shade and he sat a little more upright. "Never will I betray Roland!" he said fiercely. "I told him nothing. Nothing!" He banged his fist on the table and a bottle of mineral water danced at his elbow. The food in front of him was barely touched, but the piece of bread beside the plate had been torn to fragments.

"It's all right," Melissa said quietly. "Eat your meal." She went to the massive wooden dresser that stood in the corner and picked up a tray. His eyes followed every move she made.

"That traitor . . . he would have led our enemies to our secret refuge," he declared.

"The one beneath the cliff, near the belvedere?"

"Where else?"

"You saw him there?"

He shook his head emphatically. Hunched over the plate, he began forking the food into his mouth, one forearm resting on the table. He chewed noisily and took a swig of water from the bottle before replying, setting it down with a thump.

"I saw no one. I heard nothing." He repeated the words as if he had learned them by rote. Suddenly, he shot out a hand and grabbed her own in hard, powerful fingers, staring up at her with a feverish light in his eyes.

"We must remain watchful!" he said urgently.

A frisson of fear clawed at her stomach, but she managed

to keep her voice level as she replied, "Yes, indeed we must."

Juliette came bustling in with a laden tray. The sight of Melissa in conversation with her brother brought a frown to her face.

"Haven't you finished yet?" she scolded him. "It's time you were out of my kitchen—you are in the way!"

He started, withdrew his hand and half rose, looking as guilty as a child caught stealing jam. Melissa returned to the terrace to fill her tray; when she came back, Fernand had gone and Juliette was loading a large dishwasher. She was plainly ill at ease; several times she took a quick breath and opened her mouth as if to speak, then turned back to her task, frowning and biting her lips.

Melissa took the bull by the horns. "Your brother has some strange fancies," she said. "Has he always had this obsession with the Camisards?"

For a moment, she regretted speaking. Tears sprang into Juliette's eyes and her mouth trembled, but she managed to control herself.

"Oh, the Camisards," she murmured with a sad little grimace that seemed intended as a smile. "That was a game we used to play with our friends as children. The boys acted all the grown-up characters in turn; myself, I always had the role of the page-boy of Villars—you know the story?"

"Of how Villars disguised himself as a sort of divine messenger and his page as a magical shepherd boy? I was reading about it only this morning, in the Musée du Désert."

"Then no doubt you know that Roland, one of the Camisard leaders, did not believe the promise that the wrongs of the Protestants would be righted. He thought it was a trap and fought on for a while with a few followers, but in the end he was betrayed. It is a story of treachery, but also of great courage. Fernand was fascinated by it—almost obsessed, as you say, Madame—when he was young."

"Roland is his hero, isn't he?"

Again, Juliette seemed to be struggling with tears. "The Roland of whom he speaks is not the ancient Camisard leader, but our elder brother who was tortured and shot by the Gestapo," she said huskily, pulling a handkerchief from her apron pocket and dabbing her eyes. It was a full minute before she was able to speak again.

"Our Roland was just sixteen when he joined the Maquis, the youngest of the group. They had a hiding place—a cave beneath the cliff—where they used to meet and store their weapons. Sometimes they would conceal a refugee there and Roland would act as their guide. Fernand was too young to join the group, but he would take food to them. He could slip through the forest as silently as a cat!"

"That must be the secret refuge that he spoke to me about?"

"Yes. In our family, only he and Roland knew where it was."

"He seems to think I know where it is."

"You must have said something . . . he is confused in his mind, Madame, and when one considers what he suffered, who can wonder at it?" Juliette fiddled with the controls of the dishwasher, surreptitiously dabbing her cheeks. "Those who had been concealed there knew of the existence of the refuge, but of course they kept silent," she continued. "All save one, a spy, who betrayed our brother to the Gestapo." At the memory, her strong features hardened as if cast in concrete and bitter hatred flared in her eyes. When she spoke again her voice had a new, rasping note that brought a tingle to Melissa's spine.

"To learn of its whereabouts and the names of his comrades they tortured Roland, but he would not speak. Then the commandant had the fiendish inspiration to use his younger brother as a weapon. Soldiers came to the house and tore Fernand from our mother's arms. Never, never will I forget that terrible day!" Anguish contorted her features.

Melissa, too, felt close to tears at the sight of the other woman's pain and she reached for her hand. It felt like ice. "Don't say any more if it distresses you," she whispered.

"Yes, yes! I must tell the whole story to make you understand. My brother is a gentle man, he would hurt no one. But he has these fancies and I am afraid they will one day get him into serious trouble. That accident . . . it would not surprise me if, in his mind, that poor young man was the one whose treachery led to the death of our brother."

"Yes, he referred to him as a traitor just now," Melissa agreed thoughtfully. "And Officer Hassan seems very anxious to prove that the death of Mr. Klein was not accidental, even though the *médecin légiste* thinks it was."

Juliette gave a contemptuous snort; had she been a man, Melissa felt, she would have spat on the ground. "That stupid *flic*! Trying to impress his superiors, no doubt . . . but Fernand will tell him nothing. It would be to him like betraying Roland and all their comrades in the Maquis. But I swear to you, Madame, my brother would not harm any living creature. Even in our childish games, he would never be the one to take a life."

For a moment Juliette's face grew soft as she remembered those far-off days of innocent pleasure.

"You were speaking of the day the Gestapo took him," Melissa reminded her gently.

"Ah, yes, that dreadful day. Fernand seldom speaks of it himself; in fact, he did not speak a word for many days after, but the pain in the eyes of that child . . . I cannot describe it." Juliette covered her eyes and drew deep, racking breaths in her struggle not to break down.

Melissa led her to a chair and she sank into it, staring into emptiness, her clasped hands lying on the table.

"Only some weeks later did we learn from an escaped prisoner exactly what had happened." Her voice took on a remote quality, like someone speaking from the grave. "They took Fernand to the prison where they were holding Roland, to the exercise yard, and made all the other prisoners watch while they brought him before them. He could barely stand, they had beaten him so badly. Fernand gave a terrible cry and tried to run to him, but the soldiers held him back. Then the commandant told him that unless he revealed the secret of the refuge, his brother would be shot, there and then, before his eyes."

"The monster!" Outrage took Melissa by the throat, as if it would drag her physically into the other woman's world of grief and bitter memories. "To do that to a little boy! How old was he?"

"Not quite nine years old, Madame, and so small for his age."

"Hardly more than a baby." Melissa had a sudden vision of her own son Simon at that age, secure and happy, his world untroubled by war or threats of violence. Tears of mingled pity and anger filled her eyes, but she made no effort to brush them away.

"What did he do?" she whispered. "Did he speak?"

"No, Madame, he did not." Proudly, Juliette lifted her head. "The commandant shouted questions and threats at him while the soldiers held their rifles trained on his brother. He stood there, bewildered and terrified, and all of a sudden Roland cried out: 'Say nothing! I, your leader Roland, command you to remain silent!' "

"As if they were playing their game about the Camisards?"

"Yes, Madame."

"And then?"

"The commandant seemed to realise that he had failed. He gave the order to fire."

There was a long interval. In the background, the dishwasher whirred and splashed; from outside came the sound of a tractor starting up. At length, Juliette got to her feet.

"I must not detain you any longer, Madame," she said. "Thank you for listening."

"I am honoured that you should confide in me. Does Monsieur Bonard know?"

"Who would tell him? It is a story from the past."

"But he must be aware of some of the strange things that Fernand says?"

Juliette dismissed the notion with a shrug. "Why should a gentleman like Monsieur Bonard concern himself with our affairs?" It was evident that she held old-fashioned ideas on the relationship between master and servants.

"What about Monsieur Gebrec?"

"He speaks only to give orders—but, since he is so highly thought of by our employer . . ." Her lip curled, suggesting that, for whatever reason, her respect for Philippe Bonard did not extend to his aide.

It occurred to Melissa that if Hassan knew the circumstances of Roland Morlay's death, he might see it as a motive for murder: a half-crazed younger brother mistaking for an enemy the unfortunate young German who had shown an innocent interest in the "secret refuge." His sister had taken an extraordinary risk by confiding in her.

Juliette seemed to have read her thoughts. "I tell you these things, Madame, because I know my brother trusts you," she said. "It is unlikely that he will speak of them to you, but if he should do so, if you did not know the truth, you might feel it necessary to tell the police. If that *flic* should hear the story . . ."

"He will not hear it from me." Melissa gave the promise without a moment's reflection. "I have not even told the officer of my conversation with Fernand yesterday in the woods, only that I saw him working there."

"God bless you, Madame!" said Juliette huskily.

Five

MOST OF THE ASPIRING ARTISTS AND the students of language, literature and culture had fallen victim to the seductive somnolence of a hot afternoon. Singly or in small clusters, they lay in chairs on the terrace or sprawled on rugs under the trees, some unashamedly asleep, others nodding over books, all as immobile as figures on a set of *The Sleeping Beauty*.

The exceptions were Dora Lavender, Rose Kettle and Dieter Erdle. The former had taken a golf-club to a smooth, level patch of grass a short distance from the house which Philippe Bonard, anxious to cater for his clients' leisure needs as well as their thirst for learning, had laid out as a green; she had donned a pair of heavy-framed spectacles and was practising putting. Rose and Dieter were watching from the shade of a chestnut tree, chatting in low voices and giggling. From where she stood, Melissa could see them only in profile, but she had a shrewd idea that they were holding hands and that Dora's apparent indifference to their presence was concealing a mounting irritation.

"Well done!" called Rose after Dora had sunk six putts in a row.

"Yes, well done indeed!" echoed Dieter, ostentatiously clapping his hands. "Your friend is an impressive player," he said to Rose.

Dora retrieved her ball without a glance in their direction and marched to the far edge of the green.

"She's a scratch player," said Rose, raising her voice

slightly, as if anxious to appease her friend. "She plays in tournaments, you know. Everyone says her swing is superb."

Dieter bent to whisper something in her ear, at which she gave a squeal of laughter.

Watching Dora, Melissa observed her stiffen and tighten her grip on the putter, her arm muscles clenched below the rolled-up sleeves of her blouse. She took her stance and struck the ball; it sped across the grass like a bullet, struck the rim of the hole and shot out again.

"Bad luck, Dora!" called Rose.

"Perhaps you hit it a little too hard?" suggested Dieter.

As if they were inaudible and invisible, Dora picked up her ball and stalked past them, heading for the car. The two observers exchanged amused glances and then wandered away under the trees. Undoubtedly they were holding hands.

"I'll bet she'd like *him* to end up at the foot of the cliff," said a voice. Turning, Melissa found Jack standing beside her.

"Or put him there," she agreed wryly. "She thinks her friend is making a fool of herself and she's seriously worried about her."

"I'd say she had every reason to be." He spoke softly, with a hint of a West Country burr.

Dora flung open the boot of the Sierra and thrust the putter into her golf-bag. She closed the lid; when the catch failed to operate, she slammed it a second time with a violence that made several of the slumberers lift their heads. She marched across the courtyard into the house, her eyes stony and her jaw set.

Jack glanced at his watch. "Another half an hour before school starts again," he observed. "Shall we sit down?"

Melissa hesitated. "Well, actually, I was thinking of driving into Anduze," she said. "I want to visit the Protestant temple."

"Ah yes, I was forgetting. You're researching a novel, aren't you? And I believe you're a friend of Iris's?" There was a studied casualness in his tone that made Melissa prick up her ears.

"We're next-door neighbours."

"In Gloucestershire, isn't it?"

"That's right."

"I'm a Somerset man myself."

"I'd never have guessed!"

He laughed, a warm, comfortable sound that reminded her of homely, rustic things like sleek cattle and woolly sheep grazing on a West Country hillside. "Can't disguise the accent, can I? Iris spotted it at once."

"Where is Iris, by the way? I came out here to look for her, but she seems to have disappeared."

"She said she was going off somewhere to meditate before the afternoon session. I'm sure she needs a bit of time to recharge after giving so much of herself this morning."

"Oh, Iris swears by her yoga," agreed Melissa. "Did you have a productive session, by the way?" she added, thinking that it would be nice to have some favourable comments to pass on to Iris.

"Absolutely splendid!" Jack's eyes glowed. "Your friend has so much talent and she's so . . ." he waved his hands as if trying to snatch words from the air, ". . . she has this gift of firing one's imagination without talking too much. Some tutors just love the sound of their own voices."

"That must be a relief," said Melissa, smiling at this positive tribute to Iris's minimalist use of language. "It sounds as if you've made a promising start. By the way, when she reappears, would you mind telling her I'll be back to pick her up at the end of this afternoon?"

"Of course." He appeared delighted at the prospect. "You're staying at the Auberge de la Fontaine, aren't you?"

"That's right. And you?"

"The Lion d'Or. Not exactly five star, but the food's okay and it's got a pretty terrace bar overlooking the river. Perhaps you and Iris would care to join me there for a drink one evening?"

"That sounds a nice idea. Will you fix it with her?"

"It'll be a pleasure!" he said warmly and Melissa thought what an attractive smile he had. "Well, I mustn't keep you. I hope to see you again soon."

"I look forward to it."

Iris, you've got an admirer, murmured Melissa to herself as

she got into the car. Much more suitable than your precious Philippe Bonard, too.

The interior of the Protestant temple at Anduze was light, spacious and blissfully cool. Melissa found its clean, uncluttered lines at once calming and uplifting, and she stood for a few moments just inside the door, absorbing the tranquil atmosphere.

A number of people were walking quietly to and fro, studying the architecture, referring to guide-books and conversing in low voices. A small party had gathered round an elderly woman who had apparently been showing them round. As Melissa entered, the guide stepped back with outspread hands that seemed to invite her small audience to scatter and enjoy the building at their leisure. Then her eyes fell on Melissa and she came forward to greet her.

"*Bonjour*, Madame. Welcome to our temple. Would you like to learn something of our history?" From a plain wooden table spread with literature she picked up a booklet and offered it to Melissa, who took it with some hesitation.

"Actually, I already know quite a bit about it from the guide-books," she began. "And this morning . . ."

"Ah, the guide-books," interrupted the woman with a condescending smile. "They tell you only about the big names and the famous dates. This lady has spent many years studying the life of the people who lived in these parts in former times."

"I learned a great deal from my visit to the museum this morning," commented Melissa, glancing at the booklet as she spoke. The name of the author caught her eye. "Antoinette Gebrec—is that a common name round here?"

The woman looked at her curiously. "You mean Gebrec? Not so common. Why do you ask?"

"There is a man called Alain Gebrec who works at the Centre Cévenol d'Etudes in Roziac."

"Alain? But of course, that would be Antoinette's son!"

"You know the family?"

"I know Antoinette very well. You are a student at the centre, Madame?"

"No, not exactly." Once more, Melissa explained her interest in the region.

"But you must visit Antoinette!" exclaimed the guide. "She will love to assist you in your researches. It is a passion of hers, the history of the Camisards. She lives not far from here, in Alès. Let me give you her address and telephone number." She rummaged in her handbag, found a pencil and notebook, and began scribbling.

"Are you sure she won't mind a total stranger calling on her?" asked Melissa doubtfully as she took the proffered piece of paper.

"But of course not. There is nothing she enjoys more than to talk on her favourite subject. Tell her Gabrielle Delon sent you. You wish to buy her book?" the woman added hopefully.

"Yes, of course." Melissa took out a fifty-franc note. "And please keep the change as a donation to your temple."

"Oh, thank you, Madame. Excuse me, here come more visitors." With a bobbing movement that was almost a curtsey, Madame Delon hurried away.

"Had a good day?" asked Iris as she settled into the Golf to be driven back to the *auberge* at the end of the afternoon.

"Very interesting indeed." Melissa gave a brief account of her activities but without reference to her conversation with Juliette. "How about you?"

"Super."

"Jack seems a nice man."

"They're all nice. Going to be a good week." After a pause, Iris added smugly, "Philippe's delighted."

"So he should be—he's getting your services for peanuts." In an unguarded moment, Iris had let drop that, while Bonard was paying her expenses, she was receiving no fee to run the course.

"New venture," Iris reminded her. "Doing what I can to help it off the ground."

"Philippe doesn't give me the impression of being exactly hard up," retorted Melissa, thinking of the designer suits and the new luxury Peugeot in the garage.

"Capital at risk," Iris insisted. "Stands to lose a lot if things go wrong."

Melissa abandoned this unsatisfactory topic and reverted to her original one. "I was chatting to Jack after lunch." There was no response. "He said something about our having a drink with him one evening."

Iris's expression did not change as she murmured, "Who did?"

"Jack, of course. Didn't he mention it to you?"

"Said something about it."

"And?"

Iris yawned, put her hands behind her head and gazed out of the window. "Maybe later this week. Too tired this evening."

As soon as they were back at the *auberge*, Iris vanished into their minuscule *en suite* bathroom. She emerged a couple of minutes later clad in her black leotard, unfolded a blanket and spread it on the floor in the far corner of the bedroom. They had been given a family room, from which Monsieur Gauthier had obligingly removed one of the three single beds in order to provide the space Iris required for her daily yoga session.

"So good of Philippe to organise this for me," said Iris, sinking gracefully into a supine position. "Went to endless trouble to organise my diet as well."

"He's a businessman," Melissa pointed out, having heard this eulogy several times already. "He knew your name would bring in the customers and . . ."

"Going into relaxation now," murmured Iris, closing her eyes and spreading her arms and legs like a starfish.

"Don't worry, I shan't disturb you. I've got notes to write up and Madame Gebrec's book to read."

A couple of hours later, having showered and changed, they went downstairs to dinner. As they passed through the reception area on their way to the restaurant, they caught a glimpse of a dark green car with a German number plate driving away.

"Seen that before," commented Iris. "Guess who won't be dining here this evening."

The guess proved accurate. Dora appeared late, alone and in obvious ill-humour. The two friends tactfully refrained from enquiring after Rose, but Monsieur Gauthier had no such reservations.

"Your friend, she is not with you?" he enquired, with a solicitous bob first at Dora and then towards the door. "She is not unwell, I hope."

"She is perfectly well, but she has gone out," said Dora in a tone which discouraged further comment. She took the menu, scowled at it as if every dish carried a health warning, chose a couple at random and handed it back. When her food arrived, she appeared to eat without appetite, made little or no response to any attempts at conversation and left the table without taking dessert or coffee.

"Poor Dora, she can't wait for this week to be over," Melissa remarked.

Iris, tucking into her slice of *Tarte Tatin*, waved her fork in agreement. "Bet she wishes it was the dashing Dieter who'd gone over the cliff!" she said cheerfully.

"Funny you should say that. Jack made a similar comment earlier on."

"Oh, yes?"

"He thinks you're a great teacher, by the way."

"That's good. Perhaps he'll recommend the course. Philippe wants me to run it again in October."

"Well, I hope you'll charge him a proper fee next time. I'll bet he can afford it." Melissa was becoming more and more irritated at the constant references to Bonard. "Just on a point of interest, what's his main line of business? It must be pretty lucrative to enable him to buy Les Châtaigniers."

"Wholesale fruit and vegetables."

"That would appeal to you, of course," said Melissa dryly.

Iris ignored the taunt. "Family business—never really wanted to do it, but father made him." She leaned on an elbow and stirred her coffee, an absent expression softening her sharp features. "Lifetime ambition, setting up this school," she said dreamily.

"So you keep telling me."

"Don't like him, do you?" Iris faced Melissa with an accusing glint in her eyes. "What's he done to you?"

"Nothing. And you're wrong. I do like him, I think he's charming. It's just that ... you seem a bit too keen on him ..."

Iris flushed. "So what's wrong with that? Think he likes me too." There was a wistful note in her voice that went to Melissa's heart. Despite the strength of her misgivings, she could not bring herself to voice them.

At least the art course looked like being a success. Not that Melissa cared two hoots whether it was making money for Bonard or not—whatever Iris might claim, he was certainly not strapped for cash—but it was essential for Iris's self-esteem that it should go well. So she kept her doubts to herself, merely remarking that everyone knew what Frenchmen were like and turning the whole thing into a rather laboured joke in which Iris eventually joined.

They were sitting on the terrace admiring the sunset when Monsieur Gauthier announced with distaste that "that *flic*" was in reception and had requested a word with Melissa. She found him behind a tall potted plant in the far corner where, she suspected, he had been deliberately steered by the proprietor in order that as few people as possible should be aware of his presence in the establishment.

The precaution seemed unnecessary, since Hassan was evidently off duty. Instead of the blue uniform, which sat well on his big frame, he was sporting a hideous shirt patterned with palm trees and his plump buttocks were compressed into a pair of fawn slacks, the cut of which would have flattered a slimmer figure but was less than kind to his own. With a gallant wave of one hand he invited Melissa to sit down and with the other placed a small pile of well-thumbed paperbacks on a table in front of her. He spread them out in the manner of a dealer displaying merchandise for inspection by a client and then sat down facing her, his huge mouth stretched in a smile of pure delight.

"As you see, Madame, I have your complete *oeuvres*," he said proudly. "And I have read all the stories many times." He picked up the books one by one, opening them at the title page, watching every movement of her pen as she signed them and commenting on the brilliance of each individual plot.

"How I should enjoy meeting your Inspector Nathan Latimer, Madame!" he sighed when she had finished. "We who work in the provinces rarely have the opportunity to encounter detectives of such distinction!"

"I'm very glad that my books give you such pleasure," responded Melissa with total sincerity. "By the way, how is your own case progressing?"

"You mean the death of Monsieur Klein?" Hassan's face fell. "Alas, Madame, I have no case. My commandant accepts the conclusions of the *médecin légiste* and instructs me to abandon my enquiries." His liquid eyes were sorrowful and the ends of his moustache drooped.

"That must be rather frustrating for you," said Melissa politely. But what a relief for Juliette and for Fernand, she thought.

"For the moment, yes, but . . ." He began gathering the books together, handling them with exaggerated care and opening them a second time to gaze at Melissa's signature. He placed them in a neat pile, patting them into position with his large hands, frowning slightly. She had the impression that he had something on his mind and was uncertain whether or not he should speak of it.

After a moment he lifted his eyes from the books, leaned forward and spoke in a lowered voice. "In my opinion, we have not seen the last of this matter."

"Whatever do you mean?"

He pursed his lips and wagged his head. "Things are not as they seem . . . I have an instinct," he said.

Any moment now, thought Melissa, he'll be tapping his nose and giving mysterious glances. It was a struggle to hide her smile as he fulfilled her expectations. "An instinct," he repeated.

"Oh dear, I do hope there aren't going to be any more . . . accidents," she said. From the corner of her eye, she spotted Iris hovering by the entrance. "Will you please excuse me now? My friend is waiting for me."

"But of course." He scrambled to his feet, clutching the books to his chest.

"It's been a pleasure seeing you again, Officer," said Melissa.

"Assuredly, we shall meet again soon!" he said meaningfully and marched out, bowing to Iris as he passed.

"Like something out of a kid's lesson book, isn't he?" chuckled Iris.

Melissa agreed, but behind her smile lay a certain unease. It was illogical, but she had a premonition that Officer Hassan's instinct would prove correct.

Six

THE FOLLOWING MORNING, AFTER dropping Iris at Les Châtaigniers for the second day of her course, Melissa returned to the *auberge* and telephoned Antoinette Gebrec. As Madame Delon had predicted, her enquiry met with a cordial response followed by an unexpected invitation to lunch.

It promised to be another brilliant day. There was little traffic on the picturesque road from Roziac to Alès and Melissa drove slowly, stopping once or twice along the way to contemplate the magnificent scenery. There was something about this part of France that made a powerful appeal to her imagination and emotions. The people were so strong in the faith for which their forebears had fought and suffered; their steadfastness and courage, handed down through the ages, lived on in the men and women who only a few years ago had defied the invader of their homeland. She thought of Juliette and Fernand and their martyred brother, namesake of their hero, and in some indefinable way felt at one with them.

She arrived in Alès with an hour in hand and left the Golf in a car park alongside the Gardon, which encircles the city centre on three sides in a broad loop. She leaned for a few minutes on the stone parapet overlooking the river, shading her eyes against the glitter of sunlight on the water and feeling its warmth soaking into her bones, before crossing the road and plunging into the narrow streets of the old town.

She found a bookshop and browsed for a while. On impulse, she bought a recently published history of the region under the Occupation and took it to a pavement café, where she sat under a gaudy sunshade, idly sipping coffee and glancing through her book, but finding the passing show around her far more diverting.

Brightly-dressed children sat licking ice-creams or noisily sucking highly-coloured liquids through straws, while their parents drank coffee and ate *pâtisserie.* Evidently there was a market not far away, for there were plenty of housewives with shopping bags bulging with fresh vegetables and fruit, while here and there a businessman hurried through the crowd clutching his briefcase or sat scanning a newspaper over his coffee or cognac.

But it was the students who appealed most strongly to Melissa, sauntering past with enormous packs on their strong young shoulders, clear-eyed, tawny-limbed and confident. Her own son, now an engineer with an oil company in the States, had back-packed round Europe while at university and she remembered his homecoming, his hair bleached by the sun, seemingly taller and more mature, full of tales of the people he had met along the way. Youngsters from a dozen different countries, some of whose grandparents had fought one another in the war . . . youngsters not much older than Roland Morlay when he met his death before the terror-stricken gaze of his nine-year-old brother.

A man appeared with a guitar, wearing a black vest and the briefest of denim shorts over a deeply tanned body. He began playing a sad, haunting melody while singing of love and death in a rich Spanish tenor. When the song ended, he moved quietly among the tables, holding out his wide-brimmed black hat and coaxing money from the customers with a flash of white teeth and a sparkle of peat-brown eyes. As Melissa dropped a coin into the hat, receiving in return a courtly bow and a murmured, *"Muchas gracias, Señora,"* a nearby clock struck eleven. It was almost time for her appointment.

If Melissa had wished to create the character of an elderly Frenchwoman for one of her novels, she would surely have chosen Antoinette Gebrec as her model. Petite and vivacious, beautifully coiffured, discreetly made-up and dressed with simple elegance, she conformed in all respects to the universal concept of Gallic womanhood.

When the Golf pulled up outside her house in a quiet suburb of Alès, she was sitting beneath a pergola on the terrace overlooking the road with a book on her lap. On seeing the car, she rose immediately and came tripping down the drive to unlock the tall iron gates.

"Welcome, welcome!" she cried in English as Melissa stepped from the car. "I trust you found the house without difficulty? May I offer you a glass of wine? Or do you prefer the *citron pressé*?"

"Not wine, thank you," said Melissa with a smile, glancing back at the car.

"Of course, of course ... not during the driving. Please, take a seat. The *citron* is already prepared—I will fetch it."

She vanished into the house and was back within seconds with iced lemonade in a tall glass jug. Her carriage was graceful, her movements quick and deft; there was animation in her face and a slight catch in her voice that hinted at suppressed laughter. She reminded Melissa of champagne, full of fizz and sparkle, and thought that her son had inherited neither her looks nor her personality.

She poured the drinks, handed one to her guest and raised her own glass. "*Santé!* I am so happy to make your acquaintance. I understand you know Alain?"

"Ah, you've spoken to Madame Delon?"

"She telephoned this morning to say I might expect to hear from you. I said you had already called ... she will join us for the lunch."

"That will be lovely. Yes, I have met your son, although only briefly." Melissa explained her connection with the Centre Cévenol d'Etudes. "I expect he has told you of the tragedy?" Madame Gebrec nodded, her mobile face registering sorrow and concern. "Alain was present when we found the body—he seemed very distressed."

"He is very sensitive ... so like ..." For a moment her thoughts seemed far away and by no means happy, but she quickly recovered and gave Melissa a captivating smile.

"Now, tell me about this book you are writing. It is very exciting to meet a real author."

"But you also have written a book."

"Bah! That little thing, it is nothing! I indulge myself, it is my hobby."

"It's very interesting. I'm really fascinated by this period in your country's history." Pleasure shone in the expressive eyes. "And I want to use it in the plot for my new novel," Melissa continued. "I should so appreciate your help with the background."

"I shall be enchanted."

As Melissa explained her ideas, her hostess put down her glass and listened intently, hands clasped, head cocked on one side, now and again interjecting a word of encouragement and approval, occasionally wagging a manicured finger with an emphatic, "*Non! Ça ne va pas!* But it could be like this perhaps," illustrating her point with some jewel that she had quarried from her years of research in the mines of history. The time flew. Both women looked up in surprise when the sharp ring of a bell from the gate announced the arrival of Madame Delon.

The two Frenchwomen greeted one another with affectionate kisses and Madame Gebrec promptly went off to organise the lunch, leaving her two visitors to chat. They had barely exchanged the time of day before she was back with a trolley laden with plates of *charcuterie* and cheese, a basket of bread and a bowl of salad.

The conversation proceeded in French, since Madame Delon knew no English. The contrast in appearance between the friends was almost comical—the one so slight and elegant, the other homely, dowdily dressed and plump. Yet they had the same energetic manner of speaking: their metallic voices swooped and dived, their eyes rolled, their shoulders bounced, their hands flew in the air like birds performing a courtship dance. Melissa, struggling to follow the staccato bursts of speech that punctuated their intake of food, was so fascinated by their mannerisms that more than once she lost the thread of what they were saying and had to beg them to speak more slowly, which they did with great good humour and shrieks of tinny laughter.

The time flew and at three o'clock Madame Delon rose, saying that she must leave now to catch her bus.

"I can drive you back to Anduze," said Melissa.

"Ah, but that is so kind!" declared Madame Gebrec before her friend had a chance to speak. "That will be so much more comfortable for you, Gabrielle, and there is no need to hurry." She seemed reluctant to allow her guests to go.

Madame Delon was equally determined to stay no longer. "Just the same, I should be leaving soon," she said firmly. "Henri will be home for his supper at six o'clock and I have to do the shopping." She turned to Melissa. "If that does not inconvenience you, Madame?"

"Not at all. I have to be back as Les Châtaigniers in time to collect my friend. Perhaps I could use the toilet before we go?"

"Of course. Gabrielle, you will show Madame Craig?" Madame Gebrec began stacking plates on to the trolley.

"But certainly. This way."

The door from the terrace led directly into a long, somewhat overfurnished salon, cool and dim after the heat and brightness outside, its deep window-sills shaded by closed shutters and crowded with knick-knacks. The walls were covered with pictures; near the door was an original oil painting of the Porte des Cévennes and Melissa paused to look at it.

"Do you know who did this?" she enquired.

Madame Delon glanced over her shoulder before replying. "An old friend of Antoinette, many years ago," she said guardedly.

Melissa pointed to the small light above the picture. "May I?"

Madame Delon shrugged. "I suppose."

Melissa pressed the switch. The yellowish lamp gave the illusion of sunlight flooding the canvas and she stood back to admire the effect.

"It's good," she said after a few moments. "My friend is an artist—she would like it."

Madame Delon made no comment. She ushered Melissa

out of the room into a small entrance hall and indicated a door on the other side. "That one," she said.

On the way back from the bathroom, Melissa stopped in front of a cabinet laden with framed photographs. Most were of Alain at various stages of childhood and adolescence, some on his own, some with his mother. There was a wedding photograph as well; the passing years had faded the picture, but not the radiance of the bride's smile. Her groom, a soldier in uniform, stood stiffly at her side.

"Is Monsieur Gebrec still living?" asked Melissa softly, although she felt she already knew the answer.

"Alas no, Madame, he was killed in the war."

Madame Gebrec accompanied them to the car. The book that Melissa had bought earlier lay on the passenger seat; as she went to remove it, it slipped from its wrappings. Madame Gebrec gave a sharp exclamation.

"You buy that book?" The black eyes that had been sparkling with good humour a moment before had become hard, almost angry.

"Yes, I got it this morning in Alès," said Melissa, surprised at the reaction. "Do you know it?"

"I know it."

"Perhaps you don't recommend it? The assistant in the bookshop said . . . "

"Bah, it is well enough." Madame Gebrec screwed up her mouth and made a dismissive gesture, as if to avoid contact with something unpleasant. "The author is an historian respected by many but his so-called facts, he does not always verify them. I too am writing a book about this period . . . it will be more accurate than this one, I assure you."

"I shall make a point of buying a copy." Melissa hastily pushed the book back into the crumpled wrapping and put it out of sight, then held out her hand. "Thank you very much for your help, Madame, and your hospitality. It's been a great pleasure to meet you."

"It has been a pleasure for me also," said Madame Gebrec. She spoke warmly, but her smile of farewell did not reach her eyes and there were hard lines round her mouth.

Any hope Melissa might have entertained of learning from

Madame Delon what lay behind Madame Gebrec's outburst
came to nothing. The discreet feelers that she put out during
the drive back to Anduze met with monosyllabic replies that
indicated, firmly but politely, that the matter was no concern
of hers.

She would have liked to know just which passages in the
book her hostess found objectionable, but it was plain that
the only way to find out was to study it for herself. Even so,
she had no means of recognising them and to wade through
three hundred-odd pages in search of some unidentified reference would be a formidable task and probably not worth the
effort. It was an unsatisfactory conclusion to an otherwise
profitable visit.

She dropped her passenger in the centre of Anduze and
made her way back to Roziac. There was still an hour left before the classes finished, so she parked the Golf in the courtyard and picked up the book, then changed her mind and took
her camera from the glove compartment instead. She had not
had it with her on Sunday during the walk to the belvedere
and although it might now be too late in the day to catch the
best of the light, it would be useful to have a few shots to
help with descriptions of the scenery when she came to write
her novel.

It had turned somewhat cooler, with a light but refreshing
breeze. She soon found the path and began the climb. The
way was now wide enough for two people to walk abreast
and the largest of the loose stones had been thrown aside.
Here and there, a fragment of plastic ribbon fluttered from a
low branch, a mute reminder of the recent tragedy and the police activity that had followed.

Ahead, a series of clattering bumps that sounded like wood
falling against wood echoed through the trees; no doubt
Fernand was once more busy with the task of repairing the
guard-rail. Shortly after she became aware of the sounds, they
stopped; a moment later she came to the clearing where she
had first seen and spoken to him. The tractor was there with
the trailer attached, its tailboard unfastened. A few sections of
rail were lying on the bottom, several more were scattered on
the ground and one was propped against the end of the trailer

as if whoever had been in the act of loading or unloading had abandoned it in a hurry. There was no sign of Fernand.

Melissa stopped short, uncertain what to do. Perhaps he had stepped behind a tree to relieve himself. If she went on, there might be an embarrassing confrontation. She stood for several seconds, fingering her camera, staring up at the trees, glancing down the path and listening for the sound of trampling in the undergrowth that would herald Fernand's return to his task. Nothing. No human movement. Apart from bird calls, the rustling of leaves in the wind and the faint sound of rushing water in the distance, there was silence.

Turning, she found Fernand at her side, as if he had risen out of the earth. She gave a startled gasp; he laid a warning finger on his lips and put a hand on her arm.

"Were you seen? Were you followed?" he asked in a whisper.

Melissa shook her head, suppressing a smile. "No," she whispered back.

"Are you sure?" His grip tightened a shade.

Melissa glanced down at the powerful fingers with the powdering of sawdust round the nails and then up into the fierce black eyes, and her heart began to thump. No need to be scared, just play along with him, she told herself. As long as he believes you're on his side while he acts out his fantasy, he won't harm you. But if he gets it into his head that you're a spy . . .

She glanced back down the path and then leaned forward so that her lips almost touched his ear. "I took every precaution . . . I saw no one."

"It is well." He thought for a moment, then tugged at her arm. "We must take no risks . . . let us go to the refuge. If anyone should come, we shall hear them, but they will never find us. Tread quietly!"

Before Melissa realised what was happening, he had led her off the path and in among the trees. He moved lightly over the rough ground, dodging round bushes, avoiding every loose stone and broken twig. Melissa recalled Juliette's words: "He could slip through the forest as silently as a cat."

Hardly aware of what she was doing, she tried to do the same, thankful that her shoes had soft soles.

Soon there were no more trees and the sound of tumbling water grew louder. A wooden rail at waist height barred their way; they must be very close to the edge of the cliff. Fernand let go of Melissa's hand, vaulted over the rail and beckoned urgently to her to follow.

It was her opportunity to escape from this crazy and possibly dangerous game of let's pretend. But even as the idea occurred to her, she dismissed it; from the athletic way Fernand had cleared the rail it was likely that his legs were as strong and muscular as his sinewy arms and he would probably catch her long before she reached the house. Her flight would have convinced him that she was on her way to betray him and who knew what it would enter his confused mind to do to her? Without a word, she clambered over the rail, rather awkwardly because of the camera dangling from her wrist.

Now the sound of the river seemed to come from beneath their feet. They must be almost at the edge of the cliff. She remembered Alain Gebrec's warning that parts of it were unstable; a vision of the shattered body of Wolfgang Klein swam before her eyes, her stomach contracted and her legs turned to cotton wool. When, without warning, Fernand dropped on to all fours beside a huge outcrop of bare rock, she all but fell on top of him. He glanced back as if looking for signs of pursuit.

"We must move quickly now, before we are seen," he whispered and began to crawl forward round the rock. His head and shoulders disappeared; only his backside and his long legs in the coarse blue trousers were visible. Melissa felt a wild desire to laugh at the thought of herself, a sane Englishwoman in her forties, playing a sort of eighteenth-century game of cops and robbers with a simple-minded Frenchman suffering from delusions. It was utterly ludicrous. It scared her to death.

Fernand had completely vanished, giving her a second chance to escape, yet, almost without hesitation, she began to follow. She felt certain that he intended her no harm and her fear began to recede, its place taken by a surge of excitement and anticipation. She was being led to a place that many people had heard about, but only a handful of desperate, hunted souls had actually seen.

Reaching the point where Fernand had disappeared, she crawled round the angle of rock. Before her was a narrow ledge, scarcely more than a metre wide. On the left was the overhanging face of the cliff, beneath which it would be impossible to stand upright. On the right was a sheer drop into nothing.

"Don't look down. Come to me!"

Almost transfixed with terror, Melissa dragged her eyes from the edge. Fernand was crouched in a cleft in the rock, a little above her and less than three metres away. Her entire body was shaking, yet the sight of his brown arm reaching out towards her and the confident ring in his voice gave her courage. She began inching towards him, hugging the face of the cliff, praying that the rock beneath her would hold. She almost wept with relief as his strong fingers closed round her hand and guided her to the safety of a broad platform of stone, where at last it was possible to stand upright. He bowed ceremonially and gestured into the black cavern behind them.

"Welcome to the secret refuge!" he said proudly.

Seven

A FEW YEARS PREVIOUSLY, MELISSA had been in the Cévennes on a motoring holiday with her parents-in-law. Margaret and Arthur Craig were, strictly speaking, her parents-out-of-law, since their son, Guy, had died in a car accident without even knowing that she was pregnant, let alone considering marriage. Distraught with grief and shock, rejected by her own mother and father, Melissa had been taken by the warm-hearted Craigs into their own home; the small matter of illegitimacy had been discreetly dealt with by a statutory change of name and a wedding-ring, and the bereaved parents had found consolation for the loss of their only child in caring for his son.

It was during that holiday that the notion had first come to Melissa of setting a novel in the region. They had been visiting Trabuc and their guide had made reference to the use of the famous grottoes as a meeting-place by the Camisards. At the time, the term meant nothing to her, but she had been intrigued, read the references to the religious wars in the regional guide-book and mentally filed the information for future use.

The grottoes themselves she had found disappointing. She had been reminded of a school outing, with the guide leading the party in a crocodile down man-made stairways protected by iron railings, stopping every few yards to bombard his audience with statistics or manipulate the complex lighting and communication system. There had been high spots, of course—particularly the *grand couloir*, with its subterranean lake and its vast stalactites and overhanging the uncannily still green water—but the presence of so much technology and the chattering tourists had the effect of reducing a natural wonder to the level of a modern theme park.

She recalled trying to imagine the feelings of the fugitives in those far-off times as they waited—perhaps round a guttering lamp, perhaps in total darkness—while a rapacious enemy combed the countryside above their heads, thirsty for blood. For once, her imagination had failed her, stifled by the chorus of predictable questions, the exclamations of wonder and admiration, the admonitions of anxious parents to overventuresome children.

Now, standing beside Fernand in the mouth of a gash in the cliff, with the river raging beneath their feet and an ink-dark cavern ahead, she experienced a tingle of awe and anticipation that swept away the fear and the vertigo.

"Wait here a moment!" Fernand disappeared into the cave; an instant later there was a click and a powerful torch drove a beam into the darkness. Slowly, it moved upwards among jagged folds of rock hanging like petrified curtains above their heads; it swung to the right and travelled downwards, glistening on a myriad crystalline particles in the rock face; it moved across to the left and traced a black line where the stone floor ended abruptly just short of the far wall.

"Never go over there," warned Fernand. "That way, it is death!" Like a pebble in a well-shaft, the words fell into the void and then came rushing back from invisible walls, echoing above the roar of the water: "it is death . . . is death . . . is death!"

Melissa closed her eyes and swallowed the knot in her throat.

"I'll remember," she said faintly.

"Come!" He moved forward, shining the torch ahead of them.

Glancing over her shoulder, Melissa saw that the entrance had already shrunk to a slit. With an effort, she drove from her mind the thought of the return journey, filling it instead with the experience of the moment, absorbing the sights, the impressions and sensations, storing them in her brain, wishing she had a notebook with her so that she could record them in all their vividness and immediacy.

Fernand stopped and set the torch upright on a ledge. There was a scraping sound, the flare of a match and a whiff of paraffin, then the soft yellow light of a storm lantern replaced the harsh electric beam.

"Now, we can penetrate to the refuge itself!" His voice was hushed, almost reverent. Melissa felt as if she were about to enter a church.

They moved beneath an archway of stalactites. There were no corresponding accretions on the floor, no moisture dripped from overhead. Aeons ago, the waters must have taken a different path and the men who discovered the cave had chipped away the stalagmites to make a passage into the gallery beyond, the gallery where Melissa and Fernand now stood.

She stared incredulously about her. The place was furnished; there were chairs, a deal table, a couple of mattresses. There was even a worn rug spread on the uneven stones and a heap of blankets and pillows.

For a full minute, neither of them spoke. The sound of the water had become muted; like background music, it receded from consciousness, becoming almost a part of the stillness and the silence.

Fernand set his lantern on the table and indicated one of the chairs. "Will you sit down, Madame?" He might have been receiving her in the best parlour on a Sunday afternoon. Facing him across the bleached wooden plank, Melissa became aware of an extraordinary change in his manner. His dark eyes no longer burned with fanaticism, nor were they watchful or mistrustful, but warm, friendly, almost humorous. "I regret, I cannot offer any refreshment, Madame," he said with a smile. "I was not expecting a visitor!"

"Please, don't apologise," she murmured, wondering if this was another phase of the game, yet sensing that it was not. Her pulse rate had slowed to somewhere near normal; she sat back in the creaking wooden chair in a deliberate effort to appear relaxed, and returned his smile. "I would never have believed such a place existed," she continued, glancing around the cave. "When was it discovered?"

"It has been known to our people for centuries. The Camisards took refuge here from the Catholic armies . . . and the Maquis used it as a hiding place for their weapons during the Occupation."

"And the Germans never found it?"

"Never. Sometimes, when the Gestapo came in search of one of our refugees, the men of the Maquis were able to conceal him here until the danger was past."

"Your refugees?" Melissa remembered what Rose had said. "Do you mean foreigners?"

"But yes. Before the war, they came from many lands to escape from the Nazis—Czechs, Poles, Hungarians, Yugoslavs, even some Germans who were against Hitler. Many went to Paris to find work, but after the fall of France they began making their way to the cities of the south, where they could live in safety. But, in 1942, the Wermacht moved into the whole of our country and things changed."

"And the refugees fled to the mountains?"

"Not at first. At first, things were not so bad. The Germans were more interested at that time in hunting Communists, but later came the Gestapo and then things became much more dangerous. It was then that the city pastors began asking their brethren in the mountain villages to organise sanctuary for the refugees. We gave them food and shelter, and in return they worked on our farms, helped tend the flocks, bring in the harvest . . ."

"You mean, they lived here openly? Didn't anyone inform on them?"

Fernand drew himself erect in his chair and lifted his head.

"That is not our way," he said simply. "The people of the Cévennes have always given refuge to the oppressed."

"And they lived here in safety throughout the war?"

"Alas, not always in safety. Among the so-called refugees, there were spies sent by the Germans. One such betrayed some of our best men."

A shadow fell over his face and he became silent, as if at some disturbing memory. Recalling the tragedy of which Juliette had spoken and which had had such a devastating effect on his mind, Melissa felt uneasy. She sensed that it might take but a tiny jolt to send him back into his fantasy world. She glanced at her watch; already it was well past four and Iris would be expecting her at five.

"Perhaps . . ." she began, but Fernand was speaking again. It was as if she was no longer there; his eyes were unfocused and his voice expressionless.

"Many died because of his treachery, some of them his own countrymen . . . and Roland . . . Roland!" His voice broke and a spasm of pain contorted his face.

Overwhelmed with compassion, Melissa put out a hand and laid it on his arm. A single tear fell on it before he regained control and said with quiet pride, "The traitor escaped our justice, but our refuge remained a secret."

"Thank you for bringing me here," she said. "I feel very privileged."

"I bring you because I know you to be one of us."

The final words, and something in the tone of his voice, sent a chill up Melissa's spine. Up to now she had been so enthralled by the adventure that, despite being clad in only a cotton shirt and slacks, she had hardly noticed the cold. She shivered and rubbed her arms, trying to conceal her rising agitation.

Fernand stood up. "Forgive me, Madame. I regret, the central heating does not work!" He was back in the present, outwardly rational, with a flash of wry humour. "We must return."

He picked up the lantern and led the way. When they reached the next chamber he extinguished it and exchanged it for the torch. In silence, they made their way back to where the sunlight pierced the cliff. The cleft in the rock made a dramatic framework to the distant mountains, reminding Melissa of her initial reason for this expedition. She glanced at the automatic camera attached to her wrist; all this time she had been clutching it without giving it a thought.

Leaving the torch on its ledge, Fernand moved towards the entrance and then stopped, half-turned and gestured to the far wall and the sinister shadow that marked the emptiness below.

"Remember my warning, if you should ever have need to return here."

"I'll remember," faltered Melissa, aware once more of the sound of the river echoing round the cavern. Her head swam; she shut her eyes and pressed herself against the wall, fighting to steady herself for the return trip, struggling to contain an urge to vomit.

When she opened her eyes, Fernand had gone. She peered out and saw him crawling on hands and knees along the ledge. It took more courage than she knew she possessed to follow him. With clenched teeth, keeping her head low and her eyes half-closed, she hugged the cliff-face and inched her way along. Her outstretched hand disturbed a fragment of loose rock, sending it tumbling over the precipice; for one hideous moment she fancied the entire ledge was on the move and about to hurl her into the chasm. When at last she was able to stand upright in safety, her knees buckled and her body was drenched with sweat.

She heard the distant sound of the tractor starting up, which meant that Fernand had no intention of waiting for her. It was no matter, she knew the way back. She stopped for a moment to brush the dust from her hands and clothes and set off back to the house. It was a quarter to five when she reached it.

There was still no sign of the others. Melissa slipped indoors to wash her face and hands; it was important to appear normal, as any hint of agitation would be pounced on by Iris and lead to a cross-examination. She went back to the car, put away the camera, fetched her book and settled in a chair by the pool to wait. A few minutes later she heard the tractor clattering into the yard. Through the archway she saw Fernand jump down, open the door of the shed, then climb up again and drive in. She wondered if he would tell Juliette of their visit to the refuge. Perhaps the memory was already buried in some corner of his mind.

She began idly turning the pages of the book. Moments later a shadow fell across it. Philippe Bonard was standing beside her.

"You permit?" He gestured toward an empty chair.

"Of course."

"Thank you." He pulled the chair round to face hers and sat down.

It was easy to see why Iris found the man so attractive. He had a magnetic quality which would have drawn attention even without the good looks, the hand-made clothes and impeccable grooming. It was impossible not to respond to his smile.

"Where are your students?" she asked. "Surely you haven't deserted them?"

"By no means. They are in the library, preparing for tomorrow's exercise."

"What exercise is that?"

"I have made arrangements with certain people in the neighbourhood—a pastor, a doctor, business people, a local historian and so on—to receive my students from time to time and talk about their work. It helps to give my students"—he reiterated the words with an almost fatherly affection—"an insight into the minds, the outlook, the culture of the French people . . . and, of course, it provides excellent opportunities for them to improve their French." Hands and shoulders swam to and fro, emphasising each point.

"I'm sure it's very useful experience," said Melissa politely.

"It is a good principle, you know," Bonard continued, warming to his theme, "especially for mature students, to leave the classroom and work in the environment." His eyes shone with the enthusiasm of a man who has found his vocation. "Your good friend Iris, she shares my philosophy. Each day, she takes her class out of doors to experience Nature and learn from her wisdom. Today, for example, they are down by the river, observing the wildlife, the vegetation, the reflections in the water." He sat back in his chair, beaming with pride as he added, "The pure water of our French rivers is unsurpassed in the entire world!"

"You almost make me wish I had enrolled on your course," said Melissa, with a certain lack of sincerity. Patriotism was all very well, but she felt this was going over the top. When mounted on his hobby-horse, Philippe Bonard had the makings of a thundering bore.

"It would have been a privilege to have you as a student . . . ah, but your French is already of so excellent a quality . . . and you are occupied with your researches. Have you had a profitable day?"

"Very, thank you," she said, wondering what his reaction would be if he knew how she had spent the past hour. "By the way, you mentioned a local historian. Would that by chance be Antoinette Gebrec, Alain's mother?"

"But yes! She is one of several on whose services I may call from time to time. You know her?"

"I met her today. She has very kindly been helping me with my research."

"But that is so delightful! Alain will be enchanted when he hears." He glanced round as the throb of a diesel engine sounded in the yard. "There he comes now. He went to fetch Iris and her class in the minibus."

"He seems to have been quite badly affected by the tragedy," said Melissa. "Was Wolfgang Klein a close friend?"

Bonard waved a dismissive hand. "They were drinking companions, that is all. But Alain, he is so sensitive, he has taken the affair to heart. He insisted on being the one to break the news to the young man's family, despite his own distress." He spoke almost apologetically, like a father excusing the whims of a favourite child. He got to his feet. "Will you kindly excuse me for a moment? I must go and enquire if the artists have had a successful afternoon."

He went to meet them as they scrambled from the bus, hand extended in welcome, greeting them individually by name and exchanging a few words with each one. He spent a short time in conversation with Iris, who looked at him in a way that made Melissa want to shake her. Eventually she managed to catch her friend's eye; Iris waved and mouthed, "Five minutes," before following the others into the house. Gebrec returned from putting the bus away and Bonard took him by the arm and led him to the terrace.

"Your charming mother has been helping Melissa with her researches," he said. "Is not that delightful?"

"Really?" Gebrec smiled politely, but Melissa had the impression that the announcement gave him no particular pleasure. "I did not know you were acquainted with Maman."

Briefly, Melissa explained how the meeting had come about. "She very kindly invited me to lunch and she has given me a lot of useful information."

"I am pleased to hear it." Again, the flat tone that seemed to contradict his words. His eye fell on the book on her lap and his expression darkened. "She did not recommend that!" he exclaimed.

"No, I found it for myself," she said, trying not to show her irritation. Mentally, she was demanding: who do you people think you are? First your mother, now you, trying to dictate what I should read. Aloud, she said: "I have your mother's book on the Camisards as well, of course—that is the period that interests me particularly—but I want to learn about more recent history as well."

"Maman is writing an account of that period. It will be much better than this . . . rubbish!"

"I'm sure your mother's book will be excellent," said Melissa crisply. "When it is published, I shall order a copy. It will be interesting to make comparisons."

Gebrec was not placated. "My advice to you is not to waste your time reading that one," he said rudely.

"Alain! Melissa will make her own decision about what she will read." The mild reproach in Bonard's tone did not match the anger in his eyes. Gebrec stared coldly back at him and Melissa sensed that they were on the verge of a confrontation, but Bonard's attention was diverted by the approach of the members of his class, who had begun to emerge from the house. At their head was Dieter Erdle; Melissa guessed from the gleam of amusement in his eye that he had overheard the rather heated exchange.

"I see you have been studying local history, Melissa," he observed, indicating the book. "It is a fascinating subject, is it not?"

He had not asked if he might use her first name, but it seemed to be the practice here and she had no reason to ob-

ject. "It certainly is," she agreed. "Rose tells me it is one of
your interests."

"That is so. I have learned many things I did not know
about events in this region." The glance he directed at Gebrec
held a hint of malice and was greeted with an angry frown.
"Perhaps we can have a talk some time?"

"Yes, why not?" It might be interesting; he was obviously
intelligent and well-educated, and the fact that both Dora and
Iris had written him off as a fortune-hunter caused her no
particular misgivings.

"Tomorrow?" he suggested. "We missed you at lunch
today . . . we understood you might be joining us."

"Philippe very kindly gave me an open invitation, but today I was in Alès, as the guest of Alain's mother." She half-
turned towards Gebrec, who was still standing beside her,
glowering.

"Ah, yes, the famous local historian. But that is not one of
her works, I think." Erdle indicated the book that had caused
the recent controversy, still clutched in Melissa's hand; now,
he was smiling, openly taunting Gebrec. "You'll find that interesting reading, Melissa. There is one passage in particular
. . . may I?"

He reached out for the book, but before Melissa could give
it to him, Gebrec snatched it from her.

"It is rubbish, I tell you!" He flung the book to the ground
and stormed back towards the house, leaving Melissa open-
mouthed.

"Tut-tut! *Böse Junge!*" murmured Erdle with undisguised
glee. He retrieved the book and handed it back to her. "We
will talk more tomorrow. Your friend awaits you, I think," he
added, nodding towards the courtyard where Iris was standing
beside Melissa's car, and speaking for the first time in faultless English instead of French.

"You're quite a linguist," she said.

"It is necessary for business purposes that I speak the
major languages of Europe. I have tried to persuade our excit-
able friend that he should do the same." His smile was contemptuous. "Until tomorrow!"

Eight

"SO WHAT HAVE YOU BEEN DOING TO-
day?" asked Iris.

Melissa fastened her safety belt and reached for the igni-
tion. "Having lunch with Madame Gebrec." She backed the
Golf round and headed for the exit. Jack Hammond, who was
walking towards his car, smiled and raised a hand in greeting
as they passed. "How's he getting on?" she asked.

"Very well. A real nature-lover ... has an original eye."
After a pause, Iris added casually, "Invited us both for a drink
after dinner."

"That's nice. Did you accept?"

"Didn't see why not. You seemed all for it. What's Madame Gebrec like?"

"Absolutely charming, bubbling over with enthusiasm."

Iris grunted. "More than you can say for her son."

"He is a down-beat sort of character, isn't he?"

"Perhaps he takes after his father. Did you meet him too?"

"Hardly. He was killed in the war."

Iris tilted her head back and yawned. "Learn anything useful from Mum?"

"Oh yes, she's very clued up about the Camisards. She's
writing another book, by the way, about the Occupation."
Melissa gave a chuckle. "I'd unwittingly bought one by a ri-
val historian and you should have seen the way she turned
her nose up at it. Her son reacted even more strongly—he
was downright rude."

"Professional jealousy, I suppose."

"I guess so. I got the impression that there's one bit they particularly object to. Dieter Erdle must have read it—he seems to know what it is."

"Blowing the gaff about a black marketeer in the family?" suggested Iris with a mischievous grin.

"That's a thought. I've only glanced through the book, but it contains a lot of personal recollections. Maybe some people took the chance of paying off old scores."

"Not easy after so long to guarantee accuracy. Where is it anyway?"

"The book? In the glove compartment." They had reached the *auberge*; Melissa turned into the car park and switched off the engine.

Iris rummaged. "Your camera's here as well. Want it?"

"Might as well. The view from our balcony's worth a shot."

They went up to their room. Melissa kicked off her shoes, dumped her handbag on the floor, flopped on her bed and closed her eyes. It had been quite a day.

Iris was moving around, opening and closing drawers. "Hullo, what happened to this?" she demanded suddenly.

Melissa opened her eyes. "What happened to what?"

"Your camera case." Iris held it in front of her nose, showing the scratches and scuff marks it had collected during the nerve-racking passage to Fernand's cave. The memory made her heart skip a beat.

"I . . . I must have dropped it," she said weakly.

"Now pull the other one! You've been up to something. And how did you get *them* so filthy?" Like a heat-seeking missile, Iris's gaze homed on the knees of Melissa's blue cotton slacks and the smudges of grey dust which had resisted her hasty brushing. "Taken up bird-watching?"

"I went up towards the belvedere to take some pictures, that's all. I . . . tripped on a rock and fell over." She wasn't in the habit of lying to Iris and knew she wasn't making a particularly good job of it.

Iris cocked a sceptical eyebrow. "Saw the nutter, didn't you?"

"If you mean Fernand, he was working up there, yes. He didn't try to rape me, if that's what's worrying you!"

Iris ignored the feeble attempt at humour. "You promised you'd stay away from him," she scolded.

"For goodness' sake, Iris, stop banging on about Fernand. We had a very interesting chat and he was as normal as could be. There's no harm in him at all."

"That's what you think. Never know what goes on in a nutter's mind. Don't say I didn't warn you!" Iris yanked her leotard from a drawer and headed for the bathroom. "Going to get changed and do my yoga."

"I'll have a shower when you've finished in there."

With the noise of the water splashing round her head and drumming into the bath, Melissa found herself reliving the time she had spent with Fernand in that dark, echoing cavern. Despite her confident assertion, she knew that Iris had a point. It was not only physical wounds that left scars; damage to the mind could throb and fester in secret over many years, and some flash of memory could trigger unexpected, possibly violent reactions.

Yet Fernand had spoken openly of the war and of his brother's death without showing a trace of rancour or a desire for revenge. She recalled, with a lump in her throat, the slow tears gathering, glistening in the light of the lantern as they slid down the furrows in his cheeks. There had been suffering, but no hatred, in those eyes.

Just the same, she had experienced an uneasy moment when he spoke of the unnamed traitor who had brought about his brother's death. There was no doubt that the tragedy was as fresh in his mind as the day it had happened. So, what if Wolfgang Klein's innocent enquiries about hidden caves and grottoes had churned up bitter memories of accounts still unsettled? Hadn't Monsieur Gauthier hinted as much, spoken of how Fernand was always "looking over his shoulder for Germans"? And what about Dieter Erdle—could he possibly also represent a threat in the mind of someone suffering that kind of delusion? Should she forget her promise to Juliette and tell Hassan what she knew?

"No!" She spoke the word aloud as she turned off the water and began rubbing herself furiously with a towel. Fernand had witnessed death, but he was not a violent man. She recalled his sister's words: "Even in our childish games, he would never be the one to take a life." If she were to break her word, the big gendarme would go rushing off to his commandant with his "fresh evidence," demanding to be allowed to treat Klein's death as murder; he would harass and bully brother and sister, tearing open wounds that at best were only half-healed, forcing them to relive the pain and terror of the past.

"Not if I have anything to do with it," she muttered as she plugged in her hair-dryer. "Fernand might have the odd screw loose, but I'd swear he'd never hurt anyone."

At dinner that evening, Rose and Dora were full of their "projects" and the appointments arranged for the following morning. It was obvious that Bonard had been to considerable trouble to arrange for the members of his class to meet people with similar interests to their own. Dora had asked about sporting facilities in the region and been promised an interview with the manager of a leisure complex in Alès; Rose, who belonged to an amateur drama group in Carshalton, was to meet the director of a forthcoming performance of *"son et lumière"* whose office was in Anduze. Since they would be going in different directions and at different times, Dora would use their car and another member of the group would give Rose a lift.

"It all sounds highly organised," said Melissa, piling whipped cream on her *fromage blanc* and pretending not to hear Iris's scathing comments about cholesterol. It had been a good dinner and the *réserve maison* had sent pleasant messages around her system, signifying that after the adventures of the day, all was now well.

"Oh, it is," agreed Dora. "I must say, Philippe Bonard has some excellent ideas. He deserves to make a success of his school."

"Glad you think so." Iris glowed as if she had received a personal compliment.

"I imagine Dieter Erdle is doing some sort of history project?" said Melissa unthinkingly between mouthfuls.

Dora stiffened and made no comment, but Rose reacted with enthusiasm. "No, actually, he's got a meeting with the manager of some factory or other. He's got to polish up his business French for his job, you know. History is just a hobby for him."

"Yes, you told me. As a matter of fact, I was talking to him briefly this afternoon and we agreed we'd have a chat some time. Alain Gebrec seemed less than enthusiastic, though."

"Why was that, do you think?"

"Some disagreement as to whose version of something or other is the authentic one. Alain was getting quite hot under the collar and Dieter seemed to be winding him up on purpose."

"Oh, I'm sure he didn't mean it." Rose was quick to defend her young admirer.

Dora sniffed disdainfully. "I'm quite sure he did. He's that sort of person." Rose flushed with annoyance and seemed about to make a sharp retort.

"We have to go," said Iris, getting to her feet. "Come on, Melissa, I told Jack half-past eight and it's nearly that already."

"Made a hash of that, didn't I?" said Melissa when they got outside.

"You did give things a bit of a stir," Iris agreed. "Shouldn't let it worry you. They've probably had words before now."

"I suspect they'll be having a few more."

"More than likely."

After the business of the day and the more important business of the evening meal, the inhabitants of Roziac were enjoying a few hours of leisure in the open air. On their way to the Lion d'Or, where they were to meet Jack, Iris and Melissa passed old women knitting and gossiping in doorways or leaning out of windows, young women sauntering along with babies in perambulators, and leather-clad youths astride shiny motorbikes parked at the kerbside while they chatted up their mini-skirted girls.

In the central square a game of *boules* was in progress under the critical gaze of a group of shirt-sleeved men in baggy trousers, cropped heads enveloped in the pungent smoke from their Gauloises, glasses clutched in brawny fists. In between swigs they expressed approval or disparagement of the play with drawn-out exclamations of "Ooooh!" and "Aaaah!" and—from those whose hands were not otherwise encumbered—the occasional burst of applause. Moths fluttered in the light of lamps hanging from the trees as if dancing to the soft, rhythmic jingle of the cicadas.

"Picturesque!" commented Iris. "Unspoilt, too. Not like the Côte d'Azur."

"It's a lot colder than the Côte d'Azur in winter," Melissa reminded her as they strolled on.

On the terrace of the Lion d'Or, Jack was sitting alone at one of the round white tables, a spare chair tilted forward on either side of him. When he spied his guests, he jumped to his feet and called a greeting, straightening the chairs and holding them one after the other to steady them on the uneven gravel while they sat down. Melissa had the distinct impression that he held Iris's chair for a fraction longer than her own.

He asked what they would like to drink and they asked for coffee, declining his offer of liqueurs. They sat sipping the strong, dark brew and chatted idly about nothing in particular, enjoying the warm velvety air, the star-dusted turquoise sky slowly changing to amethyst and the heady-sweet scent from a clump of yellow broom. Immediately below the terrace was the Mauzère, wider and deeper here than at Les Châtaigniers and flowing less swiftly. A flotilla of ducks paddled past, their wakes forming arrowheads on the darkening surface of the water.

"How's that for one of 'Nature's Designs'?" suggested Jack.

Iris gave a nod of approval. "Funny you should say that. Thought I might make the next course 'Patterns of Light and Shade.' "

"You're giving another course?" Jack leaned forward, his eyes alive with interest. "When?"

"Not sure. Philippe mentioned October, but it's not definite. Would you come?"

"Sure, if I can. I might bring one or two others from my art club. When I tell them what a great teacher you are, they'll be dead keen to join."

Iris beamed. "That'd be splendid. Philippe'd be delighted." Her train of thought was now firmly targeted on Bonard. She turned to Melissa. "Has he said anything to you about giving a creative writing course?" she asked. "I did suggest . . ."

"No, and I doubt if he will." Melissa set down her empty cup and began fiddling with her necklace. She felt suddenly irritable. "When it comes to purveying language and literature, he's only interested in the home-grown variety," she declared. "He's very charming and all that, but he really is an out-and-out chauvinist. Besides," she added, cutting short a protest from Iris, "I doubt if he'd be willing to pay the sort of fee Joe Martin would insist on."

"That agent of yours is a money-grubber," Iris complained. "Can't you stretch a point for a friend?"

Melissa was about to retort that as she had only known Bonard for three days he could hardly be described as a friend of hers, when a surprised, "Well, what do you know?" from Jack made them both glance round. Dieter Erdle had just arrived with Rose Kettle clinging to his arm. They waved across before making for an empty table in the far corner. They did not immediately sit down, but leaned on the low parapet and gazed out over the river and the mountains, she with her head inclined towards his, he with a hand resting on her shoulder.

"Rosie and the toy-boy!" commented Iris. "Bet Dora's fuming!"

Jack gave a disapproving shake of the head. "A young chap like that shouldn't play on an older woman's susceptibilities."

"Maybe he really likes her," suggested Melissa. She thought such a possibility unlikely, but she was feeling perverse. She had a shrewd notion what Iris's views on the subject would be—a notion that lady promptly confirmed.

"Rubbish!" she said stoutly, with a glance of approval for Jack. "Agree absolutely. No business to lead her on like that."

Melissa, detecting a spark of comradeship between them, decided to fan it a little. "He may not be leading her on. Young men do sometimes fall for older women," she said.

"Sometimes," Jack agreed, "but not in this case, I think."

"You can't be sure."

"Course he can. You're quite right, Jack. Tell me," Iris leaned forward in her seat, "this 'Patterns of Light and Shade' thing . . . do you think . . . ?"

Melissa sat back and let her mind wander elsewhere while they talked shop.

When Iris announced that it was time for them to return, Jack insisted on walking them back. After a few minutes Dieter's car overtook them; when they arrived at the *auberge*, it was parked in the shadows a short distance away with two dim shapes close together in the front seats. Nobody commented; after brief thanks and farewells, Jack departed and the two friends went indoors.

Madame Gauthier was perched on a stool at the reception desk, making up her accounts. They were exchanging goodnights when Rose came in looking flushed and happy, but a trifle agitated.

"Had a good evening?" Iris's voice was heavily laced with irony, but Rose either did not notice or was too excited to be offended.

"Oh, lively, thank you!" She looked enquiringly from one to the other. "I don't suppose . . . I mean . . . could I possibly have a word with you?"

Iris's response was immediate and uncompromising. "If it's advice about your love life you want, pack him up before he ditches you!"

Melissa saw Rose wince. "Iris," she admonished, "let Rose tell us what she wants to talk about."

"I . . . I . . ." Rose was floundering.

Iris stifled a yawn. "If you don't mind, I'll leave you to it.

No need for two agony aunts." She marched down the passage towards the staircase.

"Don't mind her—she doesn't mean to be hurtful," said Melissa. "How about seeing if there's anyone in the salon? We could talk there."

They sat on a couch in the empty room and Rose stared at her feet. "Your friend doesn't approve of me, does she?" she said. "She thinks the same as Dora, that Dieter's only interested in me because I've got money. But it isn't like that, he really cares!"

"How can you be sure of that?"

"I just know!" Rose lifted her head and looked Melissa full in the face. Despite the lines round her mouth and the flecks of grey in her hair, there was a bloom in her cheeks and her eyes shone like those of a girl who has fallen in love for the first time. Melissa's heart went out to her. If only it were true.

"How long have you known him?" she asked gently.

"Ten days. This is our second week at the centre. That's the problem . . . you see, Dieter's enrolled for a third week and . . . I'd like to stay on as well."

"But aren't you and Dora supposed to be visiting friends in Antibes next week?"

"I don't really want to go. They're her friends, not mine, and they talk about nothing but golf. They bore me stiff."

"I thought you were keen on golf too."

"I'm not half so keen as she is—she's absolutely dedicated. You've probably noticed how she spends every spare minute practising her putting. Anyway, I'm not all that good—I just play to keep her company. She's . . . not an easy person in some ways. Apart from her golf, she hasn't got many interests. I persuaded her to come on this course because I thought it would be a change for us both."

"I see."

"I just don't know what to do. I'd much rather stay here another week, but I don't suppose she'd hear of it."

"Well, if that's what you really want, you'll have to tell her. You could always join her later."

"That would be the sensible thing, wouldn't it? The trouble is, I know she wouldn't go without me."

"She does rather manage your life, doesn't she? Or perhaps I shouldn't have said that . . ." Melissa half expected a vigorous defence of Dora's protective friendship, but the reaction was precisely the opposite.

"How right you are! I let her share my house because she could only afford a tiny flat of her own, and she bosses me around as if she's the one with the money."

Melissa was beginning to wish the conversation had never started; the last thing she wanted was to become embroiled in a dispute between two women she hardly knew, but Rose was looking her squarely in the eye as if demanding a response to her outburst.

"Well, it seems to me you'll have to talk it over with her," she said, determined to be non-partisan. "After all, if Dora wanted to change her plans, you'd expect her to discuss them with you, wouldn't you?"

It was doubtful if Rose heard the last part of her remark. She was on her feet, wearing a look of steely determination that sat oddly on her girlish features.

"You're right. I'm going to tell her this minute what I've decided. Thank you for your advice, Melissa. Goodnight." She almost ran from the room, as if afraid that her newly found resolve would melt away if she did not immediately put it into practice.

Melissa made her way slowly upstairs, wondering whether or not she had inadvertently made matters worse. She found Iris in her pyjamas, sitting cross-legged on her bed and scribbling in a notebook. She was looking distinctly pleased with herself.

"Some ideas for 'Patterns of Light and Shade,' " she explained without looking up.

"I noticed you and Jack brain-storming. Did he come up with anything useful?"

"Quite a bit. Can't wait to talk to Philippe." She put notebook and pencil aside. "Was I right?"

"About what?"

"You know what. Rosie and her German gigolo. Wanted you to tell her to follow her heart, or some such rubbish."

"You're a fine one to talk."

Iris's smug expression vanished. "Meaning?"

"Meaning you're just as soft about your Philippe as Rose is over Dieter."

I wish I hadn't said that, thought Melissa, seeing Iris flinch. The two cases are quite different. Iris has known Philippe for quite a long time. Some people would say they had a lot in common and no doubt in some ways they have . . . except I'm sure that Philippe . . .

Iris was staring in front of her with a set expression, making no response. After a minute she uncrossed her legs, stood up and made her way past Melissa to the bathroom without meeting her eye. There followed several minutes of unusually energetic teeth-scrubbing, loo-flushing and hand-washing before she returned, lay down and switched off her bedside lamp, still without uttering a word.

In an effort to mend her fences, Melissa asked, "So what are you doing tomorrow?"

"Taking the class to the bamboo forest," muttered Iris with seeming reluctance.

"Well, that should bamboozle them."

It wasn't much of a joke and it didn't get a laugh. It didn't get any response at all. Feeling weary and depressed, Melissa got ready for bed. The evening had started so well and ended so badly.

She wondered if things were any better between Rose and Dora; if anything, she thought, they were probably worse. As she switched off her own lamp she called, "Goodnight," but Iris did not reply. "Oh blast!" she mumbled into her pillow. "Tomorrow's going to be one hell of a day."

Nine

MELISSA SLEPT FITFULLY AND AWOKE
with a headache. Iris was already up and splashing in the
bath. When she emerged, she responded with a grunt to Melissa's, "Good morning," and began wrestling with the bar
that controlled the window shutters. Mechanical things were
not her strong point; after watching her for a couple of minutes, Melissa could stand it no longer. She got out of bed and
marched across the room.

"Here, let me do that before you bust a gut!"

Iris relinquished the handle without argument. Melissa began turning it and the heavy metal blind inched upwards, admitting a broadening band of sparkling light. Outside, the
early sun slanted across the mountains and filtered through
the delicate green tracery of the forest.

"Isn't that bliss!" Forgetting for a moment the strained atmosphere of the previous evening, Melissa slid back the glass
door and stepped out on to the balcony. It was only seven
o'clock, yet the air was mild enough to stand there in her
nightdress. "Just come and look at these clouds—they've got
to be one of Nature's perfect designs!"

"Hmm?" Iris, seated at the dressing-table, paused in the act
of brushing her short, mouse-brown hair, glanced briefly
through the window and turned back to the mirror without
comment.

Melissa sighed and went into the bathroom. When she
came out, Iris was on the balcony doing her morning routine
of breathing exercises, straight-backed, the sleeves of her cot-

ton robe falling away from her thin arms as they rose and fell in time with the rhythmic and somewhat noisy intake and expulsion of air. By the time she had finished, Melissa was fully dressed and busy with her make-up.

"I'm going for a walk before breakfast," she said as Iris stepped past her to reach the wardrobe. "I'll see you on the terrace."

Iris, rummaging for clothes, muttered, "Right," without showing her face.

This was ridiculous. They'd snapped at one another before—more often than not, Melissa recalled, over the involvement of one with a man considered unsuitable by the other—but any irritation had always been short-lived and apologies barely necessary. This time, it seemed, was different.

"Look, Iris, I'm sorry . . ." she began.

"Forget it."

"I didn't mean to hurt your feelings."

"Don't want to talk about it."

"All right then. See you later."

There was no reply.

Perhaps it hadn't been a good idea after all to come on this trip together. They weren't used to the cheek-by-jowl contact it entailed; the notion of living in the state of interdependence that bound Dora Lavender and Rose Kettle would have horrified them both. As next-door neighbours in their snug Cotswold cottages, they enjoyed a comfortable, undemanding relationship: discussing their work, exchanging local gossip or swapping recipes and gardening tips over coffee-breaks and the occasional meal, but always respecting each other's privacy, never invading each other's space.

It was the realisation that Roziac lay in the heart of Camisard country that had revived Melissa's idea for a novel set in the region. She had casually mentioned it while glancing through Philippe Bonard's brochure. Iris, who had spoken in glowing terms of the man and his ambitious undertaking, revealed that she had agreed to tutor a week's art course for him and immediately suggested that Melissa should accompany her.

Melissa had been intrigued to know what kind of man could persuade Iris to leave her beloved garden for the best part of a fortnight at the height of the growing season. This curiosity, as much as the prospect of a week's field research in one of the wildest and loveliest parts of France, had helped to make up her mind.

Mulling it over as she strolled along in the morning sunshine, passed occasionally by a battered Renault or a woman on a pushbike with a basket of *baguettes* swinging from the handlebars, Melissa felt more and more uneasy at her friend's obvious emotional commitment to Bonard. It wasn't that she had anything against him personally; he was a charming and clever man, dedicated to his school, an entrepreneur who was using the fruits of his success to fulfil a lifetime's dream—and good luck to him, she thought. But Iris, so shrewd in some ways, was hopelessly unworldly in others. The notion that Bonard's sexual inclinations were more likely to be directed towards Alain Gebrec than herself might not enter her head.

Returning to the *auberge*, Melissa went straight to the terrace for breakfast. She had hoped for the opportunity of a quiet word with Iris, of trying to smooth her ruffled feelings before the day's work, but to her surprise and annoyance she found Rose Kettle at their table and Brigitte laying a third place, while Dora, stony-faced, was sitting alone in the farthest corner.

"I do hope you don't mind," pleaded Rose, while Brigitte bustled off to fetch more croissants. "She's still cross with me and the atmosphere is quite unpleasant, so I asked Iris if I could join you. And I wonder," she went on as Melissa murmured a polite and hypocritical response, "if you'd be so kind as to give me a lift to the school this morning? Dora's appointment isn't till eleven so she says she isn't in a hurry. She's doing it on purpose, of course—I know she's planning to do some more of her wretched putting practice. There are times"—Rose's face took on the fierce expression of a schoolgirl talking about her most hated teacher—"when I'd like to brain her with one of her own golf-clubs!"

"Shouldn't talk like that. She's only thinking of your good," said Iris, helping herself to apricot jam.

"Oh, I know—I don't mean it, of course. Only, I do wish she wouldn't be so horrid about Dieter. I expect she's jealous really, because it's me he's interested in and not her."

"Of course we'll give you a lift," said Melissa hastily, noting the contemptuous curl of Iris's lip and anxious to forestall any blunt comment that might sour the atmosphere still further. "But I do hope you and Dora soon settle your difference." She did not ask the outcome of last night's argument and was relieved when Rose did not offer to tell her. Just at the moment she had her own anxieties without being expected to worry about other people's.

When the three of them got up to leave, Melissa glanced across at Dora and met a look of concentrated malevolence that took her by surprise. She probably thinks I encouraged Rose to defy her, she thought uneasily as she followed the others to the car park.

When they reached Les Châtaigniers, most of Iris's class were already assembled. Their enthusiastic welcome brought a smile to her face for the first time that morning. She immediately fell into conversation with Jack as they waited to board the mini-bus that stood in the centre of the courtyard, ready to transport them to the Parc de Prafance with its famous forest of bamboo.

Alain Gebrec was standing at the entrance to one of the outhouses, hectoring someone inside. After a moment Fernand emerged, an expression of sullen resentment on his face and a heavy crowbar in his hand. For a few minutes there were heated exchanges between the two; Melissa could not catch the words, but it appeared that Gebrec was giving instructions which Fernand appeared reluctant to carry out. Both men were making angry gestures and at one point Fernand brandished the crowbar under Gebrec's nose before flinging it to the ground in a melodramatic gesture of apparent capitulation.

Meanwhile, Philippe Bonard had emerged from the house and was greeting Iris and her group, now installed in the mini-bus and waiting for Gebrec to drive them. He saluted

Melissa with a smile that faded as he became aware of the argument going on across the yard. When Gebrec approached, he took him by the arm and murmured something which Melissa took to be a mild reproof. Gebrec began expostulating and pointing in Fernand's direction; Bonard patted his arm and wagged a finger, glancing towards the bus as if saying something like "Not in front of the children." Gebrec shrugged, climbed aboard, started the engine and drove out of the yard.

Most of the other students had foregathered by this time and were awaiting their final briefing from their tutor. It seemed that the appointments were at varying times, some quite early, others later in the day. It had already been arranged that Eric and Daphne Lovell would drive Rose to her destination before going on to their own and would pick her up later for the return trip. Several other people had arranged to share cars and after a good deal of last-minute discussion and instructions, they were at last on their way. Dora Lavender had still not appeared, nor had Dieter Erdle.

Melissa was about to get back into her car when Bonard called her name and came over to speak to her.

"What plans have you today, Melissa?" There was a warmth in his manner that invested the polite enquiry with a genuine interest.

"I'm going to Alès to work in the municipal library," she replied. "Madame Gebrec has recommended some books."

Bonard nodded approvingly. "I am sure her advice is excellent. Will you be joining us for lunch? I have to instruct Juliette."

Melissa hesitated. "I've no idea what time I'll be back. Perhaps I'd better say no for today, thank you all the same."

"There is no need for thanks. My house is at your disposal. If you wish at any time to take a swim in the pool or use the library—it is always quiet, ideal for writing—you are most welcome."

"You are very hospitable."

"But it is a pleasure to entertain a lady from another country who has such a love of France and of the French language." There followed another brief eulogy of his mother-tongue, of its pre-eminence in the civilised world and of the importance of preserving its purity, during which Melissa felt her smile glazing over. "And of course," he finished, reverting to his normal voice, "as you are such a close friend of dear Iris . . ."

"Yes, Iris is a *very* dear friend of mine." Involuntarily, Melissa spoke with an emphasis that took her by surprise. She sensed that Bonard was aware of it; although his smile did not waver, his eyes registered in quick succession a question, a realisation and a reassurance.

"Believe me, I too value her friendship," he said with obvious sincerity. "I value it most highly." He stood back and gave a little bow. "It is always a pleasure to talk to you, but I must not detain you. I wish you a profitable day."

It was as if a subliminal message had passed between them; as if she had said aloud, "Look, I understand how things are between you and Alain Gebrec, but Iris doesn't seem to and I don't want her upset," and as if he had responded, "Do not worry, I will not say or do anything to hurt her." She set off for Alès feeling comforted.

In the municipal library, after consultation with an assistant, Melissa settled at a table in a quiet corner with two or three of the books that Antoinette Gebrec had recommended. She soon became absorbed, oblivious to the passage of time, and was startled when she was politely informed that the doors would shortly be closed for the midday break. She gathered her pages of notes and went out into the sunlit streets. Every clock in the city seemed to be booming the hour.

Crossing the Place Henri Barbusse, Melissa went in search of somewhere to eat. She was studying the menu outside a restaurant when someone called her name. Looking round, she saw Madame Gebrec waving from the other side of the narrow street. Nimbly dodging cars, vans and packs of youngsters on bicycles streaming homewards for their midday meal, the Frenchwoman skipped across and shook Melissa energetically by the hand.

"You seek lunch?" she said in English. "Bah, do not go there! The cooking, it is execrable. Come, I show you." She steered Melissa round a corner, along a narrow passage and through a net-curtained door. In no time they were installed at a table by the window and being attended by a stately woman with an enormous bosom and a monument of granite-coloured hair. She was evidently an old acquaintance of Madame Gebrec, who addressed her as Huguette and made solicitous enquiries about her varicose veins before the two of them began a lively discussion of the menu. Eventually, and after due consultation with Melissa, the *plat du jour* of lamb spiced with juniper was agreed upon and a bottle of mineral water requested, whereupon Huguette moved majestically towards the kitchen.

"Always I eat here when I have business in town," Madame Gebrec explained. "The chef is the husband of Huguette. His cooking is superb." She lowered her voice and leaned towards Melissa. "Madame Craig, I am so happy to have this opportunity to speak to you."

"I'm happy to see you, too. I've just been in the library, studying some of the books you recommended. I'm so grateful for your help."

"But it is nothing. It is a pleasure to be of service." Madame Gebrec's face became serious; she took a sip of water, put down her glass and fiddled with the stem as if she had something on her mind. After a moment, she said, "I wish to apologise, Madame, for Alain's rudeness to you yesterday. Oh, yes, I am sure he was most impolite," she hurried on as Melissa murmured a conventional disclaimer. "He telephoned to tell me about it . . . he was very angry when he saw you with that book and I could tell that he had said things he should not have said."

"Look, it doesn't matter . . ."

"I ask you to believe that in normal circumstances he would not behave like that, but he is still not quite himself . . . the death of his friend, you know . . ."

"Please," Melissa urged, "there's no need to say any more," but Madame Gebrec continued as if she had not spoken.

"The Occupation . . . it was a bitter time for us all . . . even though Alain was not born until shortly before the Liberation, he did not escape unscarred. The times that followed, they were almost as bad ... and as he grew older, he became aware of the deep wounds his mother had suffered. Anything that causes me distress ..." Her voice trembled and almost broke.

"Don't upset yourself," said Melissa. "I quite understand."

Madame Gebrec shook her head. "But no, Madame, it is impossible that you understand. You have not known, you could not know, what it was like to live under the Occupation. One was always afraid, there were spies everywhere and one could never be sure who were one's friends. Not everyone was *patriote*, and when it was finished and the enemy had left our soil, there were those who did not speak the truth about what happened."

"I can well believe that," said Melissa.

Madame Gebrec gazed earnestly at her across the table. Her dark eyes, which seemed almost too large for her small features, held an expression of great sadness. She hesitated for a moment before asking in a low voice: "The book you bought yesterday—you have read it?"

Melissa shook her head. "I've hardly had time to open it yet. When I do get round to reading it, I'll remember what you've been saying." She was burning with curiosity and would have liked to question Madame Gebrec, but it was obvious that to do so would arouse painful memories.

There was an awkward silence, relieved by the arrival of Huguette with their food. She laid the plates before them, wished them *"Bon appétit,"* clasped her hands and stood in an attitude of expectation, awaiting their comments.

"It's delicious," Melissa assured her after the first mouthful.

"Your husband is a true artist of the kitchen," declared Madame Gebrec and Huguette withdrew, beaming.

"Speaking of artists," said Melissa, "I think I mentioned that my friend is a well-known painter and textile designer."

"Yes, indeed. How is it going with her course?"

"Very well, I think. I hear very favourable reports from her students. I wonder," Melissa hesitated, unsure of how her request would be received, "Iris is always interested in the

work of little-known artists and I believe ... Madame Delon
mentioned that the person who painted that view of the Porte
des Cévennes, the one hanging in your salon, is a friend of
yours?"

Once again the great eyes grew sombre, but this time the
sorrow was mingled with love and pride.

"He was, indeed, a very dear friend," she murmured.
"Alas, since many years he is no longer with us."

"Have you any more of his work?"

"Just a few canvases. They are not for sale," she added
sharply and Melissa was at pains to reassure her.

"No ... no, I don't want to buy them ... it was just ...
that is, would it be possible for us to see them?"

"But of course—I should be delighted! When would you
like to come? They are best seen in daylight, naturally."

"Perhaps one afternoon, after the class is finished?"

"Why not? Let us say tomorrow? You will take an apéritif
with me, no?"

It was an occasion to look forward to. Neither could have
foreseen the circumstances under which it would take place.

Ten

AFTER PARTING FROM MADAME
Gebrec, Melissa returned to the library with the intention of
working there for the rest of the afternoon, but time and again
she found her mind straying from the accounts of former religious wars and the acts of unbelievable cruelty committed
by both sides to the more recent clash of ideologies which, it
seemed to her, differed from the old in little but the relative
sophistication of the weaponry. Even the deeds of valour, so
proudly recorded, only added to her depression as she reminded herself that each was committed in response to yet
one more example of man's inhumanity to man. After an hour
or so, wearied—as the combatants themselves had at last
become—by the futility of it all, she abandoned her task and
drove back to Roziac.

The afternoon was hot and still. Remembering Philippe
Bonard's invitation to use the pool whenever she wished, she
decided to call in at the Auberge de la Fontaine and pick up
her swimming costume. She calculated that there would be
time for a quick dip before afternoon tea, which Juliette normally served at a quarter to four.

She arrived at Les Châtaigniers shortly before half-past
three, expecting to find the garden and the pool deserted. Instead, several members of Bonard's class, including Rose,
Daphne and Eric, were already in the water, others were sitting on the terrace making notes. Presumably, after carrying
out their assignments, they had been returning at irregular in-
tervals and were now preparing their reports for the final ses-

sion of the afternoon. There was no sign of Bonard or his assistant.

The water was cool and refreshing; Melissa found it a relief to stretch and exercise her limbs after the hours spent poring over books. After swimming a few lengths of the pool, she turned and floated on her back, enjoying the warmth of the sun on her half-submerged body, listening to the splashing of the other swimmers, their laughing voices, the harsh cries of magpies in the nearby forest, the occasional insect droning past. The vague sense of depression that had settled over her in the library began to slip away. She decided that she had done enough research; it was time to start detailed plotting of her novel.

Somebody called, "Tea's ready," and the bathers scrambled out of the water and began drying themselves. Rose picked up a tube of sun-cream and held it out to Daphne.

"Will you do my back for me?" she asked.

"Certainly." Daphne took the tube, squeezed a white worm of cream on to Rose's shoulders and began spreading it with her large, plump hands.

The contrast between the two as they stood one behind the other struck Melissa as comical. They're like the "before" and "after" pictures in an advertisement for a slimming programme, she thought. Daphne's huge bosom and vast posterior looked as if they were about to burst from her too-tight black costume; Rose, small-boned and slender, looked remarkably young and pretty in an aquamarine bikini that suited her fair colouring. Melissa, remembering the events of the previous evening, was beginning to believe that it was not impossible for Dieter Erdle to be genuinely attracted to her. She wondered idly why Rose had not asked him to apply the sun-cream and then realised that he was not among the swimmers. Perhaps he had not yet returned from his interview.

Her reflections were interrupted by Dora, whom she had vaguely noticed rummaging in the boot of their car when she arrived and who now came striding towards them.

"Rose, my nine iron is missing," she said. Receiving nothing but a blank look, she raised her voice and repeated impatiently, "My nine iron, I can't find it."

"I'm not deaf," said Rose pettishly.

"Well, have you taken it?"

"Oh, for goodness' sake!" Rose took her tube of cream from Daphne and began anointing her arms and legs. "Why do you suppose I'd do that? You must have left it at home."

"I tell you I didn't."

At that moment, the art group emerged and headed for the tea-table. Iris spotted Melissa and came straight across to her.

"Has Gebrec come back yet? Have you seen Philippe?" she asked.

"I haven't seen either of them but I've only been back a little while," replied Melissa. "Is there a problem?" she added, seeing the anxiety in her friend's face.

"Gebrec's taken off."

"What do you mean?"

"Supposed to pick us up at lunchtime and never turned up. Philippe's very worried."

"Hasn't he any idea where he's gone?"

"Seems not. He didn't take his car or the mini-bus."

"There's Philippe now."

Bonard had just emerged on to the terrace. It was evident from his preoccupied expression and the abstracted way he ran his fingers through his thatch of silver hair that Gebrec had still not returned. The news that something was amiss quickly spread to the rest of the group, who gathered round him to hear the latest developments.

"I am most concerned," he was saying in French as Iris and Melissa joined them. "He was in a somewhat distressed state when he came to see me after taking Iris and her students to the Parc de Prafance."

"He seemed all right to me," commented Chrissie, after Melissa had interpreted. "Did you notice anything, Merv?"

"Mmm . . . he seemed a bit quiet," said Mervyn. "I wouldn't have said distressed . . . more preoccupied. He certainly didn't have much to say for himself."

"He had a slanging match with Fernand before we set off," said Jack. "Perhaps that upset him?"

"Oh, that is nothing extraordinary." Bonard's shoulders lifted dismissively. "They have many differences. Fernand was employed by the previous owner and does not always see eye to eye with Alain on the way the estate should be managed, but no . . ."

"So what do you suppose it was?" asked Chrissie.

"He would not tell me. We had some business to discuss, but his mind seemed to be elsewhere. I asked if there was anything wrong and he said 'No,' but I could tell that he was keeping something back. So I asked him again, asked if I could help, and he became very agitated. He said, 'No one can help,' and rushed out of the room. I have not seen him since."

"Is he in his room, perhaps?" suggested Mervyn.

"He is not in the house. I have searched thoroughly."

There was a pause, during which Dora was heard to mutter, "A lot of fuss about nothing. Why do the French have to make such a drama out of everything?" In the uncomfortable silence that followed, while the others were trying to think of something tactful to say, the sound of a car pulling into the courtyard sounded unnaturally loud. A door slammed, footsteps approached, and Dieter Erdle walked through the archway on to the terrace.

His arrival seemed to break a spell. The group fragmented and re-formed in twos and threes, speculating on possible reasons for Gebrec's disappearance. Rose went scuttling off to intercept Dieter; she grabbed him by the hand and drew him towards the tea-table, her bird-like voice rising above the general chatter as she told him what had happened.

Hearing what sounded like a muttered exclamation of fury at her elbow, Melissa looked around and saw Dora turn on her heel and march off into the orchard, where she stopped under an apple tree and stared up into the branches as if inspecting its heavy crop of fruit. Even at that distance, her stance indicated suppressed rage and frustration.

The men of the party were discussing the situation and it was plain that, unlike Dora, they were taking it seriously. Melissa was intrigued to notice that Jack Hammond seemed to have taken charge, with Dieter Erdle as his lieutenant. Together with Iris and several others, she moved closer to listen.

"Wherever he went, he was on foot," said Jack. "His car,

Philippe's Peugeot and the 2CV that Fernand uses are all in their usual places. We don't even know which direction he took."

"Didn't anyone at all see him go out?" asked Mervyn. "Fernand or Juliette, for example?"

"Apparently Fernand was out too. He went to the supermarket to do some shopping for Juliette. She doesn't know anything either."

"What about Philippe's secretary?" asked Dieter.

"Never thought to ask. I don't think I've ever set eyes on her," said Jack.

"Marie-Claire," Dieter explained. "She works in a cubbyhole next to his office in the turret. She hardly ever shows her face downstairs."

"Has Philippe talked to her about Gebrec's disappearance?"

"I don't know."

"Would you care to ask him?"

"Sure." Dieter went off and returned a few minutes later with the information that Marie-Claire never came in on a Wednesday because her children's school was closed on that day.

"So she's no help," said Jack. "Wasn't anyone here at all, besides Philippe and Juliette?"

"It seems not."

"So, what do we do?" asked Mervyn.

"If Gebrec was upset or worried about something and just wanted to be alone to think things over," said Jack, "he might have gone up to the belvedere, or down by the river where we went yesterday to do our painting."

"You'd think he'd be back by now," said Mervyn.

"Unless he's had an accident or been taken ill."

"D'you think we should form a search party?"

"I've just had a dreadful thought," said Chrissie, her eyes wide with foreboding and an ominous throb in her voice which seemed for once totally natural. "Supposing he's ill . . . really ill, I mean, with something awful . . . something incurable?" She slipped her hand into Mervyn's and moved closer to him, as if for protection against some unnamed horror. "Suppose he felt he couldn't face it and . . ."

The temperature seemed to fall several degrees as the implication sank in.

"I think," said Jack, "we'd better get on and search." Everyone looked at him, waiting for instructions. "Dieter, will you come with me? We'll go up to the belvedere. Mervyn, I suggest you, Eric and the rest of the men go down to the river. Split into two parties when you get there and look a reasonable distance in both directions. Perhaps the ladies could check the gardens and the outhouses, although I doubt if you'll find him there."

"I'm staying with Merv," Chrissie declared, clinging firmly to his hand.

"I'll go and tell Philippe what we're doing," said Iris.

Jack nodded. "Good idea. All right, everyone? See you later, back here."

They scattered and Melissa found herself left with Rose, Daphne, and the two girls Sue and Janey. Just as the men had turned to Jack for leadership, so these four seemed to expect her to take charge of them.

"Where do we start?" asked Rose.

"Some of us could try the woods on either side of the track leading down to the road—away from the belvedere."

"You mean, near the clearing where Fernand was unloading his rails?"

"That's right."

"Where is Fernand?" asked Daphne.

"I don't know," replied Melissa uneasily. "I heard Alain this morning tell him to clear some dead timber. That was when they had the argument. I haven't seen him this afternoon."

"I heard a chain-saw going a while ago," said Daphne.

"Is that what it was? It sounded like a motorbike," said Janey.

"Fernand went off in the tractor soon after lunch," said Sue. "I saw him getting it out when I went to the car to get a book I'd left there. Listen, that sounds like him now."

As she spoke, the tractor came snorting into the yard in a

cloud of fumes with the trailer, piled high with logs, rattling and bumping behind it.

"Well, it looks as if he did what he was told after all. I'll go and have a word with him." Melissa crossed the yard and waited while Fernand backed the trailer into a corner, switched off the tractor engine and jumped down. His face lit up when he saw her.

"Madame, ça va?"

"Fernand, have you seen Monsieur Gebrec?"

"Yes, at nine o'clock this morning. He ordered me to cut this lot *immediately*"—he laid heavy stress on the word, his mouth twisted in a sardonic grin—"and I told him it would have to wait till this afternoon." Fernand seemed in a high good humour at the thought of putting one over on Monsieur Gebrec. He unhitched the side of the trailer and a quantity of logs fell clattering to the ground.

"Monsieur Gebrec has not been seen since nine-thirty this morning," said Melissa. "Do you know where he might be? Monsieur Bonard is very concerned."

"No idea, Madame. Perhaps in Alès, visiting his mother?"

"I don't think so. His car is still here."

Fernand indicated with outspread hands and a jerk of his shoulders that the whereabouts of Monsieur Gebrec were a matter of total indifference to him. He went into the shed where he kept the tractor and came back with his crowbar, with which he began levering more logs from the trailer to the ground. The sun was pouring into the courtyard and his brawny arms glistened with sweat. Melissa watched for a few seconds as he worked, apparently impervious to the heat, then turned back to where the others were waiting.

"He doesn't seem to know anything," she told them. "Let's get started. Daphne, will you take Janey and Sue and search the woods?" Obediently, the three set off. Melissa turned to Rose. "Shall we check the gardens and outhouses? Where's Dora, by the way?"

"How should I know?" said Rose with a shrug. "She's hardly speaking to me at the moment—except to accuse me of stealing her golf-clubs."

"Because of Dieter, I suppose?"

"Why else?"

They crossed the courtyard and went into the garden. From the far side of the swimming pool they caught sight of Dora sitting on the terrace, reading. She lifted her head and stared across, her face expressionless.

"One of us should go and tell her what's happening, don't you think?" suggested Melissa. "It'd seem a bit rude to walk past without saying anything."

"She'd only have herself to thank," said Rose waspishly, then added, with a smile suggestive of a cat with newly sharpened claws, "Anyway, I doubt if she'd know who it was with her reading glasses on."

"Just the same, I think I'll put her in the picture."

Dora, her eyes hard and her face wooden, received the information with a curt nod.

"Well, she didn't exactly overreact," said Melissa as she rejoined Rose.

"All these years I've known her and I never realised what a nasty temper she has," said Rose.

"Perhaps you've never crossed her before?"

Rose gave a gleeful chuckle. "That's what Dieter says. Do you know what she said last night, after I'd told her what Dieter and I were planning for next week? She said, 'I'd like to break that bloody Kraut's neck!' She actually swore—and she makes out she's such a lady!" She turned to Melissa with a beseeching expression. "I'm entitled to another chance of happiness, aren't I?"

"I . . . well, yes, I suppose so," said Melissa, reluctant to be inveigled into taking sides. "Perhaps for the moment we'd better get on with this search."

"Yes, of course. I was forgetting."

Their tour of the gardens and orchard revealed nothing. They had just returned to the courtyard and were about to examine the various outbuildings when they heard the sound of running footsteps. The next minute, Jack and Dieter appeared, streaming with sweat and obviously agitated.

"Something's happened!" said Melissa, hurrying to meet them.

"We think ... we've found him!" Jack's normally ruddy face was the colour of putty.

"Oh, dear, where?" faltered Rose.

Dieter, looking even more shaken, struggled to regain his breath. "On the rocks ... close to where we found Wolfgang Klein," he panted.

"Is he dead?"

"It looks like it."

"My God!" Melissa stared in horror. "Perhaps Chrissie was right!"

The period that followed seemed to Melissa to have an unreal, almost nightmarish quality. It was like some ghoulish re-run of Sunday afternoon, as if the same sequence in a film was being shot for a second time under a different director.

Rose burst into tears and was escorted indoors by Dieter. Dora was summoned; her appearance, announcing that she was taking her protégée back to the *auberge* without delay, did nothing to help matters. Rose clung to Dieter's hand and refused to budge; there followed a heated altercation between Dora and Dieter until Jack intervened and managed, using a quiet diplomacy that further increased Melissa's respect for him, to persuade them both to withdraw.

Meanwhile, the second search party returned and joined the others on the terrace. It was there that Philippe Bonard learned the news of Gebrec's death. At first, he appeared stunned and unable to grasp what had happened. Then, he let out a groan and sank into a chair, his hands over his face and his shoulders heaving as he made superhuman efforts to contain his shock and grief. After a few minutes he raised his head and was now sitting motionless, pale and haggard but controlled, while Iris, her eyes moist with sympathetic tears, stood silently and helplessly by.

"The police must be informed," said Jack. "My French isn't up to it, I'm afraid—will you phone them, Melissa?"

"Yes, of course." She went into the house and made her way to the small suite of rooms that Bonard and his staff of two used as offices. She put in an urgent call to the local gendarmerie, wondering as she did so whether Officer Hassan would take charge of the case. She pictured him, tapping away at his nose and almost gleefully saying, "I told you so," and felt sick. Her heart went out to Antoinette Gebrec, as yet happily ignorant of the fate of her son, and to Philippe Bonard, whose long-cherished dream had turned to a nightmare, while the man they both loved was lying in a broken, bloody heap at the foot of the cliff.

She left the room and plodded wearily back. On her way she passed the kitchen. The door was open and she saw Juliette standing alone by the table with a tray-load of crockery in her hands. She appeared mesmerised, as if unable to put it down; her eyes were staring and her face deathly white. Melissa went and stood beside her.

"Juliette, this is terrible news."

Juliette started violently and several cups toppled to the floor and smashed to pieces. Melissa took the tray from her and carried it to the buffet, while Juliette covered her face with a towel.

"There is a curse on this place!" she moaned. "What is to become of us?" She began rocking to and fro, whimpering softly.

"Try not to distress yourself," said Melissa. "You shouldn't be alone . . . shall I find Fernand and ask him to come to you?"

The suggestion seemed to agitate Juliette still further. "Oh, *mon Dieu*, the *flics* will be here again with their endless questions. Who knows what my crazy brother will say to them?" She grasped Melissa by the hand. "Madame, you will not betray our secret?" she implored.

"Of course not, but surely . . ."

"If the police knew, they might imagine . . ."

"Juliette, don't worry! Why should anyone suspect your brother of harming Monsieur Gebrec? What connection could there possibly be between him and what happened to Roland so long ago?"

"None at all, Madame, but you know what the police are like, especially that idiot Hassan. After Monsieur Klein's death he asked Fernand a lot of stupid questions, just because of some village gossip."

"But that was because Monsieur Klein was German, and everyone knew Fernand was suspicious of Germans."

Juliette bent down and began picking up the smashed pieces of china. "Perhaps you are right, Madame."

"Monsieur Gebrec's death was probably nothing more than a tragic accident," Melissa went on, "but"—she hesitated for a moment before saying—"there is some talk of suicide." It might not have been her place to reveal such a suspicion, but it could help to relieve Juliette's fears on her brother's behalf. In any case it would soon become common knowledge.

Juliette appeared bemused by the suggestion. "Suicide?" she repeated. "Why would he do such a thing?"

"It is, of course, only a suspicion and I'm sure you will say nothing until we know for certain. Monsieur Bonard told us that Monsieur Gebrec left the house in some distress this morning. He never came back—that's all we know at present."

Juliette picked up the tray of crockery and carried it to the dishwasher. "I must not detain you any longer, Madame." It was plain that she had said all she was going to say.

Melissa went outside to rejoin the others. "The police should be here soon," she told Jack. "They'll want to talk to you and Dieter right away, of course, as you found the . . . as you found Alain." Just in time, out of consideration for Philippe Bonard's feelings, she checked herself from saying "the body," although it was doubtful if he would have heard. He was still sitting in the same chair, staring into space like a man in a trance.

"What about the others?" asked Dieter. "Rose is still very upset—shall I take her back to her hotel?" His eyes sought Dora as if throwing down a challenge and Melissa saw her draw herself upright, her nostrils flaring. Like a war-horse about to charge into battle, she thought. Any minute now and they'll be at each other's throats again.

"I can't see any need for everyone to wait around," said Jack hastily. He too had read the signals. "If we get them to write down their names and where they're staying, they might as well go back to their hotels. Will you see to that, Dieter?

If the police want to talk to any of them, they'll know where to find them."

There was a moment's hesitation before Dieter said, "Okay," and went indoors to fetch pen and paper. Dora glared after him for a few seconds before turning away and striding across the garden towards the orchard.

The minute they were both out of earshot, Melissa said, "Jack, what are we going to do about Rose? For some reason or other, she won't have Dora near her at present."

"Perhaps you could take her back to the *auberge*?"

"Yes, of course. Should I have a word with Dora first?"

"I suppose you ought to, but," Jack gave an unexpected grin and for a moment the atmosphere of gloom lightened a little, "let's make sure we keep Dora and Dieter apart or we'll have a third death on our hands!"

Eleven

AFTER THE TRAUMA OF THE DISCOVERY of Gebrec's body and Dora's subsequent clash with Dieter, the exit from Les Châtaigniers was accomplished with minimum fuss, thanks to Jack's decisiveness and air of quiet authority to which everyone willingly submitted. Melissa drove a pale and silent Rose back to the *auberge*, and Dora followed a few minutes later. Iris elected to remain with Philippe Bonard for the time being and Jack undertook to drive her back when she was ready.

As soon as they arrived at the *auberge*, Rose announced her intention of having a long soak in the bath followed by a lie down. She also made it clear that she preferred to be alone. Sensing that Dora was about to protest, and to avoid further argument, Melissa said hastily, "Come along to my room and we'll have a drink."

Monsieur Gauthier obligingly produced a bottle of Côtes du Rhône from his cellar and Melissa led Dora upstairs and installed her in a chair on the balcony. The *auberge* was built on a knoll and the tops of the nearest trees were below eye level, their foliage a green sea ruffled into waves by the breeze, the rugged backdrop of the mountains softened to a warm gold by the evening sunlight. It was a view to inspire a poet, but its beauty was entirely lost on Dora who, between mouthfuls of wine, stared moodily down at her feet.

"We should never have come," she muttered after a long silence, "and if I had my way, we'd leave here tomorrow. No, tonight . . . right away. I feel as if there's a curse on this place."

"That's exactly what Juliette said," replied Melissa. "I suppose it's a normal reaction in the circumstances. Have some more wine."

"Thank you." Dora held out Iris's tooth-mug, which was doing duty as a wine-glass. "This is very kind of you, Melissa."

"Not at all. I felt in need of a snort myself."

"We should never have come," repeated Dora.

"What made you decide on this trip?" It was an idle question; Melissa's mind was far away but, for the second time in three days, she recognised Dora's need to confide.

"It was Rose's idea, but I went along with it willingly enough. How was I to know she'd meet that wretched man? The minute she set eyes on him, she seemed to take leave of her senses—and he's been playing up to her the whole time. Can't she see what a fool she's making of herself?"

"I agree it doesn't seem an ideal relationship, but surely, the more you oppose it, the more . . ."

"She's always taken my advice before." Dora's mouth compressed into an aggressive wedge. "I've never known her to be so obstinate. And now this absurd notion of staying at the centre for an extra week, just to be with him! Well, after this latest upset, I'm going to be firm with her. We'll leave in the morning. The course can't possibly go on after what's happened today, so we shan't miss anything. I'll speak to Bonard before we go about a refund for tomorrow and Friday."

Melissa stared at her in disbelief. "You're not serious!" she protested. "You can't pester the poor man about money just after he's had such a dreadful shock!"

"Business is business," said Dora. "His fees are steep enough to start with and two days out of ten means we're losing twenty per cent of our course."

Melissa was fast running out of sympathy with the redoubtable Dora. No doubt Bonard was as hard-headed as the next man in matters of business, but to tackle anyone so obviously grief-stricken on such a comparatively trivial point seemed to her nothing short of callous. She found herself pleading on his behalf.

"Don't you think, in the circumstances . . . perhaps if you

were to write when you get home . . . I mean, Gebrec wasn't just a colleague, he was a close friend."

"Yes, and we know what sort of friend, don't we? Oh, I can read the signs as well as anyone," Dora went on in a sudden surge of indignation as Melissa's eyebrows lifted. "If you ask me, that story about Gebrec having something on his mind was just a cover-up. There's more to this than meets the eye."

"Whatever do you mean? You're not suggesting . . . ?"

"That Bonard killed Gebrec? Of course not, he might soil his expensive suit!" Dora's lip curled; her eyes were savage. It was plain she begrudged Bonard his affluence. "What I mean is, they probably had some sort of . . . lover's quarrel, Gebrec went storming out in a rage and charged up to the belvedere to cool off. Either he was so upset that he didn't look where he was going, or he really did jump on purpose."

"You could be right." Melissa, at first sceptical, saw that there might be some truth in Dora's theory. "Maybe Bonard was trying to end the relationship altogether. We may never know for certain."

"No, I don't suppose we shall." Dora's tone was dismissive, as if the cause of Gebrec's death was of only passing interest. She stood up and began pacing restlessly to and fro along the balcony. "I wonder how long Rose is going to be. I could do with a bath myself before dinner."

"Would you like me to pop along and see if she's finished?"

"Would you? I'm afraid, if I go, she'll only get upset again. It's so unfair—she knows I always have her best interests at heart." The grim set of Dora's features belied the hurt in her eyes.

"I'm sure it's only the shock," said Melissa, aware that it sounded unconvincing.

"No, it's all this wretched business over Dieter Erdle. I've made up my mind—I'm going to tell him myself that this nonsense has got to end once and for all. I tried to catch him this morning, before we went to our appointments, but he wouldn't speak to me. I called to him, but he didn't even turn round . . . pretended not to hear!"

"From what I've seen of him, I'd say he's got rather a perverse sense of humour and enjoys winding people up," said Melissa, remembering in particular his brush with Alain Gebrec the previous afternoon over the controversial book.

"Well, he's not having any more fun at my expense," said Dora flatly. "I know where he's staying and I'm going to tackle him this evening."

"It's up to you, of course," said Melissa doubtfully. She got up and went to the door. She was on the point of saying that interfering could do more harm than good, but, knowing it would be pointless, she kept silent. She was thinking, as she went on her errand, less of the Rose-Dora-Dieter triangle than of Iris and her hapless devotion to Philippe Bonard.

Rose, apparently calm and relaxed, greeted her with a smile. "Do come in," she said.

"How are you feeling?" asked Melissa.

"Much better, thank you. Where's Dora?"

"She's in my room, having a drink. I felt we both needed it."

"Poor Dora, I'm afraid I've been rather beastly to her. Is she very upset?"

"I think she is a bit."

"I can't think what got into me. I felt suddenly . . . afraid of her." Rose's face crinkled in bewilderment. "When we heard about poor Alain Gebrec being dead, I had a sudden vision of Dora looking furiously angry . . . you know how she sometimes glares at Dieter . . . and I thought for a moment . . . supposing it had been Dieter who'd been killed . . . it might have been Dora who had . . . oh, I know it's dreadful of me to think these things, but she hates him so much."

"Don't worry about it. Shock plays funny tricks on people."

"We were so looking forward to this trip and it's been awful," Rose whispered, sadly shaking her head. "First poor Wolfgang and now Alain. They ought to shut the path up to that terrible cliff for good."

"Perhaps they will."

"What will happen now, do you think?"

"Much the same as before, I suppose. A police enquiry, formal identification . . ." Melissa bit her lip at the thought of the ordeal facing Antoinette Gebrec and wondered who, if anyone, would be there to give comfort and support.

"I mean about us? Will the course go on?"

"Dora thinks not." Melissa tried to keep her voice even. "She was talking about leaving here first thing tomorrow."

"But we can't do that!" Rose showed signs of renewed agitation. "I have to see Dieter . . . we've got a lot to talk about."

"I'm sure he'll get in touch with you as soon as he can," said Melissa, trying not to allow her irritation to get the better of her. "The best thing you can do is stay quietly here with Dora for the rest of the evening. Shall I go and fetch her? She's really very concerned about you."

"Oh, yes . . . I suppose so," said Rose sulkily.

"And do try not to have any more unpleasantness."

There was an uncompromising set to Rose's mouth as she said, "That's up to her."

"All clear," said Melissa when she rejoined Dora. "At least she isn't going to throw another wobbly the second she sets eyes on you . . . but she's not going to like the idea of leaving tomorrow."

"You told her?" Dora's expression was accusing. "Really, Melissa, that would have been better coming directly from me."

"I'm sorry, but she raised it herself. Do give her the chance of a night's rest before you have it out with her."

"I'll make up my own mind about that, thank you very much," Dora snapped and flounced out of the room.

The telephone rang; Jack was on the line. "We're leaving now," he said. "Iris is all in and I'm taking her back to the Lion d'Or for dinner. I've checked that they do vegetarian dishes. Will you join us?"

"Oh, yes, please!" said Melissa fervently. "What time?"

"Say in half an hour?"

"I'll be there."

"Iris says to tell Monsieur Gauthier not to expect you this evening."

"I'll do that." Melissa smiled fondly as she put down the phone. How typical of Iris to think of such a detail at a time like this.

The dining-room at the Lion d'Or had a modern, glass-walled extension which, like the terrace, overlooked the Mauzère.

On this warm, sunny evening the sliding doors were pushed back and the scent of broom drifted in, along with the cooling freshness of a sprinkler turning merrily in the centre of the geranium-filled garden. Music played softly in the background, haunting melodies of old Charles Trenet songs that soothed the senses, softening the harshness of chattering voices and the clinking of glass and crockery, insinuating themselves into the mind as stealthily as an incoming tide seeps into crevices between rocks.

Melissa recalled the words of one: *Je tire ma révérence*—I take my leave of you. A few hours ago, Alain Gebrec had taken his leave of everything and everyone. The thought made her skin prickle.

"It's very good of you to include me," she said when she, Iris and Jack were installed at a table, sipping apéritifs and making a show of studying the menu. "I was dreading getting caught in the fall-out from this evening's episode of the Rose-and-Dora show."

"Iris insisted she wouldn't leave you on your own," said Jack.

Melissa cocked an eyebrow. "Meaning, if you wanted Iris's company you had to put up with me as well?"

Jack looked disconcerted for a moment, then laughed. "That could have been put more tactfully, couldn't it? I didn't mean to imply . . ."

"It's all right, we're not normally inseparable," said Melissa reassuringly. She glanced at Iris, who appeared absorbed in the menu. "What happened after we left?"

"Much the same as last time. They sent a chopper and an ambulance to recover the body and there was the usual swarm of gendarmes rushing around."

"Banana Split was in charge," said Iris, without a trace of a smile. "Very subdued, very low key."

"Banana Split?" Jack looked from one to the other with a blank expression.

"Ask her. She coined the name." Iris jerked her menu in Melissa's direction.

"He wasn't doing much smiling this afternoon," said Jack

when Melissa had explained. "He seemed almost as shaken as everyone else."

"Last time I spoke to him, after Wolfgang Klein's death, he almost prophesied that something else would happen."

"You mean he was expecting another accident?"

"I'm not sure what he was expecting and I don't think he was either. He was very mysterious . . . and rather ridiculous." Melissa smiled faintly at the recollection. "He said, if I remember correctly, something like, 'We haven't heard the last of this' while beating his nose black and blue with his Biro."

"Whatever could he have meant by that?"

"At the time, he thought—no, it was almost as if he was hoping—that someone had pushed Klein off the cliff. He was chuntering on very grandly about an 'investigation' and 'interrogating the personnel.' He seemed quite miffed when it was established that it was an accident and his commandant called him off."

"He *wanted* it to be a murder? That's a bit sick, isn't it?" said Jack, frowning.

Melissa shrugged. "I imagine his very own murder enquiry is every newly promoted police inspector's dream."

Jack shook his head, evidently finding such cynicism distasteful. Iris lowered her menu and said, "At least, he didn't hassle Philippe. Saw what a state he was in. Left his 'interrogation' till tomorrow."

"Yes, how is poor old Philippe? Is anyone with him?"

"Only the servants. Wouldn't let anyone else stay. Said he wanted to be left alone." Iris's expression gave nothing away and Melissa could only guess how she was feeling.

The waiter was hovering by their table. "Perhaps we'd better order," said Jack.

The food was excellent, but none of them was hungry. When they had finished, they went out on to the terrace to drink their coffee. Already several other groups and couples were out there, the penetrating French voices and cheerful laughter sounding sharp and clear in the still air, untouched by any hint of tragedy or death.

"So, what's the state of play between Rose and Dora?" asked Jack.

"By the time I left, they were both huffy with me," said Melissa ruefully. "I seem to have said all the wrong things."

"Were they on speaking terms?"

"Just about, but there's probably blood on the walls by now. Dora's talking about leaving tomorrow."

Iris reacted sharply. "Can't do that, the course isn't finished. It'd upset Philippe no end."

"You mean, he's prepared to carry on, after what's happened?"

"Determined to. Told him people would understand if he didn't, but he said, 'They've paid their money, they're entitled.'"

"Brave man, Philippe," said Jack warmly, earning a look of gratitude from Iris.

"If he feels up to it, it's probably the best thing for him," said Melissa. "It'll help to take his mind off the tragedy." She turned to Iris. "Does he agree it might have been suicide, by the way?"

Iris stared into her empty coffee cup. "No idea what he thinks. Hardly said a word to me." She was working hard to conceal her distress, but the tremor in her voice was unmistakable.

"Would you like to go back to the *auberge*?" said Melissa gently. "You look very tired."

Without a word, Iris got to her feet. She stumbled over her chair and would have fallen, but Jack caught her arm and steadied her. "Would you like a lift back?" he offered.

"It's all right, thanks, I brought my car," said Melissa.

They settled Iris in the passenger seat of the Golf, where she sat with closed eyes. Jack hurried round to hold open the driver's door. Before getting in, Melissa put out a hand and he took it in a firm clasp.

"You'll excuse us, running off like this, won't you?" she said. "This business has knocked her for six." She hesitated for a moment before adding in a lowered voice, "She's known Philippe for quite a while, but I don't think she ever realised . . ."

"I understand," he said quickly. "It's hit her pretty hard."

"She'll get over it, but she'll need a lot of support."

He gave her hand an extra squeeze before releasing it. "You can count on me."

Iris held up until they were back in their room. The minute the door was closed she sat on the edge of her bed, covered her face with her hands and wept.

"How could I? How could I have been such a fool?" she wailed through her tears. "I really thought . . . I hoped . . . he was always so charming to me . . . so nice."

"But he is nice. Gay people often are," said Melissa. "More often than not, they're kind and gentle to everyone."

"Know that. Met lots of them before. Just didn't like to think that Philippe . . ."

"It isn't that obvious. I don't think I'd have spotted it myself if I hadn't seen the way he reacted the day we found Wolfgang Klein, when Gebrec got so upset."

"Saw that too. Suppose I'd already guessed, but didn't want to know." Iris had stopped crying and was sitting with hunched shoulders, tear-stained and dejected, but calm. She shot a glance at Melissa. "You never said anything."

"You were in enough of a state as it was over doing your course. I didn't want to upset you."

Iris managed a tremulous smile. "You're a good friend, Mel. Glad you're here."

"Me too. Now you'd better get some rest. I imagine it's business as usual for you tomorrow as well?"

"Of course. If Philippe can go on, I can."

"Good for you."

"What about Gebrec's mother? Hope someone's with her."

"Her friend, Madame Delon, is. I checked before coming out. Oh, Lord!" Melissa put a hand to her mouth. "I've just remembered. She invited us—you and me—to see some pictures tomorrow evening."

"Forget that. Poor creature won't be in the mood for social visits." Iris picked up her pyjamas and headed for the bathroom. Compassion for Antoinette Gebrec had for the time being taken her mind off her own disillusionment

Twelve

THE FOLLOWING MORNING MELISSA drove Iris as usual to Les Châtaigniers, where they found a state of confusion. All the students—even Rose and Dora, whom they had glimpsed sitting silently over their breakfast and deliberately avoiding everyone's eye—had turned up early, wanting to know what was going to happen. A pale young Frenchwoman, who turned out to be the normally invisible secretary, Marie-Claire, was assuring the assembly in a shrill voice that everything was to proceed as normal. If the group of Madame Ash required transport, Fernand would drive the mini-bus. Monsieur Bonard's students would please await him in their classroom. As soon as he was free—she gave a glance of distaste towards the police car discreetly parked in the farthest corner of the courtyard—Monsieur Bonard would proceed with their lesson. Marie-Claire then vanished into the house followed in a straggling line by the students of French. The artists were left in the courtyard, where they stood clutching their equipment with the anxious, uncertain air of a group of refugees.

Chrissie sidled up to Iris. "What are we doing this morning?" she asked in a forlorn voice. With her long hair drooping round her face and her large, mournful eyes, she looked like a lost basset-hound puppy.

Iris passed a hand over her forehead. She had slept badly and the flesh seemed to be drawn too tightly over the bones of her face. "I was planning to look at some rock formations," she said wearily. "Strata lines and so on."

"You mean, like the ones in the cliff face, opposite the bel-vedere?" Chrissie looked horror-struck. "We couldn't possibly go up there, not now!"

"There are other places."

Heads were already beginning to shake. No one, it seemed, wanted to know about rocks, no matter what cunning designs Nature had created in them.

"We don't have to stick slavishly to the programme, do we?" said Mervyn. "Perhaps a complete change would be a good idea."

"How about a train ride?" suggested Jack. "There's a little steamer that chuffs to and fro between Anduze and St-Jean-du-Gard. It goes through some wonderful scenery and St-Jean itself is quite picturesque, plenty of things to paint . . . not exactly designed by Nature I know, but . . ." He glanced round the small ring of faces, by now registering quickening interest. "What do you think, Iris?"

"Does everyone agree?" she asked. Heads nodded vigorously.

"Fine!" said Jack. "All aboard the bus, everyone; I'll go and find Fernand."

Five minutes later they had gone and Melissa was standing alone in the middle of the courtyard, wondering what to do next. She had intended to spend the day working on a preliminary plan for her novel, taking advantage of Philippe Bonard's invitation to use his library. That was out of the question now; concentration would be impossible. Eyeing the police car, she wondered whether it belonged to Officer Hassan and whether it was worth hanging around for a word with him. In the light of his melodramatic prophesy, it would be interesting to learn his reaction to this second death. Could there possibly be a link between the two? A serial killer, perhaps? It was a chilling thought.

She glanced at her watch; it was only twenty past nine. A bit too early to call Madame Gebrec. In half an hour maybe. As if the time would make any difference to a woman whose only son had just been killed. She mightn't welcome the intrusion. On the other hand . . . Perhaps Marie-Claire would let her use the office phone. She was still undecided when Officer Hassan came out of the house, marched straight across to her and saluted.

"Good morning, Madame Craig." His voice was subdued and his smile of greeting a pale reflection of its normal radiance. "This is a terrible tragedy."

"Terrible."

"I warned, did I not, that something of this nature might occur?"

That's not quite as I remember it, Melissa thought, but let the inaccuracy pass unchallenged.

"You did indeed," she said. "Does that mean that there will be a further investigation into Monsieur Klein's death?"

Rather regretfully, it seemed, Hassan shook his head. "The facts are very simple, Madame. The death of Monsieur Klein was, as the *médecin légiste* maintained at the outset and," he coughed in some embarrassment, evidently recalling his earlier insinuations, "as subsequent enquiries proved, a most tragic accident. This time, I fear, there can be no doubt— Monsieur Gebrec took his own life."

"Have you any idea why?"

"I believe so, Madame." He cleared his throat and looked down at his feet as if assessing the shine on his boots. "It seems there was a . . . relationship between Messieurs Klein and Gebrec."

"You mean a homosexual relationship?"

"Yes, Madame." He looked up and met her eye in obvious relief at her matter-of-fact response. "It would appear that the death of his friend was, for Monsieur Gebrec, an insupportable loss."

"You think he killed himself out of grief?"

"Exactly so, Madame."

"But according to Monsieur Bonard, they were scarcely more than acquaintances . . . occasional drinking companions."

"I suggest that it is not a matter which a man wishes his employer to know about."

"No, I suppose not. So what does Monsieur Bonard say about the suicide theory?"

"He is, I think, now prepared to accept it."

"Monsieur Bonard knew that something very serious was on Alain's mind, but he said he had no idea what it was. Some of us wondered if he had an illness that no one knew about."

"That possibility has already been explored. His own doctor had recently examined him and found him perfectly healthy."

Melissa sighed. "That seems pretty conclusive, I suppose."

"That is my assessment of the case, Madame, as I intend to report it to my commandant."

"Poor Madame Gebrec. She will be heartbroken."

"Alas, yes, Madame. A very brave lady. It was my unhappy duty to break the news of her son's death, which she bore with great fortitude. Now, I have to visit her one more time. It will be painful, I fear. *Au revoir*, Madame." He saluted again and marched across the yard to his car. Melissa turned and went sadly into the house.

The kitchen door stood open and on impulse she went in. She found Juliette bending over an ironing-board, busy with sponge and pressing-cloth. Behind her, on the buffet, was a tray already loaded with cups and saucers for the mid-morning coffee.

"*Bonjour*, Juliette," said Melissa. "Do you need any help?"

Juliette lowered the iron on to a pair of trousers laid out on the ironing-board, producing a hissing cloud of steam through which she stared solemnly at Melissa. In contrast to her outburst of yesterday, her manner was entirely composed.

"Thank you, no, Madame," she replied. "Everything is prepared. Will you take lunch here today?"

"Yes, if it's no trouble."

"No trouble at all."

"I have just been speaking to Officer Hassan. He confirms that Monsieur Gebrec's death was suicide."

"Indeed?" Juliette finished her task, put the trousers on a wooden hanger, hooked it over the back of a chair and unplugged the iron. It was obvious that she had no wish to discuss the opinions of Officer Hassan.

"So there is no need for you to concern yourself on your brother's behalf."

"Quite so, Madame."

There seemed nothing else to be said, and Melissa went out of the room and upstairs to the secretary's office, where, in response to her request to use the phone, Marie-Claire grudgingly pushed the instrument across her desk. "Kindly be brief, I have a number of calls to make," she said sourly.

"I shall be no longer than necessary," said Melissa. Anxiety made her speak more sharply than she had intended; she was not looking forward to telling Madame Gebrec just why Officer Hassan was about to pay her another visit and it was a relief when Madame Delon answered her call.

"I'm afraid what he has to say will cause considerable distress," she said, after explaining her reason for telephoning.

"What could be more distressing than the death of her son?" Madame Delon wanted to know.

Conscious that Marie-Claire was listening to every word, Melissa hesitated for a moment before saying, "It is believed that he took his own life."

Not a muscle moved on the secretary's pallid face. Perhaps she already knew. On the other end of the line there was a shocked gasp.

"But this is dreadful news! Antoinette will be in despair," whispered Madame Delon. "Why do they think that?"

"I cannot go into details. Officer Hassan will explain. I just want to be sure that your friend is prepared."

"That is very considerate of you, Madame. Will you come and see her soon? She is in great need of comfort."

"I'll come whenever you like. I shall be here at Les Châtaigniers this morning . . ."

"Perhaps I may call you there?"

"Please do. Goodbye." Melissa put down the receiver. "Thanks for the use of the phone. I'll be in the library for the next hour or so, if there should be a message for me."

The secretary gave no sign of having heard. She reached across the desk, grabbed the instrument and began tapping out a number with the angry, impatient air of someone who has been kept waiting for an unacceptably long time. With a shrug, Melissa left the office, fetched notebooks and a writing-pad from her car, and tried to settle down to work.

At half-past ten, the sound of voices below the library window indicated that the first lesson of the day was over and that coffee was about to be served. She went down and found Philippe Bonard with his students on the terrace. The hand that he gave her in greeting was ice-cold and his expression grave, but his appearance was as immaculate as ever and his bearing composed and dignified.

"Good morning, Melissa. May I pour you some coffee? We have been discussing *The Outsider* by Camus. You have read it, no doubt?"

"I studied his work at university," she replied, thinking that the story of a man condemned to death for murder after failing to show proper grief at his mother's funeral was not the happiest choice in the present circumstances. Yet, judging by the earnest discussion going on around her, the melancholy theme seemed to have had the effect of switching everyone's thoughts away from the actual tragedy that had happened in their midst. The quality of the French was improving too, she noted with interest, remembering how often Iris had praised Philippe Bonard's skill as a teacher.

Dieter was deep in conversation with Eric and Daphne, and Rose was talking to Janey and Sue. Only Dora stood aloof, silent and inscrutable. Melissa wondered what was passing through her mind and whether she and Rose had resolved their differences.

A sulky-looking Marie-Claire appeared and grudgingly informed Melissa that there was a telephone call for her. Madame Delon was on the line.

"Please, could you come to see Antoinette as soon as possible?" she pleaded. "She is in great distress and needs your help."

"My help? What kind of help?"

"She will explain, Madame. When can you come?"

"I'll leave in a few minutes and be with you in about half an hour. Tell Madame Gebrec I will do whatever I can." Although what that could possibly be, I have no idea, Melissa thought to herself as she put down the phone.

Melissa was prepared for signs of strain and grief, but the change in Antoinette Gebrec's appearance came as a shock.

Everything about her seemed to have shrunk except her eyes, which were huge, inky pools that dwarfed her small features. In twenty-four hours she had aged ten years.

The moment Melissa entered the house, she clutched at her with both hands. "Madame Craig, please help me! You must help me!" she begged in a voice cracking with grief and fatigue.

Melissa put an arm round her and, at a sign from Madame Delon, led her into the salon, pushed her gently on to a couch and sat down beside her.

"Yes, of course I will help you if I can," she promised. "Tell me what you want me to do."

"You know what they are saying . . . that Alain killed himself?"

"Yes, Officer Hassan told me."

"It is not true!" The small hands on Melissa's arm tightened their grip. "Never, never would he do such a thing!"

"I can understand how you must feel," said Melissa, thinking of Simon and wondering how she herself would feel on learning such terrible news, whether she could bear it, how she would cope. "I am the mother of a son myself," she went on. "The thought that he had come to that state of despair would break my heart."

"Do you not hear what I am saying? It is not true, I tell you! Alain did not take his own life, someone murdered him!" She released Melissa's arm and began beating with her fists on her lap.

Melissa took hold of the flailing hands and held them still. "Please, calm yourself," she begged with an anxious glance at Madame Delon, who responded with a grave nod.

"I share my friend's doubts," she said. "I have known Alain all his life and I find it impossible to believe that he would commit suicide. He had too much to live for."

"Have you any idea who would want to kill him, and why?"

Madame Gebrec raised her head and looked straight at Melissa. The intensity of her gaze was almost hypnotic. "That is what I ask you to find out, Madame," she whispered.

"Me?" said Melissa in alarm and astonishment. "Why me?

Surely, if you have serious reasons for doubting the police conclusions, you should approach them."

"Reasons? Does a mother need reasons? I know my son and I tell you, Madame, that he did not kill himself."

"Then, perhaps it was an accident?"

"Accident? Bah!" Madame Gebrec flung her arms in the air. "He knew every inch of that path, and how dangerous the cliff was in places. It was on his recommendation that the guardrail was rebuilt, and he constantly reminded everyone visiting the belvedere of the hazard."

Melissa shifted in her seat and looked down at her hands. "Madame Gebrec," she said hesitantly, "you know, of course, the reason why the police believe Alain killed himself?"

"Grief over the loss of his friend? Yes, I know." The small, mobile mouth trembled slightly. "Oh, I do not deny that my son was homosexual, nor that he and Wolfgang Klein were lovers. Alain was greatly distressed by his death, but," she hesitated for a moment before continuing, "he would have got over it in time. Never, never would he consider such an event so insupportable as to . . ." Her voice trailed off; it was her turn to appear uncomfortable.

"What she means," interposed Madame Delon, "is that Alain had a hard, one could almost say, a ruthless side to his nature—oh yes, he did!" she insisted as her friend was about to protest. "He was a good son to his mother and generous and loving to his . . . companions," the word was chosen with obvious care and uttered with thinly-concealed disapproval, "but he was very ambitious. Since becoming assistant to Monsieur Bonard, he has progressed rapidly in the business and only a week ago he told us of his hopes of being made a partner. So far from killing himself over Wolfgang, he would not have hesitated to end the liaison if it interfered with his plans." Melissa turned back to Madame Gebrec.

"Did he ever say anything to suggest that he felt threatened, or that his life was in danger?" she asked.

"No, never, but . . ."

"So, all you have to go on is a . . ." Melissa trawled her mental lexicon for a French equivalent of "gut reaction," failed to find one, and finished rather tamely with, "a mother's instinct."

"Exactly so, and is not that sufficient?"

Melissa was beginning to feel out of her depth. Without thinking, she had promised to give any help that lay in her power. That undertaking seemed to be developing into a commitment to conduct a private murder investigation in a foreign country. It was out of the question; she must end this bizarre interview here and now by telling Madame Gebrec, gently but firmly, that the person to whom she should confide her doubts was Officer Hassan. Yet, stirring at the back of her mind and insistently pushing its way to the fore, the ungovernable curiosity that had in the past led her into strange, sometimes dangerous but often exciting situations was threatening to override her common sense.

Common sense made one last stand and she heard herself asking, "Didn't you tell Officer Hassan of your suspicions?"

Madame Gebrec's lip curled. "Naturally, but I could see that he was merely dismissing them as the ravings of an hysterical woman. No, I can hope for no help from that quarter. That is why I ask you . . . I beg you, Madame Craig, to try and find out who murdered my son."

"I'm not a private detective, you know," Melissa pointed out, but already her mind was buzzing with possible lines of enquiry.

"But you solve crimes in your books," pleaded Madame Gebrec. "Surely . . ."

"Creating fictitious crime is one thing, solving it in real life is something else," said Melissa patiently. "Madame Gebrec, I know I said I would help you, but that was before I understood what you wanted of me. I don't see that I can do very much, but there may be some questions that, in the circumstances, the police have not thought it necessary to ask. If so, I'll try to find the answers for you. That's all I can promise for now." Madame Gebrec put out a hand. "Thank you, thank you a thousand times," she said huskily.

The look of relief and gratitude on her face brought a lump to Melissa's throat. "I must leave you now," she said. "I promised to return to Les Châtaigniers for lunch."

"You will come again? To see the pictures as we arranged?"

"Not this evening, surely?"

It had not occurred to Melissa that Madame Gebrec would even remember her invitation, let alone wish it to stand, but there was no doubt of her sincerity as she said, "No, not this evening, but another time, please. I wish to show you the work of . . . my friend."

"I'd like to see it. I'll be in Roziac for a few more days."

"And you will tell me as soon as you have news?"

If I have news, Melissa corrected mentally. Aloud, she said, "Of course, but you must not hope for too much," and made her escape.

You're quite mad, she told herself as she drove back to Roziac. You're supposed to be working on a book, not chasing around after a murderer who probably doesn't even exist. And yet . . . she thought of Officer Hassan and his belief that there had been skulduggery in the case of Wolfgang Klein. He had been proved mistaken and had probably suffered a somewhat humiliating rebuff from his superior officer. Now he was equally certain that Alain Gebrec's death was suicide. Could he once again be barking up the wrong tree?

Lunch was already served when she reached Les Châtaigniers. Immediately, she felt a change in the atmosphere. There was no buzz of conversation; most of the students had scattered with their plates of food and were sitting around eating in silence. Iris and her group were absent, it having been agreed before they set off that they would have lunch in St-Jean-du-Gard and telephone for the mini-bus from the station at Anduze on their return. Philippe Bonard was also missing.

"He's having a working lunch in his office," explained Daphne, who had returned to the table for a second helping. "Poor man, he's got a heavy load to carry with Alain gone."

"I must say, I admire the way he's soldiering on with the course," said Melissa.

"Oh, yes, he has terrific strength of character."

That's what Iris always said, thought Melissa wistfully.

Poor old Iris. At least she's got Jack to lean on. He seems really smitten with her.

Dora looked up from her chair and caught her eye. Her expression was almost welcoming and Melissa ventured to sit beside her. "How are things?" she asked.

With a slight nod, Dora directed her glance towards the opposite side of the pool, where Dieter Erdle stood staring down at the water as if engrossed in his own reflection. Rose, looking distinctly unhappy, was hovering uncertainly a few feet away, but he took no notice of her.

"Have they had words?"

Dora's smile reminded Melissa of a contented tigress. "Not exactly. He's had to change his plans, that's all. His office wants him back on Monday so his final week here is postponed indefinitely."

"That would seem to have solved your problem."

"It has." Dora put her empty plate on the ground and picked up her glass of wine. "We leave here as arranged on Saturday morning. I just hope this glorious weather holds." She looked up at the flawless blue sky, dotted with a few drifting white clouds. "I'm looking forward to some really good rounds."

"Did you find your missing golf-club, by the way?"

"No!" Dora stiffened and her look of self-satisfaction vanished. "My goodness, I'd quite forgotten . . . all the drama put it right out of my head. I can't think what's happened to it. I was doing some putting practice yesterday morning," she went on reflectively. "My appointment wasn't until eleven, so I had a bit of time to spare. After a while I thought I'd go into the orchard and practise some chip shots so I went to get my nine iron. I couldn't find it." She glared at Melissa as if holding her partly responsible.

"Could you have put it in Rose's bag instead of your own?" It seemed unlikely that anyone so competent as Dora would make such an elementary mistake, but under that fierce gaze Melissa felt bound to make some suggestion, however implausible.

Dora dismissed the notion with a sniff of contempt. "Most unlikely!" she snapped.

"Did you check?"

"Not at the time," admitted Dora grudgingly. "My watch had stopped and it was later than I thought. I'll go and look now." She strode off, returning later with a face of thunder. "I can't find it anywhere," she fumed. "Someone must have stolen it."

"Would anyone take a single club? I'd have thought any normal thief would make off with the whole bag. Unless . . ." An alarming possibility shot into Melissa's mind, but Dora could think of nothing but her own predicament.

"They might just as well have done," she said despairingly. "That iron belongs to a matched set I bought several years ago. It's irreplaceable—if it doesn't turn up, it means buying a whole new set. Of course, you're not a golfer, you wouldn't understand!"

She was becoming more and more agitated. "It's that wretched boot lid, it doesn't always shut properly. I remember now, it was open when I went back to the car. It would have been easy for anyone to reach in and yank a club out of the bag."

So it would, thought Melissa, her excitement mounting. A golf-club makes a nice handy weapon if you want to attack someone. And if your victim happens to be conveniently close to the edge of a tall cliff, by the time he's bounced down a couple of hundred metres on to the rocks, he'll be in such a mess that the injury from the blow stands a good chance of being overlooked. Was that how Alain Gebrec had died? And if so, whose hand had struck him down, and what had become of the weapon?

Thirteen

to the library, ostensibly to work on her novel, but in reality to mull over Madame Gebrec's dramatic allegations, the possible motive for an attack on Alain—if indeed, such an attack had taken place—and the significance, if any, of the missing golf-club. The afternoon tea-break arrived without her having reached any useful conclusions, despite several pages of scribbled notes well peppered with question marks.

Catching sight of Philippe Bonard, who had uncharacteristically detached himself from his students and was standing alone at the far end of the terrace, she went over to him. He was staring across at the distant mountains; he seemed to be in a reverie, unaware of her presence, and she hesitated for a moment before saying, "Could I have a word with you, please?"

"But of course." He swung round, instantly at her disposal, his head courteously inclined towards her.

"I know how upset you must feel about losing Alain," she began.

He sighed heavily. "It is a great loss, both professionally and personally."

"I understand."

"Yes, I think you do." There was gratitude in his faint, sad smile. "What can I do for you, Melissa?"

"For me, nothing, but for Alain's mother, perhaps there is something."

"Ah, yes, the poor lady. I must visit her and present my

condolences. She may be in need of advice—or perhaps financial help. I know Alain was more than generous to her."

"It wasn't money I had in mind."

"Indeed?"

"She is absolutely convinced that his death was not suicide."

Bonard bit his lip and turned his gaze once more to the horizon. "I have to admit, I too found the police version very difficult to accept," he muttered. "But it seemed inconceivable that it could have been an accident."

"She doesn't believe that either."

He looked startled. "What are you saying?" Even as he spoke, she saw the dawning horror in his eyes. "Do you mean . . . ?" He shook his head and made a movement with his hand, as if warding off some invisible threat.

"She believes he was murdered."

"Murdered? Alain? Ah, no, no! Who would kill my dear Alain?" His voice became as thin and insubstantial as a trail of smoke.

"That is what she has asked me to try and find out," said Melissa, acutely aware of how absurd it must sound.

"You? Why you?"

Melissa felt her cheeks grow warm. "I know it sounds ridiculous, but the police officer wouldn't take any notice of her—he just thought she was being hysterical. She thinks that being a crime writer makes me a detective as well. People often do," she added lamely.

"So you are going to play Sherlock Holmes and go around with a magnifying glass looking for footprints? I hardly think you will find many on the rocks." His tone was gentle, almost indulgent; it was plain that he considered the whole idea farcical, but was too polite to tell her in so many words.

"No, I wasn't planning anything quite like that. The fact is, I sort of got conned into this." Briefly, she ran through the details of the morning's interview with Madame Gebrec.

"I see." Bonard nodded gravely. "Well, ask your questions, Melissa, but I doubt if I shall be able to help."

"How long have you known Alain?"

"About five years. He came to work for my company in

Avignon as an assistant in the overseas purchasing department. He very quickly became an invaluable member of the organisation and after two years I made him manager. He and I became . . . very close." Here Bonard broke off and studied his well-kept fingernails.

"I . . . I'm not trying to pry into your personal relationship," stammered Melissa. This was becoming embarrassing; she wished she hadn't started.

"It's all right." He transferred his attention to his gold wristwatch and began fiddling with the bracelet. "I confided to Alain my ambition to establish a school such as this. I had already made an extensive study of the various methods of language teaching, purely as a hobby, and run a few short courses from my home during the holiday season. Alain was fascinated by the scheme and when at last it became a reality, he asked if he could take an active part. He has been entirely responsible for the administration of the school . . . he will be very difficult to replace."

"Was there anyone who might have felt jealous or resentful of this appointment?"

"Not that I am aware of. He was the one to approach me— none of my other employees expressed that kind of interest in the project."

"What do you know of his family history?"

"Very little. His father was killed in the war and, so far as I know, his mother is his only living relative."

"I have several times noticed a certain . . . animosity between him and Dieter Erdle. As if Erdle knew something about him, or his background, that he did not want generally known. Have you any idea what it was?"

Bonard shook his head. "You will have to ask Erdle that question, I'm afraid."

"Yes, I'll do that. By the way, did you know that Dora Lavender is claiming that a golf-club has been stolen from the boot of her car?"

He frowned. "I overheard her say to her friend that she had lost something, but she has not reported it to me. What of it?"

"It occurred to me that a golf-club can be a pretty lethal weapon."

Bonard's jaw dropped. "Melissa! What are you suggest-ing?"

"The boot of Dora's car, where she keeps her bag of clubs, has a defective catch. Anyone could have opened it, stolen one of the clubs and gone after Alain when he left the house. You said he was in a distressed frame of mind, so he proba-bly wouldn't have noticed he was being followed. A single blow on the back of the head would have stunned him, might even have killed him outright."

"Yes, I see what you mean." Bonard's look of amazement had changed to one of bewilderment. He licked his lower lip. "But the body was found at the foot of the cliff."

"He might have been standing near the edge and fallen af-ter being struck. On the other hand, he wasn't all that heavily built and a strong man—or woman, come to that—could have dragged him a short distance."

"I suppose so." He covered his eyes with a hand that shook. His voice was not quite steady as he asked, "Is there anything else you want to know?"

"Just one thing more. Do you really have no idea at all why Alain left your office in such distress?"

He made no reply, but the pain on his face told her what she wanted to know. "I mustn't take up any more of your time," she said gently. "Do I have your permission to go up to the belvedere and look around?"

"If you wish, but what do you hope to find? The police have already carried out a search."

"They weren't looking for a weapon. If that golf-club was used to attack Alain, the killer would want to get rid of it as quickly as possible."

"He might have thrown it over the cliff."

"Not if he was smart. He'd know that someone would have to go down there and recover the body and it could easily have been spotted. No, my guess is that he or she hid it somewhere in the undergrowth. That's where I'll start look-ing."

"Are you sure it wouldn't be better to tell your suspicions to the police?"

"Much better, if they'd take any notice of me," said Melissa with a grin. "From what I've seen of Officer Hassan, it would take more than a missing golf-club to prise him away from his suicide theory."

"Do you want to ask the students a lot of questions?"

"If you have no objection, I'd like to know where everyone was at the critical time. Iris and her group are eliminated straight away, of course, and most of the others had appointments which would give them alibis."

"Alibis?" He looked dismayed, as if the word conjured up a vision of a formal enquiry, with everyone being grilled about their movements and the happy atmosphere of his beloved school fouled by dark suspicions. "You will try not to alarm them?" He glanced round at the groups of people on the terrace, by the pool, strolling in the garden. His student family, the men and women who were the living embodiment of his dream. "Already much damage has been done," he said sorrowfully.

"I'll be as discreet as I can," she promised.

Melissa slipped out behind the house, through the gate in the perimeter fence and up the path leading to the belvedere. Looking at the tangle of bushes on either side, she soon realised that to make a thorough search of the undergrowth was out of the question. It was the kind of operation that needed a squad of policemen with metal detectors to carry out. Unless the hypothetical killer had been careless enough to leave part of Dora's golf-club visible, her chances of finding it must be virtually nil. Just the same, she had made a promise and would do what she could to keep it.

She reached the clearing where she had first seen Fernand. It was deserted; evidently, the work of repairing the safety barrier was complete. There was no sign of anything untoward: grass and a few bushes flattened by the weight of wood recently heaped on them; some traces of sawdust lying on the ground; nothing more. There had been no rain for several weeks and the earth was hard, barely showing marks of the tractor wheels.

She decided that her best hope was to go up to the belvedere and see if she could find any indication at all that some-

one else had been involved in Gebrec's death. It was
unlikely; any obvious signs of a struggle would have been
noted by the police. On the other hand, if foul play had not
been suspected, even the overzealous Hassan might not have
examined the spot too closely. It was worth a try.

She was getting close to the river; the sound of the tumbling water increased steadily from a gentle rushing to an in-
sistent roar. She felt a nervous spasm in her stomach as she
passed the point where Fernand had led her from the path to
show her his secret refuge. She wondered now, in cold blood,
just how she had found the courage to undertake the terrifying trip along that narrow ledge and told herself that nothing
would ever induce her to go near it again.

Reaching the head of the path, she inspected the new safety
barrier. It followed an arc some two metres from the edge of
the cliff and was a simple structure of uprights and a double
row of horizontals, about waist-high to a person of average
build. The wood was roughly finished; Melissa ran a hand
along one of the top rails, collected a splinter in her thumb
and stood sucking it while considering the possibilities.

Jack and Dieter had stated quite clearly that Alain Gebrec
had been lying on the rocks below the belvedere. Therefore,
if he had killed himself, he must have either climbed over or
through the barrier somewhere near this point. The searchers
had probably done the same as, from where Melissa was
standing, only the middle and the far side of the river bed
were visible. On the other hand, from a different vantage
point they might have seen the body without having to go
right to the edge. She was wasting her time; without knowing
exactly where it had been lying, there was no means of iden-
tifying the spot from where it had fallen. Nor was there anything to be gained by a closer look but . . . all the same, as
she was here . . . she might as well . . . before she knew
what she was doing, Melissa ducked through the rails.

As she straightened up, something caught her eye: a wisp
of blue thread clinging to one of the tiny plants that somehow
managed to exist in the thin soil on top of the cliff. She
picked it up, laid it on the palm of her hand, and considered.

Gebrec had been wearing blue slacks yesterday morning. If

this thread had come from them, it could have happened in two ways. If he had crawled under the rails in order to throw himself off the cliff, then he could easily have caught his slacks on something and left the thread behind. If, on the other hand, someone had dragged his unconscious body after slugging him with Dora's missing golf-club, there might be other shreds of cloth lying about.

Keeping well away from the edge and steeling herself against a spasm of vertigo, Melissa searched for several minutes, but found nothing further. Then, remembering her damaged thumb, she went back and examined the top rail, exclaiming aloud in excitement as she found a second thread clinging to the rough wood. With a feeling of triumph she placed both threads inside a paper tissue, folded it carefully and put it in her pocket.

Conscious that she had been crawling around in the hot sunshine for some time without a hat, she retired a short distance to the shade of some trees, sat down on a convenient boulder and tried to conjecture how Alain Gebrec might have spent his last moments. If he had indeed come up here determined to end his life, then he might have climbed over the guard rail, leaving a scrap of thread behind as he did so. Perhaps the second fragment had become detached at the same time and simply fallen to the ground where she had picked it up. From there, two or three strides would have taken him over the edge and into oblivion.

But if he had been murdered? Perhaps he had been standing at that spot, gazing out over the river towards the mountains or maybe with bowed head, grieving for his lover. If an assailant had struck from behind, he would have toppled forward over the rail. What then? To make it look like suicide, the killer would have to get the unconscious—or possibly already dead—man across two metres of rough, stony ground. First, take the legs and heave them up and over; then grab the body by the arms or legs and drag it to the edge . . . no, that wouldn't be practicable, that way the killer would be moving backwards and be the first to fall. He would have had to roll the body away from himself until he was close enough, with one final shove, to send it plunging down. To do a proper search, Melissa would have to follow his tracks and simulate that gruesome task.

Swallowing hard, she crawled once more under the rail and inched forward, keeping her eyes on the ground as she went. The noise from below battered her eardrums until it felt as if a high-speed train was roaring through her head. All the nerves in her chest and stomach tightened into one solid knot that seemed about to burst out of her throat. She recalled Alain Gebrec's warning that the edge was unstable in places; panic threatened to take over; she was on the point of abandoning the whole insane exercise when, almost at the very edge of the cliff, she spotted something that gleamed in the sun. She stretched out a hand and retrieved a small pearl button.

Fourteen

house, it was nearly a quarter past five. Iris and Jack were in the courtyard, talking to Philippe Bonard; everyone else seemed to have left.

Iris hurried to meet her. "Got worried about you!" she said reproachfully. "What kept you so long?"

"Sorry, I forgot the time."

"Jack wanted to leave a message and take me back to the *auberge*. Wouldn't go without you. You all right?" she added, with a keen look.

"Of course I am—why shouldn't I be?"

"You look very hot. Should wear a hat in this sun."

"I'm quite all right, really," Melissa insisted.

"But empty-handed, I see," said Bonard.

"I'm afraid so." She gave him an enquiring glance, uncertain as to how much the others knew of the reason for her absence.

He gave a nod of reassurance. "I told our friends here the gist of our conversation—no doubt you will fill in the details. I presume your next unhappy task will be to inform Madame Gebrec that you have found nothing to support her contention?"

"Not just yet. I've still got some other ideas to follow up."

"You will tell me if you learn anything significant? If I can be of any help . . . since we had our talk, I too have begun to have doubts. I should like to know for certain how . . . Alain died."

His voice wavered. Iris put a hand on his arm. Jack cleared his throat and looked from one to the other. "Perhaps we'd better leave you now, Philippe," he said. "We'll see you in the morning."

"Yes, of course." Bonard drew himself upright and shook hands with everyone, once again the courteous, attentive head of the establishment. "I wish you all good evening."

Back in their room at the *auberge*, Melissa took the tissue from her pocket and spread it with its contents on the table. Iris stared with her mouth open as she described how she had found them.

"Why didn't you tell Philippe?" she demanded.

"Because they might not have come from Alain's clothing at all and I didn't want to upset him unnecessarily."

"Where else could they have come from?"

"Several places. Alain wasn't the only person to wear blue yesterday. Fernand wears his *bleu de travail* every day and he must have handled that rail umpteen times—the threads could have come from him. And Dieter—I've seen him in similar clothes to the ones Alain wore yesterday, blue slacks and a white shirt. He might have lost those threads when he climbed over the rail during the search."

"He was wearing fawn slacks yesterday," said Iris.

"Are you sure?"

"Positive. Noticed when he came back in the afternoon, while he was talking to Rose. Her dress was almost the same colour, sort of café au lait, only hers had flowers on it."

"That narrows it down a bit, but we'd need a forensic scientist to establish whether the threads came from Alain's slacks or not."

"Hmm." Iris sat on the edge of her bed with her chin in her hands. "What about the button?"

"If Alain was murdered and pushed over the edge the way I figured, then it could easily have been torn off. On the other hand, it might have been loose anyway and just fallen off. It's all very circumstantial."

"It's a very ordinary button." Iris examined it thoughtfully. "Might not be from his shirt at all."

"The only way to find out would be to get the police to check it against the one he was wearing when they found him."

"You're going to the police?"

Melissa rewrapped the tissue and put it in a drawer. "I haven't decided yet."

Iris gave her an appraising look. "Planning a bit more private sleuthing, are we?"

"Maybe."

"Wish you wouldn't. Could be dangerous."

"I'll be careful," promised Melissa. "It's just that I don't want Officer Banana-Split Hassan to start harassing Fernand unnecessarily."

"Fernand? Why should he be involved?"

"Hassan strongly suspected that he had something to do with Wolfgang Klein's death. He was mortally disappointed when it was officially declared an accident and there's nothing he'd like better than to find some excuse to start ferreting round and upsetting everyone with his 'interrogations.'"

"Philippe would hate that," said Iris, as if this was sufficient reason for leaving Hassan with his suicide theory for the time being. "Anyway," she said with a frown, "I don't see how there could be a connection. It's Germans that get Fernand's goat. Now, if Erdle had been the victim . . ."

"Dora Lavender would be suspect number one!" said Melissa dryly. "And that would have been ironic, wouldn't it, now he's been posted back to HQ. I wonder if Rose will be down to dinner?"

"Dressed in mourning?" Iris gave an unsympathetic cackle. "Can't say we didn't warn her."

The atmosphere at the dinner table could have been worse—for most of the meal, at any rate. Dora, naturally, was in good spirits and with Fortune on her side she could afford to be magnanimous. She made no reference to either Dieter's recall or the coming week of golf in Antibes; instead, in response to a question from Melissa, she gave an account of her visit to the sports centre the previous day and then encouraged

Rose to talk about her experiences in the world of *son et lumière*.

Rose responded bravely, but her manner was artificially bright and brittle. Like Dora, she too avoided any mention of Dieter. It was a chance remark that caught her off guard.

"Your interviews seem to have been a great success," said Melissa casually as she helped herself to cheese. "Did everyone fare as well?"

"I think so," said Dora. "Everyone seemed very pleased with the arrangements Philippe had made, didn't they, Rose?"

"Dieter was a bit put out." Rose had evidently spoken without thinking. Her colour deepened and she bit her lip and looked down at her plate.

"Why? What went wrong?" asked Dora gently.

"Nothing really . . . I mean, it was a good interview. It was just that the man he went to see kept him waiting from nine o'clock until almost ten. Something to do with a piece of machinery breaking down."

"These things happen," said Dora. "Monsieur Tollet at the sports centre had to leave me several times to deal with queries."

"Just a minute," said Melissa. "Dora, didn't you say something to me about trying to have a word with Dieter yesterday morning, before you went off to your interview?"

Dora thought for a moment. "That's right, I did. He was in the garden and I called out to him, but he didn't answer. Wouldn't answer, more likely," she added tartly, forgetting her role as peacemaker and earning a resentful glance from Rose.

"What time would this have been?"

"Oh, I don't know. Half-past nine, perhaps. I didn't look at my watch, but I found out later it had stopped so it would have been wrong anyway. Everyone else had gone and I was practising on the putting green. I saw him go through the gate into the woods . . ."

"You couldn't have done," Rose interrupted. "He was waiting to see that man at the factory long before then. Anyway, why did you want to speak to him? You usually avoid him like the plague." The cordial atmosphere was crumbling fast.

"Does it matter?"

"Of course it matters. You were going to interfere, weren't you?" Rose's voice shook, the pitch growing higher with each word. "Trying to come between him and me? Well, it won't work. And don't imagine that just because he's got to go back on Saturday, we shan't be seeing one another again." She leapt to her feet and glared at Dora, her chin thrust forward, her eyes hard and angry.

"Rose, do calm down. Everyone's looking at you."

"Let them look. I'm not staying here with you another minute!" Almost in tears now, Rose rushed out of the dining-room, narrowly avoiding a collision with Monsieur Gauthier bearing a loaded tray.

Dora was about to follow, but Iris stopped her with a gesture. "No point," she said laconically. "Only lead to another bust-up. Have a liqueur with your coffee." She beckoned to Monsieur Gauthier, who came bobbing across to their table.

When he had gone to fetch their order, Melissa said, "Dora, are you absolutely certain you saw Dieter Erdle in the garden yesterday morning?"

"Of course I am. He was going into the woods."

"Did you happen to notice what he was wearing?"

Dora looked surprised, thought for a moment and said, "Blue trousers and a white shirt, I think." Iris opened her mouth to contradict, but Melissa nudged her under the table. Dora looked at them curiously and said, "Why do you ask?"

"I just wondered . . . you said this was about nine-thirty. Would that have been about the time you went back to the car to look for your nine iron?"

"No, that was later. I went back and carried on with my putting practice for a while. What did I do next?" Dora traced an abstract pattern with her finger on the table-cloth, as if she felt it would help the process of recall. "Oh, yes, I thought perhaps I'd try to intercept Erdle on his way back. I hung around for a while . . . now I come to think of it, I walked a short way along the path, looking for him."

"But you didn't see him?"

"No, I came to the conclusion that he must have gone the other way, along the track leading to the road."

"Weren't you surprised to have seen him in the first place? I mean, didn't you know he was supposed to be in Anduze at nine o'clock?"

"Why should I? We were given the details of our appointments individually. I simply assumed his was for later on, like mine."

"So, when you failed to find him, you gave up and went back to the car to look for your nine iron?"

"That's right. I couldn't find it, but I didn't search thoroughly just then."

"Because you realised your watch had stopped and it was later than you thought?"

"Yes. I checked the car clock and it was twenty past ten. My appointment was in Alès at eleven and I wanted to give myself plenty of time to find the place, so I decided to leave straight away. Why are you asking all these questions, Melissa? Do you suppose it was Erdle who stole my iron?"

"I've no reason to think so, but I'm trying to consider all possibilities." Remembering her promise to Bonard and anxious not to excite any alarmist speculation, Melissa kept her tone casual, but the damage had been done.

Dora jerked her head like a horse shying at a pheasant. "Well, I have every reason to think so!" she declared. "I see it now—it's that stupid young fool's idea of a joke, to pay me out for objecting to the way he's been behaving towards Rose! Just wait till I get hold of him!" Her face registered gathering anger and her tone a blistering contempt. "I've a good mind to go and have it out with him here and now. I know where to find him—he's staying at the Lion d'Or."

"Hang on a minute," said Melissa, restraining Dora in the act of leaping to her feet. "What proof have you got?"

"What proof do I need? Who else would play a trick like that on me? I wouldn't be surprised if Rose put him up to it!" She was becoming increasingly agitated, glaring at Melissa as if in some way holding her responsible.

"Take it easy," said Iris. "This is getting out of hand."

Dora ignored the intervention. "There's something funny

going on," she insisted. "What was Erdle doing in the woods this morning, I'd like to know?" She stabbed the air with her forefinger. "I'll tell you what he was doing. He was looking for somewhere to hide my iron. He might even have thrown it over the cliff. If he has, it'll be ruined!"

"Please, Dora, be reasonable!" urged Melissa. "According to Rose, he was at a factory in Anduze by nine and spent the rest of the morning there. He couldn't be in two places at once."

"His contact didn't show up till nearly ten. He had plenty of time to come back."

"But Rose said . . ."

"Rose will believe anything that man tells her," fumed Dora. "All I know is, I saw him, I followed him, but he disappeared into the woods. What he did after that, I've no idea. Unless," her hand shot to her mouth and her eyes dilated, "unless he was going after Alain Gebrec. Perhaps that poor man didn't kill himself after all!" Her voice faded to a barely audible whisper. "Perhaps Dieter Erdle murdered him . . . with my nine iron! Oh, how dreadful!"

"If I were you, I wouldn't go spreading accusations like that around," said Melissa, alarmed at the turn the conversation was taking. "You could find yourself in serious trouble."

"I don't need your advice on how to conduct myself, thank you," said Dora through her teeth.

Further acrimony was prevented by the arrival of Monsieur Gauthier with the liqueurs. Immediately, Dora put her expression to rights, even squeezing out a polite smile of thanks as he set her glass in front of her, the epitome of a well-bred Englishwoman who never reveals her feelings before servants or foreigners.

"Your friend, she does not return?" he enquired, with a bob towards Rose's empty chair.

"She is tired and has gone to her room. I'll go up and see how she is. I'll take this with me." Dora stood up with the glass in her hand. "Will you get another one, please?"

"Well, what do you make of that?" murmured Melissa as soon as Dora was out of earshot.

"Couldn't have been Erdle she saw," replied Iris. "Wrong colour trousers."

"He might have changed them." Melissa's brain was in overdrive. "Suppose Dora's right and he did kill Gebrec? Crawling about disposing of the body, he could have got them dusty."

"Suppose so. Or bloodstained. A bash on the head with a golf-club'd make a nasty mess."

"In that case there'd have been blood on the ground," Melissa pointed out. "The fuzz would have been on to that straight away. No, if there's anything in the golf-club theory, it's more likely the victim was merely stunned."

"So you reckon Erdle might have done it?"

Melissa shook her head doubtfully. "There is the problem of time. If what he told Rose was true, he couldn't have been at the belvedere after about a quarter to nine. We know Gebrec was alive at least half an hour after that. It should be the easiest of alibis to check."

"Oh, yes? Like how, Madame Poirot?"

Melissa shrugged. "You tell me. I've got no authority to go asking questions of complete strangers."

Iris's eyes sparkled. "Knowing you, you'll think of something!"

Melissa grinned back at her. "I'm delighted to know you have such faith in me!" They clinked glasses and sipped their liqueurs in a companionable silence, forgetting for a minute or two the gruesome nature of their discussion. Then Melissa said, "Motive. Let's think about motive."

"Any ideas?"

"Nothing very positive, but Erdle was constantly needling him, wasn't he?"

"More like a motive for him to bump off Erdle than t'other way round."

"That's a point. And there's that book I bought—gosh, I keep forgetting about that! Both Gebrecs were furious about something in there, and Erdle knows what it is. He offered to show me, but Alain nearly went berserk and then we got interrupted. I started to flip through it, but I didn't know where

to begin. It's got over three hundred pages, all heavily anno-
tated."

"Tried the index?"

"Of course." Melissa looked pained. "First thing I did."
She finished her drink and got up from the table. "There's
only one person who can answer this."

"You mean Erdle? Not going to tackle him about this business of Dora's golf-club, are you?"

"Of course I'm not."

"What about Madame G?"

Slowly, Melissa sat down. "Yes, of course, she knows," she
mused. "But when I asked her if she knew of anyone who
might have a motive for killing Alain, it didn't seem to ring
any bells."

"Revenge?" suggested Iris. "Long-standing grudge . . . one
generation settling the previous one's accounts?"

"Mm, could well be. I can't bother Madame Gebrec this
evening, she's far too upset. But I can talk to Erdle." Melissa
stood up again.

Iris did the same. "I'll come with you."

Melissa eyed her with something like suspicion. "This is a
change of heart for you, isn't it? You usually do your
darnedest to talk me out of getting involved in this sort of
thing."

"Learned my lesson, haven't I? Can't stop you poking your
nose in, but I can keep an eye on you."

"Okay," sighed Melissa. "Come if you insist—but please,
let me do the talking."

When they reached the Lion d'Or, the first person they saw
was Jack Hammond sitting in a corner of the terrace. He hurried across to greet them, his ruddy face alight with pleasure.

"I was just thinking about you," he said. His glance briefly
included Melissa, but settled, beaming, on Iris. "Will you
have a drink with me? Dieter said he'd be along presently."

Iris hesitated, but Melissa jumped in quickly. "You two
wait here for me and I'll join you in a minute or two," she
said. Over Jack's shoulder, she caught her friend's eye and
put a finger to her lips. There was no particular reason why

he should not know what she was up to, but she instinctively felt an urge to keep it quiet for the moment.

She intercepted Dieter just as he was emerging on to the terrace. He looked surprised at her request for a word in private, but readily agreed and led her across the hotel reception hall, out through a door at the rear of the building and into the garden. There was no one about; the swings in the children's play area hung motionless and the only sound from the swimming-pool was the hum of the filtration plant. The reflections of a string of coloured lanterns danced in an ever-changing pattern on the rippling surface of the water.

"Isn't that pretty!" exclaimed Melissa.

Dieter raised an eyebrow. "You did not come out here to admire the lights, I think?"

"No."

"Then let me guess. You bring a request from Dora not to deprive her of—what is the English expression—her meal ticket?" His grin held the same hint of mocking, almost insolent provocation as when he had taunted Alain Gebrec.

Melissa was about to retort that Dora had every right to be concerned about her friend, but reminded herself that it was no business of hers and that in any case, Dora was quite capable of fighting her own battles.

"I'm quite sure Dora can do without the services of an emissary," she said coolly and his laughter echoed across the empty garden.

He was quite outrageous and she knew she should not have so much as smiled, but she found herself laughing with him. He was a handsome animal with a charm that was hard to resist; his brown hair sprang from his scalp in crisp waves, his speech was brisk, his carriage erect and his movements athletic. It was easy to see why Rose found him so attractive; whether he cared for her was another matter and nothing to do with Melissa or her present mission.

"So," he said, smiling in obvious delight at having so easily disarmed her. "What can I do for you, *gnädige Frau*?"

"You remember how angry Alain became when he saw me with that book?" she said.

"Of course." The recollection appeared to cause him further amusement.

"There's something in it that upset both Alain and his mother very much. You know what it is, don't you?"

His smile faded. "Why do you say that?"

"You offered to point it out to me. You must remember— Alain snatched the book from my hand before you had the chance."

He gave an uneasy laugh. "Just an example of my unfortunate sense of humour, I fear."

"You mean, you don't really know at all?"

He avoided her eye as he replied, "I have no idea."

"So why all the snide remarks?"

He looked at her in apparent perplexity. "What does this mean, 'snide'?"

"I think you know perfectly well," said Melissa impatiently, suspecting prevarication. "Teasing him about speaking German, wisecracks about spies . . . that sort of thing. What were you getting at?"

"Getting at?"

This time, his look of puzzlement was far too exaggerated to be genuine, but she kept her voice even as she said, "What . . . did . . . you . . . mean?"

"Ah, I understand. Well, I meant nothing at all, I assure you. Just a little joke. I told him last week that he looked more like a German than a Frenchman and he became very cross." His short laugh sounded slightly hollow. "It was quite funny."

"He didn't seem to think it was funny."

Dieter thrust his hands into his pockets and traced with the toe of one foot the outline of a damp patch on the concrete surround of the pool.

"I like to make jokes, but some people have no sense of humour, that is all," he said defensively. "Why do you ask me all these questions?"

"Alain's mother doesn't believe he committed suicide and I'm inclined to agree with her." For a moment, the foot hesitated in its rotation, then completed one more cycle and came to rest. He continued to stare at the ground as she added, "I'm just wondering who might have had a motive for killing him."

"So," he said without looking up, "you play the real-life detective for a change?"

"I promised to ask around a bit, and it occurred to me that the book might contain a clue."

"I am sorry, I cannot help you."

"That's a pity. I don't want to have to question Madame Gebrec, because I think it would upset her. Since you won't tell me, I suppose I'll just have to plod through the whole book."

He shrugged. "In your place, I would not waste my time. Have you any other questions for me?"

"No, that's all."

As they walked back through the hotel he remarked casually, "I said I'd meet Jack on the terrace for a drink."

"Yes, he told me."

"Perhaps you would care to join us?"

"As a matter of fact, he's expecting me. My friend Iris is there with him already."

"Aha! Another romance, to keep the score . . ." He moved his hands up and down, simulating a pair of scales. *"Gleich?"*

"Even," she translated and added, "I don't follow you."

"Well, we have had two deaths, so why not two love affairs—or, perhaps I should say, flirtations?"

The words were spoken with a provocative, sidelong glance and Melissa was sure that, just for the hell of it, he was trying to trick her into questioning him over his relationship with Rose. She declined to be tempted. And it had not escaped her notice that he had allowed the words, "since you won't tell me" to pass unchallenged. It might have been a weakness in his command of the language, but she did not think so.

Fifteen

IRIS AND JACK WERE SEATED AT A TA-
ble with a book of glossy coloured plates lying open in front
of them. Iris was discoursing with animation, her hands de-
scribing sweeping patterns in the air, her whole attention focused on her subject. From the way her companion was
looking at her it was easy to see that only part of his mind
was concerned with art.

Glancing at Dieter, Melissa read "What did I tell you?" in
his smile as he made a great pantomime of clearing his
throat.

"I hope we do not interrupt you?" he said with mock formality. The two looked up in surprise and Jack half rose from
his seat.

"Please, don't get up," said Melissa. She sat down in the
chair that Dieter held for her and craned her neck to peer at
the book. "What have you got there?"

"Reproductions from the Arthur Sanderson Design Ar-
chive," explained Jack. "These are from the William Morris
School. We've been looking at the contrasting features of
these two." He pushed the book across and pointed out the
swirling fronds of "Seaweed" and the stiffly formal "Sweet
Pea," while Iris looked on, nodding and chipping in with observations from time to time. Melissa detected a growing
rapport between them, and rejoiced.

Jack put the book to one side and the four of them sat chatting over a bottle of wine. The evening air was soft as silk,

cicadas sang in the trees and a few birds, black against the sunset, flew home to roost.

"Last day of the course tomorrow," said Jack with evident regret. "I understand you're going home on Saturday as well, Dieter?"

"Yes—a summons from my manager. It seems I have to make some travel abroad, but I may return later to complete my studies."

"I'm hoping to come back as well, if everything goes to plan." Jack glanced at Iris and received a nod and a smile in return.

The slight figure of a woman emerged from the hotel and stood on the steps leading down to the terrace, scanning the tables with anxious eyes and making agitated, jerky movements with her hands.

"Here's Rose," said Melissa. "Something seems to be wrong."

Rose caught sight of them and came rushing across, dodging between the tables and nearly sending a waiter flying. Dieter guided her to an empty chair; she was trembling violently and he called for brandy.

"What is the matter?" he asked, a note of resignation in his voice. "Have you had another quarrel with Dora?" She nodded without speaking. "The usual thing, I suppose?"

"No, it's much worse. Oh, Dieter, I don't know how to say this!" Her shoulders slumped and she covered her face with her hands. With some reluctance, it seemed to Melissa, Dieter put an arm round her. When at last she lifted her head, she found herself facing three pairs of curious, slightly embarrassed eyes. She appeared taken aback, as if she had only just realised that the pair of them were not alone.

Simultaneously, the others stood up. "We'll leave you now," said Jack. "I'm sure you want to have a private talk."

"No, please stay," begged Rose. "You'll hear about it soon enough anyway—Iris and Melissa probably know already."

"Know what?" asked Dieter as she seemed unable to go on.

She turned terrified eyes on him. "Dieter, can you say exactly where you were yesterday, every minute of the day until you got back to Les Châtaigniers?"

He frowned. "I am not sure about every minute. Why do you ask?"

She grabbed him by the hand, her eyes frantically searching his. "You were at that factory by nine o'clock, weren't you? It's important!"

"Yes, of course."

"When they told you you'd have to wait ... you stayed right there ... you didn't leave and then go back later?"

He frowned and said, "What a foolish question. Why should I do that?"

"You might have thought, as you had to wait ..."

"And where do you suppose I went?" he said impatiently. "Really, this is becoming quite stupid."

"How long were you at the factory?" she persisted.

"Until about twelve o'clock. Then Monsieur Coutelan invited me to lunch in a restaurant in some village. I don't know what time we came back."

"But you were with someone all the time? You do have an alibi for the whole morning?"

"Why should I need an alibi?" He forced a smile. "Has someone robbed a bank?"

"Dora thinks Alain Gebrec was murdered," said Rose in a terrified whisper. "She says ... she saw you go up to the belvedere ... and one of her golf-clubs is missing ... I'm afraid she thinks you took it ... to kill him!"

"Indeed?" Dieter withdrew his arm. "Your friend goes to great trouble to make you think ill of me." His expression was grim and a muscle above his right eye started to twitch.

"Oh, darling, you don't think I believe it, do you?"

"I hope not." His face did not relax as he picked up the brandy and handed it to her. "Perhaps you should drink this," he said.

Rose's hands were shaking so badly that some of the contents of the glass spilled on her dress. Spluttering and gulping, she mopped it with her handkerchief. "I'm sorry," she faltered. "It was such a shock when I realised what Dora was suggesting. We had a terrible quarrel . . . I was screaming at her. I don't think I can ever be friends with her again."

"You know something about this?" Dieter glared across the table at the others, his voice harsh and angry. Jack shook his head and Iris gave great attention to her glass. It was left to Melissa to reply.

"Dora took it into her head this evening that you'd pinched one of her golf-clubs as a sort of practical joke," she explained. "She insisted she'd seen you heading out through the woods at about half-past nine, shortly before she missed it. Then she suddenly got the wild idea that you might have taken it to attack Alain. I did point out that you were supposed to have been in another place at the time . . ."

"That's Dora all over," interrupted Rose with a sniff. "Once she gets an idea into her head, wild horses won't shift it." She turned to face Dieter. "I didn't believe it for a single moment, darling," she repeated earnestly. "I just wanted to be sure you had an alibi."

Dieter ignored her. He was staring at Melissa with fury in his eyes. " 'Supposed to have been in another place'—what are you suggesting?" he demanded.

She spread her hands in a conciliatory gesture. "Nothing, really . . . just a figure of speech. It seems to have been a case of mistaken identity."

"Obviously," said Dieter coldly. To Melissa's relief, he did not raise the subject of their earlier conversation.

"Then who did she see, if it wasn't Dieter?" asked Jack.

"It could have been Alain," said Melissa. "They wear similar clothes, and they are the same build and colouring when you come to think of it. You did say her eyesight isn't all that good, didn't you, Rose?"

"Of course!" Rose sat bolt upright. "If she had her putting glasses on, anything at a distance would look fuzzy. Most people with her problem wear bifocals, but not Dora, oh no!" She did not actually say, "she would have to be different," but the implication was unmistakable.

"So it was Alain all the time, and she took him for me," mused Dieter. *"Mein Doppelgänger!"* He gave a short, mirthless laugh. "How ironic," he added, almost to himself.

The cloud had vanished from Rose's face. "How silly we are not to have thought of that before," she said. "And won't Dora feel a fool when we tell her." Equally relieved at the removal of any suspicion towards Dieter and delighted at the prospect of Dora's embarrassment, she picked up her glass again and swallowed a mouthful of brandy with relish.

"Dora said she called after him, but he didn't respond," said Melissa thoughtfully. "If it was Alain—and it almost certainly was—then he might not even have heard, let alone taken any notice. Philippe said he rushed off in some distress."

"Poor chap!" said Jack sadly. Mechanically, he picked up the wine bottle and offered refills, but gloom had settled over the table and no one was interested.

"So what happens now?" asked Iris with a keen, somewhat disapproving, glance at Rose.

"I don't know." Rose turned to Dieter. "I can't go back to sharing a room with Dora, and I know the *auberge* is full." She put a hand on his arm and gave an arch smile. "Perhaps I could stay here?"

Looking anything but delighted at the prospect, he stood up. "Wait here, I'll go to ask," he said curtly.

He returned a few minutes later with the news that a room was available. "I have told them to make it ready for you," he said. "I will take you now to collect your things."

"Oh, thank you!" she said, but her smile withered at the sight of his expression and she trailed after him towards the car park without a word or a glance at the others.

"Hmm," said Jack. "Things seem a bit bumpy there, don't they?"

"Looks as if Dora's going to have the last laugh," said Iris. "I'm going to the ladies, then we'll be leaving too." She hoisted her lanky frame from her chair and Jack immediately leapt from his. "No need to fuss," she said, evading the hand he held out to assist her. She slung her bag over one shoulder and went marching across the terrace, head erect, free arm swinging. Jack's eyes followed her in admiration.

"What a woman!" he exclaimed.

"She's an independent soul," commented Melissa.

"But a rare character. I can't tell you how much I'm enjoying this week, despite all the trauma." His face grew serious. "Melissa, do you agree with Alain's mum that he was murdered? It's pretty odd, isn't it, one of Dora's clubs going missing like that. I take it your search came to nothing?"

"Well, as a matter of fact . . ." On impulse, she decided to tell him of her discoveries at the belvedere and the conclusions she had drawn from them. "I didn't say anything to Philippe because it was so inconclusive," she finished, "and I still can't decide whether it's worth taking them to the police."

"I see your point about Philippe, but I don't see why you're keeping this from the police," said Jack.

"What's the point of sending Officer Hassan flying off at half cock and upsetting a lot of people if it's all to no purpose?"

"Who do you mean by 'a lot of people'? You wouldn't be trying to protect anyone?" His eyes were shrewd. "Fernand, for example?"

"I suppose Iris has been telling you about my chats with 'the nutter,' as she calls him?"

"You can't pretend he's normal and it's no secret that he didn't see eye to eye with Alain."

"Fernand has been badly traumatised, but he's a gentle soul and wouldn't lay a finger on anyone," Melissa insisted.

Jack shook his head. "That really isn't the point, Melissa. The evidence you found may not on its own be inconsistent with the suicide theory, but just the same, it's your duty to hand it over and let the police decide if it's worth following up."

"I suppose so," she sighed. "All right, I'll give them a call in the morning. Ah, here comes Iris. We'd better be going now."

Sixteen

ON THE WAY BACK TO THE *AUBERGE*, Iris demanded to know what Melissa had managed to learn from Dieter Erdle.

"Precisely nothing," Melissa said. "He claims it was just harmless Teutonic fun at the expense of a humourless Frog."

"You believe that?"

"No."

"So what's the game?"

"I don't know, but I'm going to find out even if it means sitting up all night reading that bloody book. Hullo, what's going on in here?"

They had reached the *auberge* to find the entire Gauthier family—Monsieur, Madame and five daughters—assembled round the reception desk in excited and voluble discussion. The sound of six Frenchwomen all talking at once gave the impression of a barnyard invaded by a marauding fox, with Monsieur Gauthier rushing to and fro, beating the air with his hands like a distraught chanticleer. In the farthest corner, looking as if she would rather be anywhere else in the world at that moment, sat Dora. There was no sign of Rose or Dieter.

"Wonder what's happened," said Iris. "Can you make out what they're rabbiting on about? I'll go and talk to Dora."

Madame Gauthier, in between making intermittent, shrill contributions to the general commotion, was proceeding with her regular evening task of making up her accounts. Melissa's politely worded question was received with an unfriendly stare and a tart suggestion that "those other English" would put her in the picture. She, Madame Gauthier, wife of the proprietor, had her business to attend to, and this kind of scandal did it no good at all.

The Gauthier daughters, however, were only too ready to talk; they practically fell on Melissa as she attempted to make her way through their ranks. The two English ladies, they explained, had had a most regrettable, a most serious disagreement, during which voices had been raised and charges of murder, yes, murder, had been uttered. A French lady in an adjoining room who understood some English had become greatly alarmed and taken it upon herself to summon the police. An officer from the gendarmerie was even now interrogating the accused person.

"What accused person?" Melissa asked, but before anyone could give a coherent answer Monsieur Gauthier managed to impose some sort of order on the chaos and shooed his family, like so many cackling hens, towards the private quarters at the rear of the hotel. Only his wife remained, a scrawny figure with gold-rimmed spectacles half-way down her nose, presiding like a recording angel over her ledgers.

In the corner, Iris was sitting beside Dora, who was looking shaken. "I never dreamed it would come to this," she declared. "I tried so hard to make her see how . . . unsuitable that man is. I told her over and over again, but she wouldn't listen."

"You don't seriously believe Dieter attacked Alain Gebrec, do you?" said Melissa. "I did point out . . ."

"Why not? I did see him you know—oh, I know he's supposed to have been somewhere else, but his alibi might not be . . . anyway, I'm sure he's quite capable of it," insisted Dora in a transparent attempt at self-justification. "In any case, I was only trying to warn her. How was I to know that stupid woman would call the police?" She looked pleadingly from one to the other.

"Where is she now?" asked Melissa. "And where's Dieter?"

"Erdle's being questioned by that big gendarme and Rose is upstairs, packing her things. She's throwing herself at that man, making a complete fool of herself. He's not seriously interested in her—anyone can see that—and our holiday's ruined!" Overcome with rage and frustration, Dora jammed a fist against her mouth and gnawed at her knuckles.

"I'm just going to fetch something," said Melissa. "I'll only be a minute. If it's Hassan, don't let him leave before I get back," she added to Iris before hurrying upstairs.

On her way back she met Rose, a suitcase in her hand, her face white with fury. "Have you heard what's happened?" She almost spat out the words. "When we got back, that fool of a gendarme practically arrested Dieter on the spot. It's all Dora's fault—I'll never forgive her, never!"

"She didn't intend . . . I mean, it wasn't Dora who rang the police."

"If she hadn't been screaming all that nonsense at the top of her voice, it would never have happened. I just hope she gets arrested herself for wasting police time. It'd serve her right!"

The final words were pronounced in ringing tones as they arrived back in the hall, where Officer Hassan and Dieter were just emerging from the salon. Rose rushed at Dieter and made a grab at his wrist, as if fearing to find handcuffs dangling from it. He shook her off with an irritable gesture and turned to the gendarme.

"I take it I may go back to my hotel now?"

"Certainly, Monsieur. We will talk again tomorrow."

Without meeting Rose's eyes, Dieter took her suitcase and marched through the door. She followed at his heels. Dora half rose, then resignedly sat down again.

"Madame Craig!" Hassan rushed forward with one hand outstretched and a grin like a buttered croissant, then remembered he was on duty and saluted instead.

"Good evening, Officer," said Melissa politely. "Whatever is going on?"

"A most dramatic turn of events!" he began and then, becoming aware of Madame Gauthier's fiercely disapproving frown, he gave a conciliatory bow and said, with a meaning glance in Dora's direction, "If Madame will permit, I should like to use the salon for a few more minutes."

"I've told you everything I know," declared Dora.

"That remains to be seen." His tone held a hint of menace. "I will speak to you again in a moment, Madame. First, I should like a word with these other ladies."

"There is nothing I can tell you, Officer," said Iris in her stilted French, "but my friend has something that may interest you."

"Indeed?" His face registered delighted anticipation. "Then, if you would also remain here for a few moments, Madame Ash, perhaps Madame Craig would be so kind as to come this way?"

The moment the door closed behind them, he exclaimed, "A most extraordinary allegation has been made by Madame Lavender. She tried to persuade me someone stole one of her golf-clubs in order to attack the unfortunate Monsieur Gebrec."

"So I understand from Mrs. Kettle," said Melissa. "In the circumstances, you may find what I have here of some interest."

She unfolded the tissue, displayed its contents and explained how she had come to find them. "I hope you don't think I question the competence of your men," she said, anxious to be diplomatic. "It is plain that all the indications were that Monsieur Gebrec had taken his own life . . . it was only on account of my promise to his mother . . ."

It was doubtful if he heard the final words. He gazed at the two scraps of blue thread and the single button as if they were the contents of Aladdin's cave and then turned admiring eyes on Melissa.

"Madame Craig, you are not only the greatest living writer of the detective novel, you are also a detective yourself!"

"You think these might be significant?"

He scrutinised the items, turning the tissue this way and that under the light. "I will have these examined by our experts first thing tomorrow," he said. "In the light of Madame Lavender's statement, I will also seek permission to have the body re-examined." He folded the tissue carefully and tucked it into the back of his notebook. "Now, Madame Craig, this golf-club that is alleged to have been stolen . . . do you have any information about that?"

"Only what Mrs. Lavender has told me herself."

"You have no idea who might have taken it, or for what purpose?"

"None at all."

"Have you seen any evidence that the ladies' car or its contents have been tampered with?"

"No."

"So we have nothing but Madame Lavender's word that the article is missing?"

"I suppose so. The only other possibility is that it was never there in the first place—that she left it at home by mistake."

"I myself put that very point to her." Hassan beamed at this evidence of a meeting of minds. "She refuted the idea absolutely."

"I can well believe it," said Melissa with a smile. "She takes her golf very seriously; she told me her clubs are a matched set and I imagine they're worth quite a lot of money. I'm sure she keeps a careful check on them."

"Quite so. Now, as to the circumstances of yesterday morning. I have been over her story several times and she is quite positive that she saw Monsieur Erdle walking towards the belvedere at about half past nine, although she is unable to state the precise hour. Monsieur Erdle denies this absolutely; he has made a statement—which, of course, will be verified —accounting for his movements from nine o'clock until well past the estimated time of death."

"We were discussing this earlier," said Melissa. "There was a suggestion that it was Alain Gebrec that she saw."

"She does not accept that possibility."

"Well, I'm sure you will check everything very thoroughly," Melissa murmured tactfully. "By the way, what was the estimated time of death?"

"Some time between nine-thirty, when Gebrec left the office of Monsieur Bonard, and midday. Now," Hassan licked a forefinger and turned a page of his notebook, "you are no doubt aware that Madame Lavender has shown considerable hostility towards Monsieur Erdle on a number of occasions?"

"It is because she is very anxious about the extent of his influence over her friend," said Melissa. "She does not wish to see her hurt."

"Ah, yes." Hassan fondled his moustache. "The little Madame Kettle. She is, I think, much in love with Monsieur Erdle?"

"Mrs. Lavender is convinced that it's an infatuation that will pass once they leave here."

"And what do you think?"

"I hope for Mrs. Kettle's sake that she is right."

"Madame Lavender alleges that there was ill-feeling between Monsieur Erdle and Monsieur Gebrec. Have you observed anything of the kind?"

"Several times." Melissa recounted briefly the exchanges on the way to the belvedere and the altercation over the book. "I would have said, however, that the ill-feeling was all on Alain Gebrec's part. Erdle kept hinting that he knew of something unsavoury about him—or possibly his family—and the angrier Gebrec became, the more Erdle taunted him."

"But you did not observe any threats being exchanged?"

"No, nothing like that. As a matter of fact, I tackled Erdle about it this evening because I was curious to find the reference in the book that upset both Madame Gebrec and her son. He denied knowing anything about it, but I'm not sure I believe him."

"I will mention the point myself tomorrow." Hassan scribbled in his notebook. "It may be significant, although it hardly suggests a motive for murder. Now, Madame." He glanced round, dropped his somewhat magisterial style of questioning and leaned towards Melissa with a prurient gleam in his eyes. "My next question is a rather delicate one. I know from your books, that I admire so much, that you are a shrewd observer of human . . . er, behaviour. What, would you say, are the intentions of Monsieur Erdle towards Madame Kettle?"

"If you had asked me that question yesterday, or even this morning, I might have found it difficult to answer," said Melissa slowly. "I was prepared to believe that he was genuinely fond of her, although I don't think many of the others at the Centre would have agreed with me. But now . . ."

"Now you have doubts?" She nodded. "May I ask what made you change your opinion?"

"My conversation with him this evening made me realise that he can be quite devious, and also that he has a rather cruel sense of humour. I suspect that the relationship with Mrs. Kettle began, from his point of view, as a light-hearted flirtation—in fact, he as good as said so. He would, I think, have found Mrs. Lavender's attitude to him something of a challenge and it probably amused him to manipulate Mrs. Kettle into defying her and then to observe her reactions. Only I doubt if he realised just how seriously Mrs. Kettle was taking him."

"So you do not share Madame Lavender's conviction—almost, I would say, her obsessive fear—that Monsieur Erdle is seeking to marry Madame Kettle for her money?"

"I wouldn't like to say that such an idea has never occurred to him, but, if it has, I suspect he is having second thoughts. She is, after all, some years older than he is and inclined to be emotional, hysterical even."

"Madame Lavender, I understand, has very little fortune of her own. Such a union would cause her a certain . . . inconvenience, shall we say?"

"I don't know much about their private affairs," said Melissa guardedly, "except that they are friends of many years' standing and have shared a house since they both became widows some time ago."

Hassan's smile nearly severed the upper part of his head. "Then I have the advantage of you!" he declared. "Madame Kettle is this evening a very angry lady . . . and when people are angry, it is easy for an experienced interrogator like myself to make them talk." He tapped his nose with an air of supreme self-satisfaction.

It was not difficult to guess the direction his thoughts were taking; Melissa's own were not far behind. The idea, as yet only half formed, seemed preposterous . . . and yet . . . it would be interesting to know if he had learned something of which she was unaware. A bit of judicious flattery might bring results; after all, she thought, angry people aren't the only ones capable of indiscretion.

"Of course, a trained investigator knows all the tricks," she said, injecting a good ladleful of admiration into her tone. "People don't always realise how much they are giving away, and in the hands of an expert such as yourself . . ."

Predictably, he tapped his nose again, but it immediately became plain that she had underestimated the man.

"Exactly so," he said proudly, "but the situation is a little tricky, is it not? Until we can be sure that murder has been committed, we must tread carefully. Very carefully indeed, Madame." For the time being he was going to play this one very close to his chest.

"Then you do not now rule out the possibility of murder?" she said.

"I rule out nothing." His smile was tantamount to an un-spoken "We must hope for the best." He closed his notebook and put it in his pocket. "Thank you, Madame, that will be all for the moment, but," he bent his head close to her ear as they moved towards the door, "I would ask you to act as my eyes and ears when I am not present. Anything, anything at all that might be significant . . . you will report to me?"

"Of course," she promised, keeping her expression as solemn as his.

When they returned to the reception hall, Madame Gauthier had departed, leaving only one dim light switched on. Dora was sitting in the shadows with Iris at her side, staring at the floor. They both looked up as the tall figure of Hassan loomed over them.

"The old girl left us in the dark," said Iris with a jerk of her head towards the empty desk. "Think she was trying to tell us something."

"Madame Lavender, I should like to ask you one or two more questions," said Hassan.

"Can't it wait till tomorrow?" said Dora crossly. "I have nothing more to tell you and I'm feeling quite exhausted."

Hassan glanced at his watch, pursed his lips and nodded gravely. "Very well, Madame, provided you will give me your solemn undertaking not to leave Roziac in the meantime."

An hour or so later, Iris and Melissa collapsed, fully dressed, on to their beds, too weary to change into their nightclothes. After Hassan's departure they had escorted an abnormally subdued and submissive Dora to her room, where Iris insisted on putting her through a series of noisy deep-breathing exercises, "to calm her down," and then prepared a cup of herbal tea, "to make her sleep." Dora accepted these ministrations without protest, but Melissa thought she detected a growing restiveness and a thinly veiled relief when at last they said goodnight and returned to their own room.

"What d'you suppose he meant?" asked Iris, yawning.

Melissa turned her head without opening her eyes. "What who meant by what?"

"Banana Split. Telling Dora not to leave Roziac. Is she a key witness or something?"

"Reading between the lines," said Melissa, "I think he suspects her of killing Alain Gebrec, mistaking him for Erdle."

"Good Heavens!" Iris sat up with a jerk. "He said that?"

"Not in so many words, but I'm pretty sure that was what he was getting at."

Never loquacious, Iris was for the moment totally lost for words. She sank back and closed her eyes. "Too fantastic!" she muttered after some thought.

"Not so fantastic as you might think," said Melissa. "She admits following someone she believed was Dieter into the woods."

"Only to talk to him."

"That's what she says. Suppose her real intention was to kill him?"

"To stop him nobbling Rose and her money?"

"Something like that. From what we learned the first evening we were here, Rose is very well heeled and it's obvious that by sharing her home, Dora enjoys a lot of luxuries she could never afford by herself. If Rose were to remarry, she'd be thrown on her own resources."

"Don't suppose she'd starve. Doesn't she work in a bank or something?"

"Even so, it might mean a pretty drastic cut in her living standards."

Iris looked dubious. "So what's your theory?"

"I haven't worked it out in detail," Melissa admitted, "but I was thinking about it while you were putting her through your puff-and-blow routine . . ."

"Yoga breathing," Iris corrected firmly. "Helped you more than once."

"Only kidding. Now, how does this sound? For the past week or so Dora has been getting steadily more frustrated at the way things are going between Rose and Dieter. She's been counting the days to the end of the course in the hope that it'll be a case of out of sight, out of mind. And then what happens? Rose decides to cop out of the trip to Antibes for another week here with Dieter."

"Oh, yes." Iris gave a derisive cackle. "The last straw, losing her golfing partner. Enough to make anyone commit murder!"

"Be serious, Iris. Who knows what Rose and Dieter might start planning, here on their own? Apart from what Dora would see as a disaster for her friend, her own life-style could be on the line. She'd do anything, anything, to stop the affair going further. And then, suddenly, she sees Dieter going off on his own, and decides to have it out with him. Only it isn't Dieter, it's Alain Gebrec, but because of her dodgy eyesight she doesn't realise her mistake."

"And when she does, she lets off steam by socking him anyway!" jeered Iris. "Believe that and you'll believe anything."

"Do shut up and listen. Alain, totally absorbed in his own troubles, has reached the belvedere. The last thing he's thinking about is being followed. Maybe he's leaning on the safety rail, with his back to the path and his head bent. Dora sees him there, and suddenly realises he's at her mercy. It never enters her head that it isn't Dieter, she happens to have a golf-club in her hand and the temptation is overwhelming."

"Hmm . . . maybe." At last, Iris was beginning to listen seriously. "So far, so lethal. Now what?"

"She's got to get rid of the body. I've already explained how I think that could have been done."

"Don't tell me she still doesn't know it's Gebrec she's topped. Her sight can't be that bad."

"It's just possible, I suppose—if she keeps her head averted all the time—but I agree it's unlikely. At this stage, it doesn't make much difference. The deed is done, she's got a corpse to dispose of and there's only one way to do it."

Iris sat up again, crossed her legs and put her chin in her hands. "Over the edge with the stiff, back to the house and off to her appointment. What does she do with the weapon?"

"My guess is she hides it in the undergrowth."

"Then what?"

"She assumes that sooner or later the body'll be discovered and there'll be a hue and cry. The suicide theory won't occur to her and her common sense would tell her it's unlikely to be written off as another accident. If it's later established that death was due to a blow on the head with a blunt instrument, the police are going to find that golf-club and start asking awkward questions, so she puts it round that someone's nicked it."

"Why not put it back in the bag and say nothing? No one would suspect her of killing Gebrec?"

"Er, hadn't thought of that," admitted Melissa. "Maybe she just panicked for the moment, wanted to get rid of it as soon as possible."

Iris frowned. "Not Dora," she declared. "Not the panicky sort."

"You never know how people are going to react in that sort of crisis," Melissa insisted. "Anyway, let's assume for the moment that's what happened. She probably spent the time it took her to get to Alès working out her story. I must say, she's pretty cool. Never batted an eyelid when we were all wondering where Gebrec had got to . . . although she did react rather oddly when Dieter showed up," she added thoughtfully.

Iris was still sceptical. "Having her story ready in case

things get hot, that makes sense. But why stir up a hornet's nest by accusing Erdle when murder hasn't been mentioned?"

"That's a point. When did that first come up?"

"At dinner this evening, when you were playing detective."

It was Melissa's turn to sit up suddenly. "That's it! She twigged what I was driving at . . . that I suspected Alain had been murdered . . . and decided to get in first to throw me off the scent. How does that strike you?"

"Far-fetched." Iris rocked to and fro, clasping her ankles and shaking her head. "Might use it in one of your whodunnits, though," she added with a malicious twinkle. "Needs polishing up, but . . ."

"Oh, come on, Iris, it is feasible."

"Okay, let's think." Iris closed her eyes and began speaking slowly as if reciting a lesson. "Go after A, kill B by mistake, then have a go at throwing suspicion on A . . . hmm." She opened her eyes and said emphatically, "No good. A has an alibi."

"Assuming the alibi holds water. I thought Dieter seemed a bit evasive when Rose was questioning him."

"Normal reaction to her blathering."

"Maybe." A disturbing thought struck Melissa. "Iris, if we're on the right lines, Dora must be feeling pretty grim at the moment. Perhaps we shouldn't have left her on her own."

"You're right!" With the same thought in their minds, they hurried from the room.

When they tapped at Dora's bedroom door, a calm voice invited them to enter. She was sitting up in bed with a light shawl round her shoulders and a book on her lap, apparently quite composed.

"What is it?" she asked, with the air of a headmistress disturbed by a couple of prefects during her lunch hour.

"We just wanted to make sure you were all right," said Melissa hesitantly.

"Of course I'm all right. If Rose wants to behave like an irresponsible teenager, that's her affair. I've decided to wash my hands of her."

"You're sure you'll sleep? You wouldn't like one of us to stay with you tonight?"

Dora's eyebrows lifted. "Do you suppose I'm afraid of the dark or something?" she said frostily. "Rose is the one who has nightmares, not me."

"Sorry. Only trying to help," said Iris. "Come on, Mel, let's get to bed. I'm tuckered." Feeling vaguely foolish, the pair went back to their own room.

"She's a tough customer," remarked Melissa when they had finally settled down for the night. "If she did kill Gebrec, Banana Split will have a job getting her to admit anything."

"*If* she killed him? You're having doubts about your theory then?"

"I still think it's possible—just—but yes, I agree with you that it's unlikely. I'm beginning to think his mother's right, though. It wasn't suicide."

"What about Erdle? You were going to spend all night studying that book, remember?"

Melissa gave a deep yawn. "Tomorrow," she promised. "Tomorrow morning, for sure."

Seventeen

IT WAS FRIDAY AND THE FINAL DAY OF both courses currently running at the Centre Cévenol d'Etudes. Iris's group, their nerve restored after the successful outing to St-Jean-du-Gard, had managed to come to terms with rocks and agreed to her suggestion that they spend the morning studying strata patterns and fossil traces near Anduze. Fernand was once more pressed into service as driver—a role he appeared to relish, as Melissa commented to Juliette when she came out to water the geraniums.

"That is how it is with him," said the woman with a shrug. "He has good days and bad days. One never knows." Her eyes fell on the book which Melissa held in one hand. "You study our history, I see?"

"Yes. Have you read this?"

"I have little time for reading. Will you be here for lunch today, Madame?"

"Yes, please. I'm going to spend the morning here."

Juliette made no further comment and her manner discouraged further conversation. Melissa turned away to chat to the students as they got out of their cars and gathered in groups in the courtyard. Philippe Bonard came out to welcome them all with the customary handshake and greeting.

Dora, who had not appeared at breakfast, now drove in alone, parked facing the wall and remained in the car, the angle of her head suggesting that she was watching points in the rear-view mirror. A few minutes later Rose and Dieter arrived; the latter was in an ebullient mood, shaking hands and exchanging pleasantries all round, while his companion hardly spoke, but kept her mouth stretched in a smile that was like a tight band across her face.

Bonard detached himself from the others for a quiet word with Melissa. "I take it there have been no further developments?" he said.

"On the contrary. Didn't you notice?" She nodded across to where the students were making their way towards the house—all except Dora, who was giving unnaturally close attention to a morning-glory climbing up the wall.

Bonard gave a wry smile and shook his head. "I meant, with your detective work."

"In a way, there's a connection." Briefly, she recounted the events of the previous evening and his face grew grave. "I'm afraid there are going to be repercussions," she said. "If Officer Hassan has his way, there'll be a squad of gendarmes searching for that missing golf-club."

Bonard spread his hands and lifted his shoulders in a gesture of resignation. "So be it," he said. "I hope they keep the disturbance to a minimum. It has been a bad week for the Centre."

"Yes, it has. I'm so sorry."

"Thank you." A smile relieved his sombre expression, but could not disguise the shadows under his eyes. "Do you wish to use the library this morning?"

"If you don't mind, I'll sit on the terrace and do some reading. I've decided to give my novel a rest for this morning."

"Whatever you wish." With a brief bow he hurried after his flock.

Melissa made her way into the garden, settled herself in a comfortable chair under an umbrella and began to read. It was going to be another scorching day, with the temperature already climbing through the twenties. At first she found it difficult to concentrate and her eyes kept straying—first to the pool, sparkling like polished glass in the morning sunshine, on through the gardens and the orchard and thence upwards across the forest towards the soaring mountains and the vast blue dome of the sky. It took a strong effort of will to shut out the distracting beauty of the place and give her attention to *The Turbulent History of the Cévennes*.

The early chapters sketched in the historical background, drawing parallels between the courage and tenacity of the Camisards and their twentieth-century descendants who had shown such resolve and independence of spirit during the German occupation. This was familiar stuff and Melissa found herself skipping through it, pausing here and there to check an unfamiliar word.

Next came a chapter detailing some of the means of surveillance used by the Vichy Government, which included a systematic form of undercover censorship of communications. There had been widespread tapping of telephones and steaming open of letters, leading to the arrest of hundreds of people suspected of harbouring refugees or dealing in forged documents. This could obviously have been done only with the collaboration of French civil servants; several names were mentioned, but although Melissa read with close attention, she could find no clue to a possible link with Antoinette Gebrec.

Her concentration was beginning to flag when Fernand appeared carrying a bucket, a squeegee on a long pole and what looked like an outsize shrimping net. He waved to Melissa and called a greeting before commencing a systematic cleaning operation, scrubbing the sides and bottom of the pool and skimming leaves and dead insects from the surface of the water. He had a jaunty air; he whistled a cheerful tune and his movements as he plied the various implements were brisk and confident. It crossed Melissa's mind that here, at least, was one person who was not in mourning for Alain Gebrec. Fernand was his own man again with no one trying to teach him his job.

By the time she had, without success, ploughed through yet another chapter, Bonard's students began emerging for the mid-morning break. She could tell immediately that the strains affecting three of their number had not gone unnoticed. Eyebrows were lifted and glances exchanged as Dora retreated with her cup of coffee to the farthest corner of the terrace and ostentatiously turned her back on everyone. Rose, pale and downcast, made half-hearted responses to Daphne, who was doing her best to cheer her up without making it too obvious.

Melissa found herself next to Eric in the queue for coffee and biscuits.

"Seems like the end of the great romance," he said in a low voice, with a jerk of his head to where Dieter was responding to eager speculation from Janey and Sue as to the reasons for his sudden recall and his probable destination. "If I'm not mistaken, the further away they send him, the better he'll be pleased."

"Why do you say that?"

"Isn't it obvious? The little Kettle was coming to the boil and he was scared of getting scalded!" Eric gave a sly chuckle at his own joke.

Sipping her coffee, Melissa covertly watched the group. As usual, Dieter exuded an easy, slightly mocking charm, but it was all for the benefit of the two younger women. Not once did he glance at Rose.

Philippe Bonard, appearing several minutes after the others, immediately headed towards Melissa.

"I have just had a call from Officer Hassan," he said in a low voice. "It is as you predicted, Melissa. He will arrive shortly with a troop of his men to carry out a search. He also wishes to interview everyone about their movements on Wednesday." It was evident that the stress was beginning to tell; Bonard's face was drawn and his eyes seemed to have lost some of their lustre. "Oh, what is the point?" he went on. "What good will it do? Nothing can bring my poor Alain back to life."

"If he was murdered, you surely wouldn't wish his killer to escape justice," said Melissa gently.

He bowed his head and she saw his hands clench. "No, of course not," he whispered. After a moment he looked up and his normal, brisk manner returned. "I have informed the officer that he may use the library," he said. "I must go now and break the news to my students. I fear it will badly disrupt their last day of study."

• • •

Half an hour or so later Melissa heard a car drive into the courtyard. There was the sound of voices—Hassan's pompous, measured tones and Marie-Claire's shrill, staccato whine. Then came the scrunch of feet on gravel; shortly after that a young gendarme appeared, saluted and respectfully requested a few minutes of Madame Craig's time in the library. Feeling as if she were taking part in the plot of one of her own novels, Melissa followed him indoors.

From the other side of a table on which were ranged a carafe of water, a glass, a notebook and a manila folder, Hassan rose with a vast smile of welcome. He prayed her to be seated and, with slow and deliberate movements, opened the folder and extracted a typewritten sheet.

"The supplementary report of the *médecin légist*," he explained. "He confirms an injury just behind the jaw, not in itself the prime cause of death, but potentially fatal and sufficient to render the victim immediately unconscious. This injury could—and the report stresses 'could'—have been inflicted with an instrument such as a golf-club. The technical term for the point of impact is . . ." He hesitated, frowned and peered uncertainly at the document.

"The mastoid process?" Melissa suggested.

.Admiration radiated from Hassan's face like a sunburst. "Is there no limit to the extent of your knowledge, Madame?"

"It just so happens that I used this in one of my novels," she explained modestly. "Perhaps you remember . . ."

"But of course! *La Chute d'Humpty Dumpty!*" He pronounced it "Ermpitty Dermpitty," but she managed to keep a straight face. "It is essential, therefore," he continued as he put the paper away, "to find the golf-club that Madame Lavender alleges has been stolen. I have promised Monsieur Bonard to cause as little disturbance as possible, but if the search of the grounds and the base of the cliff reveals nothing, then it will be necessary to check all buildings and vehicles, and question everyone very closely indeed." He rubbed his hands together, plainly relishing the prospect.

"What about the button and the pieces of thread?" enquired Melissa.

"On first examination it appears that they match the victim's clothing," said Hassan gleefully. "The indications are that we almost certainly have a case of murder, Madame Craig."

"Well, I'll leave you to get on with your enquiries." Melissa stood up.

"Ah! Just one moment if you please, Madame. There is one question I have to put to you ... purely a formality in your case, of course, but I regret, I can make no exceptions." He tugged at his moustache and rolled his eyes as if too embarrassed to utter the words.

She came to his rescue. "You want to know where I went and what I was doing on Wednesday?" He nodded, dumbly grateful for her understanding and she briefly recounted her movements. He seemed vastly relieved as he penned the details in his notebook; doubtless any suggestion of a flaw in the alibi of one so eminent would have been painful beyond words.

"And one final point, Madame." He laid down his pen and leaned across the table towards her. "I should like to feel ... that is, if you could spare me a few minutes of your time later on ... the thoughts of the creator of the great Nathan Latimer would, I am sure, be of inestimable value in my enquiries."

"If I can be of any help, you only have to ask."

"Oh thank you, Madame." He hurried to the door and bowed her through it. Just wait till you hear about this, Detective Chief Inspector Harris, thought Melissa as she returned to the terrace and her interrupted reading. A detective who actually asks for my help instead of telling me to stop poking my nose into his cases. Wonders will never cease!

At midday Fernand set off in the mini-bus to collect Iris and her group. The sight of police vehicles parked along the lane drove all thoughts of Nature and her designs from their heads; they swarmed on to the terrace and buttonholed Melissa, who was helping a silent and subdued Juliette to set up the lunch table. She had barely time to explain the latest developments when Philippe Bonard's students emerged, most of them in a state of electric excitement.

"We've all been interrogated!" squeaked Janey. "Just imagine, one of our group could be a murderer!" Above the hand that she clapped over her mouth, her eyes rolled like blue marbles.

"Don't be stupid!" scolded Sue. "Why would one of us want to kill poor Alain?"

"Well, they can't possibly suspect one of our group," said Jack. "We were in the bamboo forest all Wednesday morning—it was Alain who drove us there."

"You mean, they won't even want to question us?" Chrissie spoke in tones of deep disappointment, as if the prospect of being eliminated from the enquiries without even the excitement of a police interview was not at all to her liking.

"You know," said Janey. "I think it was Fernand who ki . . ." She broke off, her colour rising, as meaning glances reminded her of Juliette's presence.

There was an embarrassed silence before Mervyn said, "Is it quite certain that Alain was murdered?"

"It looks like it—I understand they're looking for a missing golf-club," explained Eric.

Chrissie's eyes fell, almost accusingly, on Dora, who was standing apart with her back to the others. "They must think that was the murder weapon."

"They can't be sure until they find it," insisted Mervyn. "We mustn't jump to conclusions."

"Oh dear, are you quite, quite sure you didn't leave it at home, Dora?" faltered Rose. It was the first time she had spoken and everyone turned to look at her. She was in a pitiable state; the sparkle and the girlish animation that had drawn attention from the crows' feet and the sagging jaw-line were gone and with them, it seemed, every vestige of self-confidence as well. She looked old, tired and frightened.

Dora turned. Her expression was grim and her eyelids puffy, as if she had slept badly, but she was perfectly composed as she replied, "How many times must I repeat that I know I brought it with me?" in a strong, level voice. "Someone," she put a meaningful emphasis on the word and her eyes sought Dieter Erdle, "stole it from the boot of the car.

When it is found, there will no doubt be fingerprints on it and we shall know who the thief is."

Dieter returned her gaze with an air of studied nonchalance. "*If* it is found," he said mockingly. He picked up a plate and ran a critical eye over the buffet table. "We might as well eat something after Juliette has been to all this trouble," he said and began helping himself to food as if everything was perfectly normal.

"I don't think I could eat a thing," wailed Daphne, but she took the plate that her husband pushed into her plump hand and allowed him to pile it with food.

One by one, the others followed. At one point, Juliette disappeared temporarily in search of more bread; the minute she had gone, Mervyn rounded on Janey.

"You shouldn't have said that about Fernand, especially in front of Juliette!"

"Oh, what does it matter?" said Janey sulkily. "She doesn't understand English. As for Fernand—we all know that he didn't like Alain, and he's been as cheerful as a cricket since his body was found."

"That doesn't mean he killed him. Anyway, didn't he go out on Wednesday morning? He's probably got an alibi."

"I believe he went to the supermarket in Alès, but I'm sure Officer Hassan will check everyone's movements," said Melissa.

All eyes turned back to her. "Who do you think did it?" demanded Chrissie. "You're a crime writer—haven't you got a theory?"

"Of course she has—several theories, in fact," said Dieter. With a forkful of *charcuterie* poised above his plate, he grinned insolently at Melissa. "I'm sure she has discovered that any number of us have a motive, just like in one of her books. Several of us could have done it—Philippe, myself, Dora, even Rose, perhaps—no, no, not Rose, she hasn't got the nerve." Rose winced at this unfeeling remark which, judging by the exchange of glances, several people considered to be in poor taste. "I warn you," he went on, quite unabashed, "that anything you say will be conveyed to the investigating officer and may be used in evidence. Isn't that right, Melissa?"

"Anything you say, or anything I happen to read," she said coolly and had the satisfaction of seeing his smile waver. "Seriously, I don't know any more than the rest of you," she went on, "and I think Mervyn is absolutely right, it isn't certain yet that Alain was murdered and we shouldn't go jumping to conclusions."

This pronouncement seemed to put a damper on further discussion and people developed a sudden interest in the contents of their plates. The lunch break was just coming to an end when Philippe Bonard came out of the house, accompanied by a short, plump man of fifty or so clad in a shapeless grey suit that contrasted oddly with his own faultless tailoring.

"Mesdames et Messieurs, I present my colleague Roger Darmel. He has just arrived from Avignon and will take over the administration of the Centre for the time being." Bonard's eyes sought Melissa and he led the newcomer over to her. "I wonder, Melissa," he said hurriedly, "as it is time for the classes to reassemble, if you would be kind enough to explain to Monsieur Darmel the reason for the police presence and then escort him to the office of Marie-Claire? Madame Craig has the ear of the investigating officer on account of her reputation as a crime novelist," he explained, and hurried away.

Monsieur Darmel took out a handkerchief and mopped sweat from his glistening bald head. He eyed Melissa with a mixture of mistrust and disapproval.

"I regret, I am not familiar with the genre," he said stiffly, "and I am not accustomed to having contact with the police." His tone implied that those who had such contact were not the kind of people a respectable citizen expected to meet in his daily life.

"This has all been very distressing for Monsieur Bonard," said Melissa. "Until yesterday, it was believed that Alain Gebrec took his own life. That was bad enough, but now there is talk of murder."

"Murder!" Monsieur Darmel's sallow face turned a shade

paler and his mouth fell open. "Who? Why?" He plied the handkerchief again in shock and bewilderment.

"Nothing is known for certain. The police are searching for a possible weapon."

"Monsieur Bonard implied that you have information from the police."

"A little." Melissa outlined the facts, but offered no opinions. "Of course, I only met Alain last Sunday, so I have really no idea what kind of man he was. Did you know him well, Monsieur?" she added casually.

"Me?" Darmel licked his lips. "No, no, hardly at all, only as a colleague, you understand, not at all in our private lives." The words tumbled out in a nervous rush as if he felt himself under interrogation. "I mean, we had contact, attended meetings together from time to time, that sort of thing, but our departments were separate, quite separate."

"But you must have some impressions of him?"

"I assure you, I never considered the man as anyone but a business associate."

"He was in charge of the overseas purchasing department of Monsieur Bonard's company, I understand."

"That is correct."

"And you?"

"I am the administration manager."

"That must bring you into contact with the senior people in all the other departments. Did you ever notice any friction or ill-feeling between Alain Gebrec and any of his other colleagues? I know that Monsieur Bonard is very anxious to know exactly how and why he died," Melissa went on persuasively. "Anything you can remember may help to solve the mystery."

"There's nothing in particular that I can tell you. Of course, everyone knew . . ." Darmel broke off in sudden embarrassment and mopped his head yet again.

"About his relationship with Monsieur Bonard?" prompted Melissa.

"Well, yes. We called him the old man's blue-eyed boy, but it didn't cause any trouble. Monsieur Bonard's private life is his own affair. When it comes to business matters, he never shows favouritism." The last words were spoken with a sudden warmth; plainly, Philippe Bonard was highly thought of by his employees.

"And did Gebrec," Melissa hunted for the right words, "ever show any interest ... personal interest ... in anyone else in the company?"

"No, but I have heard gossip once or twice, about ... pretty boys." The corners of Darmel's mouth turned downwards. "People say he used to be seen in gay bars in Avignon and other places." He wrinkled his nose as if he had detected an unpleasant smell.

"Did Monsieur Bonard know about them ... the pretty boys?"

Darmel shrugged. "Possibly. It made no difference. For him, Gebrec could do no wrong. To be fair," he added, "Gebrec had an excellent brain and first-class managerial skills, although he was not, I think, particularly well liked among his subordinates. Several people expressed satisfaction when he left the company in Avignon to help Monsieur Bonard with his new venture."

"So Monsieur Bonard was prepared to overlook his ... shortcomings?"

"It would seem so." Darmel managed a faint smile, more at ease now that his own relationship with Alain Gebrec was no longer under scrutiny. "Perhaps, Madame, you would be kind enough to conduct me to the office of the secretary? I have much work to do, to learn my new duties."

Eighteen

over to a less than welcoming Marie-Claire, Melissa returned to her book. She began to wish she had never bought it; chapter after chapter yielded no clue and concentration became increasingly difficult. She had almost made up her mind to abandon the search when a familiar but totally unexpected name caught her eye. She read on in a state of mounting excitement, oblivious now to her surroundings, so that the young gendarme sent by Officer Hassan to request the favour of a little of her valuable time had to clear his throat twice to attract her attention.

When she entered the library, Hassan was standing by the window. He greeted her with his customary effusiveness, but she thought he looked tired and a shade dispirited.

"Madame Craig, it is so good of you to come," he began.

"Not at all." Melissa sat in the chair facing the table where he had been working, but he remained on his feet, pacing restlessly to and fro. "Have you made any progress?"

"Alas, almost none. My men have combed the area between the house and the belvedere, but they have not recovered the missing golf-club of Madame Lavender. In a search of the outbuildings, a crowbar was found which could, perhaps, have been used as a weapon. It has been sent for examination, but it is heavily soiled with grease and sawdust, and there is no reference in the report of the *médecin légiste* to either substance being found on the body. Still, we must leave no avenue unexplored."

"Of course not," agreed Melissa gravely. "What about your, er, interrogations? Have you learned anything significant?"

"That is what I should like to discuss with you, Madame. If you will kindly bear with me, I will give you a résumé of each interview and invite your comments."

"By all means." She was bursting to tell him that her reading had at last yielded some results, but decided to await the right moment. It was plain that Hassan was even more eager to share his thoughts with her and she was equally anxious to hear what, if anything, he had discovered.

"So, Madame." Hassan at last returned to his chair and picked up his notebook. He turned back a dozen or so pages, all covered with cramped handwriting. "Let us begin. I first interviewed the proprietor of this establishment, Monsieur Philippe Bonard. He declared that Gebrec returned to the Centre after driving Madame Ash and her party to the Parc de Prafance and reported to him in his office at approximately nine-twenty. During their discussion, which Monsieur Bonard insists concerned nothing but routine matters of business, Gebrec become increasingly agitated and after ten minutes or so he rushed out of the room, apparently on the verge of tears. Monsieur Bonard did not follow him, but shortly afterwards observed him from the window, hurrying towards the belvedere."

"That would be about the time that Mrs. Lavender claims to have seen Dieter Erdle going in the same direction," said Melissa.

"Just so. Now, Monsieur Bonard states that he did not follow Gebrec, nor make any attempt to find him, until some time after eleven o'clock, when he went to ask the housekeeper if she had seen him. She declared that she had not and he returned to his office. Shortly after midday, Madame Ash telephoned to say that Gebrec had not come to bring her and her students back to the Centre for lunch. Accordingly, the man Fernand Morlay, who had returned from Alès a few minutes previously, was sent on this errand."

"And there was still no sign of Gebrec?"

"No. When by four o'clock or thereabouts he had not returned, Monsieur Bonard became uneasy and was happy to accept the offer of some of the students to organise a search, the result of which, of course, you know."

"Yes, indeed," murmured Melissa. "Did you by any chance ask Monsieur Bonard why he did not himself go in search of Gebrec, if he was so concerned at his absence?"

"Naturally." There was a hint of triumph in Hassan's smile. "The question appeared to surprise him. He does not, I think, consider it the responsibility of a *patron* to pursue an employee who goes off in a huff. He would be more likely to expect that employee to return of his own volition, probably with an apology."

"Yes, I'm sure you're right. Still, in view of the close personal relationship between the two men . . ."

"Ah!" A gleam appeared in Hassan's eye. "You have some observations on that situation, Madame?"

"From remarks I have overheard it is obvious that everyone assumes . . . and according to Monsieur Darmel . . ."

"Who is he?"

Melissa explained, and repeated her conversation with Gebrec's replacement. Hassan's cheeks puffed in excitement as he made more notes. "This is very interesting, Madame. We will return to that in a moment. May I now proceed with my next interview?"

"Please."

"The man Fernand Morlay. I confess, I at first considered him a possible suspect. His antagonism towards Gebrec was observed by several people, including the fierce disagreement of Wednesday morning when he appeared to be threatening him with physical assault. However, he was absent from Les Châtaigniers during the critical period. He left at about nine-fifteen to take his car to Alès to have new tyres fitted—the work record of the garage confirms this—and then he went to a nearby supermarket to do some shopping for his sister. She was able to show the till receipt bearing the date and the time of eleven-thirty. On his way back, he called at the Bar des Sports in Roziac and was seen by several witnesses. I think we can safely eliminate him from this enquiry."

"I'm glad of that," said Melissa impulsively.

Hassan raised an eyebrow. "May I ask why, Madame?"

"I have had several conversations with him and I find him
... *sympathique*." She wondered how Hassan would react if
he knew the whole story, and was thankful that it would not
be necessary to tell him. "We share an interest in the history
of the region."

"Ah, yes, I was forgetting. Your new masterpiece—you have
begun work on it?" His eyes lit up at the recollection. "If there
is any way in which I can help your researches . . . ?"

"Thank you, I'll bear that in mind," she said and he sighed
happily.

"It would be a supreme privilege." He coughed, tugged his
moustache and referred once more to his notes. "Now, the
housekeeper, Juliette Morlay. She was performing some duties upstairs during the time Gebrec was in Monsieur
Bonard's office. She declares that both men were raising their
voices, but she could not distinguish the words. She heard a
door bang and the sound of footsteps running down the stairs,
but no more. She confirms Monsieur Bonard's statement that
he went to the kitchen later on and asked if Gebrec had been
seen. At the same time, he gave her some garments that
needed pressing and asked her to attend to them."

"I remember seeing her sponging and pressing some trousers," commented Melissa. "It was on the Thursday morning,
I think."

Hassan shrugged as if he considered the point immaterial.
"I understand that it is quite usual. Monsieur Bonard is very
particular about his clothes—you have no doubt observed that
he buys none but the very best—and he does not trust dry
cleaners."

"Juliette does a good job—he always looks immaculate."

"She declined to be drawn on the question of the relationship between her master and the victim," observed Hassan,
"but I am convinced that she is aware of it."

"I have the same impression."

"You have had conversations with her?" Hassan's expression became eager. "You can add something to my findings?"

"Not a great deal." Melissa was having a silent tussle with
her conscience. On the one hand was her duty to help unmask

the killer of Alain Gebrec, on the other her promise to Juliette to remain silent about the family tragedy. Still, Fernand was in the clear, he had a strong alibi and would not be harmed if she were to tell a little of what she knew.

"Please, try to remember." Hassan was not going to let go of this one. "What exactly did she say?"

"Nothing specific. She was telling me about life under the German Occupation. A member of their family was shot by the Gestapo and I asked if Monsieur Bonard knew about it. She said something about a gentleman not being interested in the private lives of his servants, but when I mentioned Gebrec her manner changed. She did not say in so many words that she suspected a homosexual relationship between them, but I think it's very likely."

"And this man Darmel confirms it. I think," said Hassan softly, "I must have another interview with Monsieur Bonard. Perhaps he has not told me everything."

"Surely, you don't suspect him?"

Hassan tapped his nose with a flourish. "Let us say, Madame, that I have not yet eliminated him."

Melissa felt as if the world was going topsy-turvy around her. In all the speculation and discussion that had followed the start of the police enquiry, no one had so much as hinted that Philippe Bonard might be the murderer. On the contrary, he had been the object of universal sympathy. Yet, once the possibility had been laid squarely before her, she wondered why it had not occurred to her before. Juliette had heard raised voices; wasn't it conceivable that Bonard had been tackling Gebrec about his history of infidelity, demanding an end to the succession of "pretty boys," of whom Wolfgang Klein was the most recent but would probably not have been the last? Perhaps the younger man had taunted the elder. Who could tell to what state of frustration Bonard had been driven?

Hassan was watching her intently as she sat digesting this new and disturbing line of enquiry. "May I share your thoughts, Madame?" he said at last.

"On the face of things, it appears feasible," she murmured, almost thinking aloud. "The story about Gebrec being distressed, but refusing to say what was wrong, might have been a lie. When he left the office, perhaps Bonard followed him and saw him heading towards the belvedere."

"Yes, yes," prompted Hassan as she paused, trying to picture the scene. "Please go on, Madame."

"Dora Lavender's car is standing in the courtyard with the boot open, but Dora herself isn't there, she's on the putting green." Melissa closed her eyes, bringing all her visual imagination into play. "He sees her bag of golf-clubs and impulsively grabs one and goes in pursuit of Gebrec. He finds him at the belvedere, kills him, pushes his body over the cliff and hurries back to the house."

"In other words, a *crime passionnel*, committed on the spur of the moment?"

Melissa shook her head. "I don't know," she said doubtfully. "There are quite a few unanswered questions, aren't there? What did he do with the weapon? How is it that Mrs. Lavender didn't see him? And what about Dieter Erdle? Mrs. Lavender seems quite positive that he was there too."

"I will come to Erdle in a moment. Let us first consider Mrs. Lavender's statement. She happens to glance up from her golf practice and sees someone whom she believes to be Erdle, but is in fact Gebrec. She calls to him but he does not answer. A few minutes later, Bonard leaves the house, perhaps by the rear door through the kitchen. Juliette is working upstairs, Mrs. Lavender has returned to her golf and he makes his way to the belvedere unobserved."

"And after killing Gebrec he returns to the house, again unobserved," said Melissa musingly. "By this time Mrs. Lavender has left to keep her appointment in Alès, so he can't put the weapon back where he found it. It must be hidden somewhere. Why haven't your men been able to find it?"

"Whoever committed this crime has since had plenty of time to dispose of it elsewhere. It might be lying in a ditch several kilometres away. We have to face the possibility that it may never be found—unless, of course, the guilty person can be, let us say, persuaded to lead us to it."

The last words were spoken with a hint of menace, accompanied by a tigerish smile quite unlike the combination of gleaming teeth and exuberant moustache that had caused Melissa to dub him "Banana Split." She felt a twinge in her stomach; she had heard that the methods of questioning used by the French police were sometimes less than gentle. Into her mind's eye sprang an image of Philippe Bonard under a relentless inquisition, no longer the proud, elegant, successful entrepreneur whom Iris had loved and she herself had come to admire, but a weary and vulnerable old man.

"There is one other point that occurs to me," she said, as if in a deliberate effort to divert Hassan's mind into other channels. "I have had several conversations with Monsieur Bonard and I am convinced that the Centre Cévenol d'Etudes represents for him the most important thing in his life. It is the culmination of a lifelong ambition, and Gebrec was his right-hand man."

"So?"

"So, I am asking myself which was the more important to him, the success of the Centre or to be rid of a faithless lover."

"Madame, when one is in the grip of violent sexual passion, does one stop to ask such rational questions?"

"I suppose not."

While Hassan made more notes, Melissa became aware of the book that she had been holding throughout the interview, one finger still marking the place where she had made her discovery. "May I now tell you of something that I have found out this afternoon, Officer. It may be relevant to your enquiry."

He put down his pen and spread his hands in a magnanimous gesture. "By all means, Madame."

"Before I tell you, could I ask if you spoke to Dieter Erdle about the matter we discussed yesterday evening?"

"You mean, about the book which caused the *contretemps* between him and Gebrec? Yes, I did. He insisted that he was merely having a joke at Gebrec's expense and that, so far as he is aware, it contains nothing of any significance."

"Then it would be interesting to know what he has to say about this." Melissa opened the book and placed it in front of Hassan. "This chapter concerns the activities of certain pastors of the Protestant Church who set up a network of escape routes for refugees from the Germans." She indicated a paragraph. "This passage refers to the work of Pastor Heinrich Erdle, himself a refugee from Nazi Germany, who was eventually betrayed to the Gestapo and shot."

Hassan read the passage twice, tracing the words with a surprisingly well-manicured forefinger. "You are assuming, Madame," he said after several moments' thought, "that this pastor was a relative of Dieter Erdle?"

"It seems likely, don't you agree?"

Hassan shrugged. "It may be so, but where is the connection with Gebrec?"

"Supposing it was a relative of Gebrec who betrayed Pastor Erdle?"

"You think that would provide a motive for Dieter Erdle to attack Alain Gebrec?" Hassan blew out his cheeks and slowly shook his head, plainly sceptical.

"Surely, it's possible. There was a lot of ill-feeling between them—there must have been something behind Erdle's taunts."

"Erdle was quite definite that his remarks were made without prior knowledge, and that Gebrec's reaction was a surprise to him. The fact that he continued with his taunts confirms your assessment of his character, Madame, but it does not make him a murderer."

"But," Melissa gestured towards the book, "doesn't this prove that he was lying?"

Again Hassan shook his head, this time almost apologetically. "Sad as I am to disagree with one so eminent as yourself, I see it as nothing more than a coincidence," he said. "In any case, Erdle was nowhere near the belvedere at the critical time."

"You mean, he has a cast-iron alibi?"

Hassan's eyes flickered. "I am satisfied that he was not there," he insisted.

"He had the best part of an hour to wait before his interview at the factory. Would it not have been possible for him to slip out, drive back to Les Châtaigniers . . . ?"

"Possible, yes, but highly unlikely," Hassan interposed. He thumbed through the pages of his notebook. "He reported at nine o'clock at the premises of a furniture factory, Menuiserie

Cévenole, as arranged. Unfortunately, there was a problem, a lathe had broken down, and the gentleman who was to meet him was not immediately available. At about nine-fifteen, he was informed that he might have to wait a while longer. In fact, it was in all some fifty-five minutes before Monsieur Coutelan was at last free. When the receptionist came to look for Erdle, he was still in the waiting-room where she had left him, reading a prospectus."

"But he might have gone out and returned without being seen," she repeated.

Hassan compressed his lips. It was plain that he had satisfied himself that Dieter Erdle was in the clear and was not pleased at having his judgment questioned. However, under Melissa's challenging gaze, he obviously felt obliged to justify his position.

"Theoretically, yes," he admitted. "The receptionist was busy with her duties and was called away several times for a few moments. However, ask yourself these questions, Madame. Assuming that Erdle wished, for whatever reason, to attack Alain Gebrec, how could he know where to find him at that particular time? How could he be sure of leaving the premises of Menuiserie Cévenole and returning unseen? What if Monsieur Coutelan went in search of him during his absence—how would he account for it?"

"I suppose you're right," said Melissa reluctantly, "but it does seem odd that he should be so evasive."

"About the history of his relative, you mean? That I cannot account for. Since you are so interested, why don't you ask him?"

"You wouldn't object? It wouldn't interfere with your enquiries?"

Hassan lifted both hands and the familiar smile exploded on his expressive face. "Not in the least, Madame."

"In that case, I will—just out of curiosity. Is that the end of your interviews so far?"

"There remains one person concerning whose movements I am by no means entirely satisfied. You can perhaps guess the identity of this individual?"

"Mrs. Lavender?"

"Precisely. I find her attitude quite extraordinary. She is, if you will forgive me for saying so, Madame, the archetype of your 'stiff-upper-lip' English lady." He pronounced the expression "steef-oopair-leep" and Melissa, suppressing a smile, wondered where he had got hold of it.

"I'd say that was a fair description of her," she agreed.

"She has not changed one word of her story since I questioned her yesterday. She insists that she saw Erdle walking towards the belvedere at about half-past nine on Wednesday morning and that she discovered shortly afterwards that one of her golf-clubs was missing—'stolen,' she declares, although she has no proof of this. Having observed the hostility between Erdle and Gebrec, she offers the theory that either Erdle deliberately murdered Gebrec with her golf-club, or that Gebrec attacked Erdle and accidentally fell to his death during a struggle."

"You have, of course, put it to her that it must have been Gebrec that she saw?"

"Naturally." Hassan rolled his eyes in exasperation. "She will not believe it. Or rather, she pretends not to believe it."

"Perhaps she is just too proud to admit that she made a mistake."

"Perhaps. Or perhaps there is a more sinister reason." This time, Hassan gave his face the full treatment, with pursed lips, blown out cheeks and a frantic tattoo on his nose. He leaned forward. "Suppose, Madame, that she herself killed Gebrec, in the belief that he was Erdle—the man who, she feared, was threatening to deprive her friend of her fortune and disrupt her own comfortable existence?"

"You hinted last night that such a theory had occurred to you," said Melissa. "You think it's possible that, having killed the wrong man, she persisted with her story of seeing Erdle to throw suspicion on to him?"

"Why not? After all, she had no conceivable motive for killing Alain Gebrec. If she had succeeded in killing Erdle, his fall from the cliff might have been found, as in the case of Wolfgang Klein, to be an accident. He has visited the belvedere only once and the path is known to be dangerous, but

Gebrec knew the area well. No one would believe that such an accident could happen to him."

Melissa could hardly believe her ears as he proceeded to outline a scenario identical in almost every detail to the one she had put to Iris the previous evening—and subsequently rejected.

"So," he finished, "we have two people with the motive and the opportunity."

"But no weapon," Melissa could not help pointing out.

"Alas, no. And perhaps the fact that the golf-club was probably used points rather towards Madame Lavender. I suspect her claim that it was stolen to be a fabrication and I shall therefore be questioning her again." He glanced at his watch. "My apologies, Madame, for detaining you for so long."

"Not a bit, it's been absolutely fascinating to follow your methods of enquiry," said Melissa and he almost purred with pleasure.

"I, too, have greatly benefited from your own very shrewd observations," he responded gallantly. He looked down at his papers and cleared his throat. "It has occurred to me, Madame, that as you are setting your next book in France, you may find the need for a French detective. If I can be of any assistance in the creation of such a character . . ."

The suggestion was made so artlessly that Melissa found it difficult not to laugh. She pictured him, bragging among his friends and colleagues that he, Officier de Police Judiciaire Hassan, had inspired the French opposite number of the famous fictional detective Nathan Latimer.

"I'll bear your offer in mind," she promised for the second time that afternoon as she stood up to leave. "I hope you will keep me informed of developments. And I'll do the same," she added, holding up the book.

He gave a benign smile. "You still expect to find something significant in that?"

"I can't help feeling that the key to this mystery lies somewhere in the past," she said.

"Much as I respect your judgment, Madame, I fear that I cannot agree with you," he said sorrowfully as he bowed her out of the room.

Nineteen

just as Juliette arrived with the tea-tray, closely followed by
the students. There seemed a marked contrast between the
two groups; the artists were engaged in animated discussion,
but the members of Bonard's group appeared subdued and
dispirited. Bonard himself was not there. Rose and Dora
stood side by side, but seemed to be deliberately avoiding eye
contact with one another, and Dieter Erdle immediately withdrew as far as possible from everyone and stood moodily
staring into space.

Melissa strolled over and stood beside him. The weather
showed no sign of breaking and the sun shone full on the face
of the mountains, reducing shadows to a minimum and turning the highest peaks into a two-dimensional frieze against an
intensely blue sky.

"It's a splendid view, isn't it?" she remarked.

"Splendid," he replied without turning his head.

"Very different from the landscapes in northern Germany,"
she went on, "Schleswig-Holstein, for example." She was
aware that he gave a barely perceptible start as she added in
the same conversational tone, "That is where Pastor Heinrich
Erdle came from, isn't it?"

Without taking his eyes from the panorama before them, he
gave a high-pitched, almost infantile laugh. "What a splendid
detective you are, Mel Craig! Did you go running to that stupid policeman with tales about me? If so, I fear you were
wasting your time."

"I'm aware that you claim to have an alibi," said Melissa coolly. "What intrigues me is, since that is the case, why did you pretend not to know that your relative was mentioned in the book we were discussing? He was your relative, wasn't he?" she added as he remained silent.

"My father's brother," he admitted grudgingly.

"Exactly what happened to him?"

"You've read the book. He was betrayed to the Gestapo and shot."

"Who betrayed him?"

"No one knows for certain. There are stories about a Viennese doctor called Julius Eiche, who claimed to be a refugee from the Nazis, but who was later suspected of being a spy. The Maquis were after him, but he disappeared before they got to him. The truth has never been established."

"Is that why you came here—to find out more about your uncle's death?"

"Not at all." His look of surprise seemed perfectly genuine. "I am here for one reason only—to improve my French. My company selected the school and made all the arrangements for me. When I realised where I was being sent, I thought it might be interesting to do a bit of research. That is why I bought the book."

"Did you learn anything of interest?"

"About what happened to my uncle? No."

"Or what caused Alain Gebrec to become so agitated?"

"No." She raised an eyebrow and saw him redden, but he stuck to his guns. "I tell you the truth," he said stubbornly. "I made one joke about Gebrec having a Germanic appearance and it made him very angry. I found that amusing, so I made more jokes. There are references in the book to French women having liaisons with German soldiers, and the unpleasant reprisals they suffered after the war . . ." He sniggered, like a schoolboy who has just told a smutty joke. "Perhaps that is what upset our friend . . . maybe his mother . . ."

Melissa felt her anger rising. "You really enjoy needling people, don't you?" she snapped.

"Needling?" He affected a grimace of incomprehension.

"Riling them. Getting their dander up. Hurting their feelings—you know bloody well what I mean!" she said furiously. "Is that why you carried on flirting with Rose Kettle, even when you could see the trouble it was causing? Because you found the effect it was having on Dora Lavender 'amusing'?" She had not intended to bring Rose into the conversation, and certainly not to lose her temper, but his flippancy in the face of tragedy infuriated her.

"Ach, the silly *Röslein*! How could I know that she would take me seriously? I thought her life must be so boring with her starchy friend, why not give her some fun?"

Again, Melissa was reminded of a schoolboy, whining excuses after being caught out in some classroom prank that had ended in disaster, pleading that he had meant no harm. All his sophistication had slipped away, revealing the shallowness of his nature.

"If Rose could hear you now, she'd probably find you as contemptible as I do," she retorted. "And you still haven't told me why you were so anxious to conceal your connection with Pastor Erdle."

"You disappoint me." Ignoring the insult, he made an effort to regain his cocksure manner. "I would have thought that with your knowledge of human nature . . ." His tone was deliberately provocative and she had difficulty in checking a second burst of anger.

"I suppose you're trying to tell me," she said after giving herself a moment to calm down, "that after Alain's body was found, and before it was put about that his death was suicide, it occurred to you that in the course of routine enquiries someone who knew about your uncle's fate might recognise your name and start asking questions. Some connection that you *say* you know nothing about"—here Melissa contrived, by a change of tone, to imply an unspoken "of which I'm not entirely convinced"—"between you and the Gebrec family might emerge. It might even be seen as a possible motive for murder. Especially since, until the time of death was established, you couldn't be sure you had an alibi. And of course, once it turned into a murder enquiry, there was all the more reason to say nothing."

"Bravo!" He clapped his hands in mock admiration. "You are right, it could have meant a great deal of unpleasantness for me, and my employers would not have been pleased. Now the police have accepted my alibi, the matter has no relevance."

"Probably not," she agreed with some reluctance.

"So, all the time you spent reading that boring history has, I fear, been totally wasted," he said, with the same air of derision that had so enraged Gebrec and Dora. "I trust you are now convinced of my innocence of any crime?"

"I'm convinced you didn't kill Alain Gebrec to avenge the death of your uncle, if for no other reason than that I can't imagine you capable of any feelings of family loyalty and honour," said Melissa scathingly. "But I'm by no means convinced that you've told me everything you know."

She had the satisfaction of seeing the smug expression wiped from his face before turning on her heel and walking away.

She was helping herself to a cup of tea when Iris appeared at her elbow.

"Can we talk?" she muttered.

"What is it?"

"Come away. Don't want the others to overhear."

She led the way down the steps from the terrace and stood by the pool with her hands clasped behind her and her head bent. Melissa stood beside her in silence, aware of the soft gurgle of the water through the filtration system, watching it run in ripples towards the deep end and idly thinking what a good job Fernand had made of cleaning the majolica-blue tiles. The gardens and the putting-green that Philippe Bonard had so meticulously provided for his students' recreation looked peaceful and colourful; the orchard that supplied Juliette with the fruit for her *compotes* and preserves was dappled with patches of glowing colour. Normally at this time the students would be scattered around like figures in a landscape, chatting, laughing, taking the opportunity of some gentle exercise. Today they remained close to the house, their chatter restrained, occasionally glancing over their shoulders as if half-expecting yet another summons from the intruders who had settled without warning in their midst.

"What is it?" repeated Melissa, as Iris appeared lost in thought.

"Philippe."

"What about him?"

Iris fiddled with one of the tortoiseshell slides that held her springy hair away from her face. Her colour deepened as she muttered, "Hassan asked us all ... if we knew about ... Philippe and Gebrec."

"You mean, if they were lovers."

Iris nodded, biting her lip. "Does he suspect him?"

"Look, Iris, you must understand, the police have to keep an entirely open mind. Some people can be eliminated straight away—your group, for example, and the people in Philippe's group who were away from here all that morning. Everyone else has to be considered as a possible suspect."

"But Philippe loved Alain. Why would he kill him?"

"If a wife is murdered, the husband is normally suspect number one. If a lover is murdered, I imagine the same reasoning applies. But if it's any comfort, Iris, there's at least one other person who had motive and opportunity."

"You mean Dora Lavender?" Hope lit Iris's forlorn face.

"I shouldn't be telling you this, but Hassan figures she could have done it in the way I said last night. The problem is, until he finds that missing golf-club—or some other weapon—it's all purely hypothetical."

"What about Erdle? Did you find anything in that book?"

"Yes, but it doesn't help much. Hassan is satisfied with his alibi." Melissa gave a brief account of her conversation with Erdle, but Iris had already lost interest.

"It's aged Philippe, losing Alain," she said miserably. "To be suspected of killing him must be frightful. Mel, you don't believe he did it, do you?"

"I don't know what to think. I know he loved Alain and I know how important Alain was to the success of the Centre. But I also know that Alain was unfaithful to him, not just once but many times. I'm sorry, Iris, I know how horrid this is for you. It'll be better when we're away from here."

"I'm not leaving till this is cleared up!"

"What good can you do by staying?"

"He needs support, someone who believes in him. You don't need to worry—I know the score, but I can still be his friend."

Melissa's drooping spirits rose a fraction as Jack Hammond approached.

"Have there been any developments?" he asked. The question was directed at Melissa, but his eyes were on Iris's woebegone face, and his voice and his ruddy, open countenance showed his concern for her.

"Not so far as I know," replied Melissa.

"I imagine that if anyone had inside information, it would be you," he said shrewdly.

"All I can tell you is that Hassan's men haven't yet found Dora's missing golf-club and until he lays his hands on that, or some other weapon, he's up against a blank wall. He wouldn't admit it, of course, but he can't even be sure it was murder."

"Some other weapon?" Jack turned to Iris. "Didn't we see Fernand brandishing a crowbar under Gebrec's nose that morning?"

"That's been sent away for routine examination," said Melissa, "but Fernand has been eliminated, he's got an alibi," she added, a shade too quickly.

Iris shot her a keen glance. "Alibis can be faked. Heard you say that more than once."

"Hassan seems happy with this one."

Iris opened her mouth to argue, but at that moment Marie-Claire came clicking down the stone steps from the terrace on her high heels and announced a telephone call for Madame Craig. On the way upstairs they met Philippe Bonard coming down. He stood aside, with a bow and a smile, to allow them to pass. Some of the strain appeared to have lifted from his expression, as if the arrival of his new assistant had reduced the pressure. Through the half-open door of his office Melissa caught a glimpse of Monsieur Dalmer, in shirt-sleeves, a cigarette dangling from his mouth, seated at a desk with a stack of files in front of him.

Antoinette Gebrec was on the line. She spoke in French, her voice firm and controlled, but lacking the vitality that had charmed Melissa during their earlier meetings.

"You are still interested in coming to see my pictures?"

"Well, yes, but in the circumstances . . ." Melissa found herself murmuring platitudes, but Madame Gebrec swiftly interrupted.

"Then you will take an apéritif with me at six o'clock this evening?" There was a slight but unmistakable hesitation before she added, "Your friend, also, if she wishes."

"I'm not sure if she's free, but I'll come with pleasure."

By the time Melissa returned to the terrace, the students had disappeared and Juliette was removing the tea-things. With unusual abruptness, she declined Melissa's offer of help, hurrying into the house with the laden tray as if working against the clock. She looked exhausted; her face had the colour and texture of wax and the lines on either side of her nose and mouth had deepened. Melissa imagined her lying awake at night, worrying on her brother's behalf. Perhaps she too had her doubts about his alibi. Could there be a flaw in it, as Iris had suggested? Was Hassan waiting for him to betray himself, playing a cat-and-mouse game with him, a game in which she herself was an involuntary participant?

There was an hour to wait before classes ended and still a couple of chapters of the book unread, but she found herself unable to settle. Her swimming costume and towel were in the car and on impulse she went to fetch them. Her head was aching with too much reading; a swim would help her to relax and might clear her brain.

Owing no doubt to Fernand's attentions that morning, the water was colder than she had expected and after ten minutes she was glad to get out, dry herself and lie on a chaise-longue in the sun. Within a very short time she was dozing. She began to dream. In her dream, she was playing golf with Dora. Suddenly, Dora began running, across the garden, out through the gate and up the path to the belvedere. She was calling as she ran and at first Melissa could not hear what she was saying so she ran after her. When she caught up with her, Dora gasped, "My nine iron, he's got my nine iron, he's taken it to the secret refuge!" and raced headlong towards the edge of the cliff. Melissa tried to scream a warning, but in the way of nightmares she could make no sound. Then, with a start, she awoke.

She was too hot, the sun was scorching and she hadn't bothered to apply any sun-cream. Half stupefied, she gathered up her towel and shoes and went back to the changing-room for a shower before getting dressed. The effects of the dream were still on her, the feeling of helpless terror as Dora plunged along the path that ended in that awful drop . . . in the act of turning on the water, Melissa's hand froze.

"Oh no!" she exclaimed aloud. "Not that! Please, not that!"

She wanted time to think, and time was very short. In ten minutes classes would finish and Iris would be waiting to be driven back to the *auberge*. She had to make up her mind what she was going to do, whether to tell Hassan about the secret refuge, knowing that, if Dora's golf-club had been hidden there after being used to kill Alain Gebrec, it pointed to the guilt of only one person. He would, of course, have thrown it into that hideous black void at the edge of the cave, believing that it would remain concealed there forever, but an experienced climber with the right equipment would soon be able to recover it. If it was there. If it really had been stolen, as Dora claimed, if it had been used as the murder weapon, if . . . if . . . So far from clearing after her dip, Melissa's thoughts were like a tangled skein of thread with no end and no beginning, impossible to unravel.

Returning to put away her swimming things she noticed two gaps where cars had been parked. The first, she quickly realised, had been occupied by the police car in which Officer Hassan and his young winger had arrived. So they had gone; well, that solved, or at least shelved, her immediate problem. Mentally, she ticked off the remaining vehicles and came to the conclusion that the second absentee was Dieter Erdle.

The students began emerging from the house. First came Iris with her group clustered round her, apparently discussing an arrangement to meet. Then they separated amid a chorus of, "See you later," climbed into their respective cars and drove away. Only Jack remained to help Iris load her equipment into the back of the Golf. Watching their approach, Melissa thought how relaxed her friend appeared, compared with her earlier anxiety. Something must have happened.

"Heard the news? Dora Lavender's been arrested," said Jack.

"Good Lord!" exclaimed Melissa. "How do you know?"

"Philippe told us when he came to our classroom to say goodbye."

"Have they found the weapon?"

"No idea. Philippe didn't know any details."

"Poor Rose, she must be in a dreadful state."

"Here come the others now," said Iris. "We might learn a bit more."

It was a subdued and silent group that approached. Rose was being half led, half supported by Daphne, who had one sturdy arm round her shoulders while Eric walked on her other side. She appeared to be in deep shock, her face was ashen and her mouth twitched. Almost unnoticed, Sue and Janey murmured discreet goodbyes and left.

"I suppose you've heard?" said Eric.

"About Dora's arrest, yes, but nothing else," said Melissa.

"That's all we know. Hassan sent for us all again after tea, one by one, of course. He kept Philippe longer than the rest of us, but he came back eventually. Then it was Dora's turn, and we never saw her again. It was Juliette who brought Philippe the news that she had been taken away in the police car."

"Have they found her golf-club?"

"We don't know."

"Where's Erdle?" asked Jack, glancing round as if he had only just missed him.

"Gone." Daphne spat out the word in a mixture of fury and contempt. "The minute Hassan had finished with him he said goodbye to Philippe and shook his hand, gave us all a parting wave and left." Her disgust at this cavalier treatment of Rose was clear and she gave her an encouraging squeeze. "Forget about him, dear, you're well rid of him," she said and Melissa heard herself saying, "Daphne's right," thinking that she herself would have expressed the sentiment more strongly.

"What will happen to Dora?" asked Rose in a creaky whisper, looking straight at Melissa. "What will they do to her?"

"Ask her questions, that's all."

"What right has he got to arrest her?" demanded Eric. "Isn't there anything we can do?" He too looked to Melissa for an answer.

"Hassan must have got permission from the *proc* to detain her."

"Who?"

"The *Procureur de la République*—a sort of senior magistrate. Try not to worry too much, Rose. If they can't get Dora to change her story, or find some evidence to break it, they'll have to let her go in a few hours."

"What beats me is why they should suspect her in the first place," said Eric. "I mean, what possible motive could she have had for killing Alain? She hardly knew him."

"Mistaken identity," said Melissa, and briefly explained.

"Eric, let's not hang around here any longer," said Daphne impatiently. "Rose is exhausted, she must lie down."

"Of course dear." He turned to the others. "We're staying in a rented apartment and we're taking her back with us," he explained, and followed Daphne and Rose.

"I'll see you presently," said Jack as he got into his car.

"Right," said Iris. She climbed into the Golf and fastened her seat belt.

Melissa started the engine and followed the others out through the gate. She waited for an explanation of Jack's parting remark, but, as none came, she asked casually, "Do I take it you have plans for this evening?"

"Meeting the group for a farewell drink at the Lion d'Or. Thought of asking Jack to join us for dinner at the *auberge* later. Any objection?" A hoarse catch in the voice betrayed Iris's embarrassment.

"No objection at all," said Melissa heartily. "At least, not to Jack and dinner. I'm sorry you've arranged to go out beforehand though." She explained about Madame Gebrec's invitation.

"Pity," said Iris. "Can't be helped though. You can make the right noises."

"I'll do my best."

"What about Dora? How long can they hold her?"

"I'm not all that well clued up on French procedure, but my understanding is they'll have to let her go after six or seven hours unless they can break her story. It might be what they call '*liberté conditionelle*,' which means she couldn't leave the area until either they're satisfied she's in the clear or they've got enough evidence to bring a charge."

"Banana Split must be pretty sure she did it. Do you think so?"

The question revived all the doubts and unease that had been driven to the back of Melissa's mind by the news of Dora's arrest. Unless, under Hassan's "persuasion," Dora confessed to the killing and revealed the whereabouts of the missing golf-club, was she not bound to betray Fernand and suggest the secret refuge as its possible hiding place? She wished with all her heart that he had never taken her there.

"Well, do you?" Iris broke into her reverie.

"I think she's capable of it. And if she did, and she's managed to hide that golf-club where it won't be found, she could just get away with it. Because," Melissa swung the car into the car park at the Auberge de la Fontaine and switched off the engine, "if anyone can stand up to Hassan's 'interrogation,' it's Dora Lavender."

"Well, at least it means Philippe isn't a suspect any more," said Iris with evident satisfaction.

Melissa did not have the heart to point out that this was not necessarily the case, and changed the subject. "I suppose Madame Gebrec will want to know how the enquiry is going," she said as they made their way up to their room.

"You going to tell her about Dora's arrest?"

"Iris, I can't!"

"Why not?"

"Think about it. Would you like to tell a woman her son might have been murdered by mistake?"

Twenty

ANTOINETTE GEBREC HAD MADE A SU-
preme effort to put her grief to one side to receive her guest.
Her manner was composed, her grooming flawless, her blue
silk dress simple but elegant. Only the charcoal smudges
under her eyes told of the hours of sorrow and sleeplessness.

"It is good of you to come," she said, with a brave smile that
was far more moving than tears. "Your friend, she is not with
you?" Her tone implied relief rather than disappointment.

"I'm afraid she already had an engagement that I didn't
know about when you phoned," said Melissa. "She sends her
apologies."

"It is no matter."

The sun had gone round and the shutters outside the salon
windows stood open, but the daylight did nothing to dispel
the overfurnished appearance that Melissa remembered from
her earlier visits. A space had been cleared among the clutter
of ornaments and knick-knacks on the buffet for a silver tray
bearing crystal goblets and a pale green glass bottle of an unusual spiral shape.

"May I pour for you some wine?"

It was Melissa's habit, when driving, to drink only mineral
water or fruit juice, but there was something about the arrangement of the goblets and the bottle, its cool surface filmed with
dew, that struck her as almost symbolic. The cork had already
been drawn and she sensed that it was in some way important
to Madame Gebrec that they should drink together.

"A little wine would be lovely," she replied and saw at once that it had been the right thing to say.

Madame Gebrec took up the bottle as if it were a sacred relic. "This wine," she said softly, "was the favourite of my son." She poured some into two of the goblets and handed one to Melissa. "Your very good health, Madame!"

"And yours!" Melissa responded, wondering why Madame Gebrec had chosen to speak in English. Perhaps she felt that the effort of concentration might provide a distraction, a temporary relief from her burden of sorrow. In the face of such courage, Melissa felt a sense of humility. More to conceal her emotion than out of any claim to be an oenophile, she slowly rolled the wine over her tongue before swallowing and nodding approval. "Your son was a connoisseur," she said solemnly, and was rewarded by a smile of almost unearthly radiance.

"Come, let us sit on the terrace for a while. The paintings, they are upstairs—we will see them presently."

For a few minutes they sipped their wine in silence. There was still warmth in the sun, but the oppressive heat of the day had passed and a light breeze stirred the tangle of clematis on the pergola overhead.

After a while, Madame Gebrec said quietly, "I am so grateful, Madame, that you were able to persuade the police of the justice of my statement that Alain was murdered."

"It wasn't entirely my doing." Melissa had hoped to avoid the subject of the police enquiry, but plainly it was not to be. All she could hope for was to avoid any mention of the fact that Dora Lavender was in custody.

"Ah, you are too modest. Did you know that the investigating officer came to see me this morning?"

"No, I didn't." Melissa felt rather miffed at the realisation that Hassan had taken her only partly into his confidence. "What did he want?"

For a few moments Madame Gebrec sat motionless, her wine cupped in both hands, her coral fingertips resting like delicate flower petals on the glass.

"He asked me what I knew about Alain's . . . relationships," she said at length.

"Did he question you about anyone in particular? Monsieur Bonard, for example?"

"Yes." The contents of the goblet became the object of careful scrutiny and there was an uneasy silence before she spoke again. "I know that Monsieur Bonard loved Alain. Alain had an affection for him, but I always believed it was the sentiment of a son for his father. In fact, when speaking of him he used often to say, 'Papa Bonard.' "

"Your friend, Madame Delon, told me that your husband was killed during the war."

Madam Gebrec's eyebrows lifted in surprise, but her reply came quietly enough. "That is true."

"So, as Alain never knew his own father, it would be natural for him to become attached to an older man like Monsieur Bonard, wouldn't it?"

"Yes, of course."

"And Alain never said anything to suggest . . . a different kind of relationship between them?"

"No, and I assure you there was none." Abruptly, Madame Gebrec stood up and began pacing to and fro on the terrace. She swung round to face Melissa and it was clear from her expression that the subject was painful to her. "Alain had many younger . . . friends. I think you already know this."

"But perhaps Monsieur Bonard would have liked . . . has it occurred to you that he might have been jealous of these young men?"

"Madame Craig, Monsieur Bonard is a kind man who did much to help my son in his career. I cannot believe that Alain . . ." Her voice faltered; for the first time that evening, suppressed emotion bubbled to the surface. Melissa remembered some of the words Madame Delon had used to describe Alain, despite his mother's protests: hard, ruthless, ambitious. Such a man might not scruple to accept his employer's advances if he could thereby further his own career.

"Would it surprise you," she said quietly, "to learn that Bonard is a suspect?"

"No." The monosyllable was scarcely more than a sigh of resignation.

"It has been suggested that Alain might have been attacked

with some heavy metal object such as a golf-club," said Melissa. "The problem is that, although the police have carried out an intensive search, they haven't been able to find such a weapon."

"There is a cave under the cliff. Perhaps it is hidden there?"

Melissa stared in astonishment. "I have heard of the existence of this cave," she said cautiously, "but I thought its whereabouts were a secret."

"Bah, all the people in Roziac know, although they pretend they do not."

"How did you come to hear about it?"

"Alain told me. When he and Monsieur Bonard first visited Les Châtaigniers, the agent told them of it and showed them the way to the entrance."

"Did they actually go into the cave?"

"Indeed, no. Alain said it is too dangerous. Monsieur Bonard feared an accident if anyone should attempt to enter it and made it, as you say, out of the bounds. Alas, the poor young Wolfgang learned somehow of its existence . . ." Madame Gebrec broke off and a look of horror dawned in her eyes. "Madame Craig, you do not suppose that Monsieur Bonard . . ." As if the shock of the sudden suspicion was too much to cope with, she suddenly lapsed into French. "Is it possible that he deliberately lured that poor young man to his death because he was jealous of his affair with Alain?"

"It's hard to believe he'd do such a thing," said Melissa thoughtfully. "And in any case . . ." She was about to say, "Access to the cave is easy enough provided you aren't scared of heights," but remembered just in time that the comment would invite questions she would rather not answer and changed it to, "The police are satisfied that Klein's death was an accident—part of the cliff gave way under his weight."

"I am glad to hear you say it."

Melissa's head was buzzing, but it had nothing to do with the wine. For the second time within as many hours her thoughts had moved off in a new direction, conflicting messages flashed through her brain until it seemed the interior of her skull must become red-hot. She thought of Iris, happily

deluding herself that Philippe Bonard was in the clear, and
was thankful that she had been spared hearing of this latest
development from a stranger. She longed to be on her own so
that she might think logically and quietly, but there was still
one question she needed to ask.

"Did you tell Officer Hassan about the secret . . . the cave?"

"No, why should I? He did not tell me his men were looking for a weapon."

"Just what did he tell you?"

For a moment, Madame Gebrec looked almost amused.
"He told me nothing," she said. "He asked only questions.
But I talk too much about my own problem. You are here to
look at pictures. Come."

Melissa had totally forgotten the pictures. With an effort, she
dragged her mind back to the purpose of her visit and followed
Madame Gebrec upstairs to her study. In contrast to the downstairs rooms, this one was severely functional. On a plain black
wooden desk were a word processor, an adjustable metal lamp,
a telephone, and a container for pens and paper-clips in heavy
smoke-grey glass. Against the left-hand wall stood a filing cabinet and a bookcase, and there was a second bookcase on the
right. There was no other furniture, no flowers or ornaments,
the only seating a single typist's chair. Plainly, this was a sanc-
tum to which visitors were not normally invited.

The wide, uncurtained window gave a splendid view over
the Gardon, its waters shining in the early evening light as it
made its sinuous way southwards from the mountains. Three
of the walls were bare; on the one opposite the window hung
a series of paintings in simple modern frames, all apparently
by the same artist and arranged in careful symmetry.

Melissa turned to study them; as she did so, she saw Madame Gebrec's eyes on her. There was pride in them, but
there was something else as well—a pleading, almost a hun-
ger. They were saying more eloquently than speech that this
small collection represented to its possessor something far
greater than the sum of its parts. Perhaps it was the work of
a former lover, all that remained of a relationship still precious but long past. For some reason that she herself might
have been at a loss to explain, she had been willing, in the

midst of her grief, to share her treasure with someone she hardly knew. Now she waited, almost fearfully, for a verdict.

Melissa's initial feeling was disappointment. The paintings were executed with care and craftsmanship, but even her comparatively untutored eye could see that they lacked originality and did not fulfil the promise of the single canvas that hung in the salon.

Madame Gebrec neither moved nor spoke; almost, it seemed, she had ceased to breathe, but Melissa sensed that inwardly she was crying out, "Please admire them, say they are good, say they are beautiful!" as if more than anything in the world she needed the comfort of hearing praise for what she held most dear.

Recognition of that need injected an enthusiasm that was not entirely genuine into Melissa's voice as she exclaimed, "But these are lovely!"

"They please you?" The words gushed out on a wave of relief. "Truly?"

"They're quite charming . . . really delightful." It did not matter that to a detached observer the words would sound trite, possibly insincere; they were what Madame Gebrec needed to hear. Iris would have given her an honest opinion, pointing out, in her laconic but outspoken way, the weaknesses as well as the merits of the artist's work—one more reason, Melissa thought wryly, to be thankful she was not there. It was not a detached, professional assessment of the collection that was wanted.

So she made a show of scrutinising the canvases and of praising some feature of each—the execution of a patch of cloud, a contrasting pattern of light and shade or the grouping of figures round a market stall—while Madame Gebrec hung on every word, her face glowing with pleasure and gratitude.

"Thank you for letting me see them," said Melissa at length.

"I am so happy that you like them." Madame Gebrec opened the study door and indicated with a gesture that the viewing was at an end. "They are all I have left now." The final words were barely audible.

Back in the salon, Melissa went to look once more at the

picture of the Porte des Cévennes which had caught her eye on her first visit. "I suppose this one's your favourite?"

Madame Gebrec nodded. "It is, I think, the best. Do you agree?"

"Yes, I do, it is excellent." Melissa peered at the date, inscribed in the corner. "1944—later than the others."

"Yes. Those upstairs he painted for himself. This one he painted expressly for me."

"I wonder why he didn't sign any of them?"

There was a moment's hesitation before Madame Gebrec pointed to a corner of the canvas and said in a low voice, "That small emblem, beside the date—that was his 'signature.'"

"He signed all his pictures in that way?"

"Yes."

"It looks like a pull from a blind-cord," commented Melissa. In response to Madame Gebrec's blank stare she mimed the action of pulling down a roller blind, but there was no answering smile. Fearing that she had made a *faux pas*, she glanced at her watch. "Madame, it's time I was leaving. I've arranged to meet some friends for dinner."

"I am grateful to you for coming." Madame Gebrec hesitated, as if there was something more that she wanted to say, but was doubtful how to phrase it or how it would be received. In her uncertainty, she turned and fiddled with the switch controlling the light above the painting. "The artist . . . he was very dear to me," she said in a whisper.

"I guessed as much," murmured Melissa, ashamed now of her flippancy.

"He brought me . . . for a little while . . . great happiness."

Unable to think of a suitable reply, Melissa held out her hand. "Goodbye, Madame, and thank you once again," she said, her voice suddenly husky.

"It is I who thank you. Come, I will open the gate for you."

As she drove away, Melissa heard the clang of metal on metal—the sound of Madame Gebrec locking herself into her solitary world.

Twenty-one

IT WAS WITH CONSIDERABLE RELIEF that Melissa noticed Jack Hammond's car parked outside the *auberge* and her relief increased when she found him sitting alone on the terrace, a glass of Stella Artois in one hand and a book in the other. He was so absorbed that he did not notice her until she slid into the chair beside him.

He greeted her with a cheery smile. "Hi, Melissa, I've got your book." He held up her copy of *The Turbulent History of the Cévennes*. "Iris thought it'd keep me amused—she's got a great sense of humour! You don't mind, do you?"

"Of course not. I'm impressed that your French is up to it."

"It isn't really," he admitted. "I'm just looking at the pictures. Did anything strike you about this one by any chance?"

"To be honest, I've hardly glanced at any of them. I've been more interested in the text."

The book was open at a double-page spread of photographs; Jack pointed to one of a youngish man with a high forehead and thick wavy hair. "That one. Here, I'm forgetting my manners. Would you like a drink?"

"Thanks, I'd love one of those." Wearily, she gestured towards the empty bottle on the table. While Jack caught the eye of one of the Gauthier girls, who were bustling to and fro in the background, she searched the legend at the bottom of the page. It took her several seconds to link the picture with the name: Julius Eiche.

"Looks a bit like young Erdle, don't you think?" said Jack, peering over her shoulder.

Melissa was scanning the other photographs and linking them with the names. "I think they've got a couple of them mixed up," she said after a moment.

"What makes you say that?"

"Look at this one." She showed him a portrait of a heavy-featured man with deep-set eyes.

"Looks like Rudolf Hess," commented Jack. "What about him?"

"According to the book, that is Pastor Heinrich Erdle."

Jack's brow crumpled. "Some relation to Rose's toy-boy?"

"His uncle. I got it out of him this afternoon." Melissa repeated their conversation. "My guess is that that one," she tapped the photograph that had caught Jack's eye with her forefinger, "is Heinrich Erdle. I agree, there is a resemblance."

"You reckon this sinister-looking character is Julius Eiche?"

"Well, he looks more like a spy than a respectable reverend, doesn't he—and vice versa?"

"Mmm ... perhaps. You can't always go by appearances. You say Eiche betrayed Uncle Heinrich to the Gestapo?"

"I don't think anything was ever proved. Let's see what they say about him." She turned to the index at the back of the book, but it slipped from her grasp and fell to the floor.

"You okay?" asked Jack as he straightened up from retrieving it. "You look a bit washed out."

"I ... it's been quite a day," she said shakily. The problem that had been churning in her brain during the drive back from Alès, temporarily superseded by the photographs, had suddenly resurfaced. "By the way, where's Iris?"

"Standing on her head in a corner somewhere, I believe," said Jack with a chuckle. "She said she'd be half an hour, and that was," he glanced at his watch, "nearly fifteen minutes ago."

"That's good. I'd like to talk to you before she comes down."

"Something bothering you?" He gave her an anxious look. "Are you sure you're all right? Would you like something stronger than beer?"

"No, beer'll be fine." She reached for the glass that Brigitte had set in front of her and took several long swallows. Then she put it down, leaned her elbows on the table and covered her face with her hands. She was trembling; she had not realised until that moment how dog-tired she was.

"Are you ill? Shall I go and fetch Iris?" said Jack in alarm.

"No!" she said sharply, grabbing at his arm as he half rose. "I need your advice. I think I know who killed Alain Gebrec and it's going to be a blow for Iris. I don't know how to tell her."

"Philippe Bonard?" he asked in a low voice.

"Yes." She told him of her conversation with Madame Gebrec and the revelation that Bonard had known all along of the cave under the cliff. His face registered first puzzlement, then surprise, and finally consternation as she admitted having visited Fernand's "secret refuge."

"I'm not surprised that Iris worries about you if that's the sort of thing you get up to," he said grimly. "Why the hell didn't you tell your gendarme as soon as you knew he was hunting for a weapon?"

"It didn't enter my head at the time that it might be hidden in the cave. In any case, I thought the only person who knew where it was and how to reach it was Fernand, and he had an alibi."

"Which could be phoney," Jack pointed out.

"Fernand didn't kill Alain," said Melissa stubbornly.

"You reckon Philippe Bonard did?"

"It looks very much like it, don't you agree? Either through jealousy or some other motive that we don't know about. The indications are that under that rather willowy exterior, Alain Grebec was pretty hard nosed. Maybe he was blackmailing Bonard. Or maybe . . ."

"Maybe you should just call Officer Hassan, tell him what you've learned and let him do the investigating. It is his job, after all."

"Meaning I should keep my nose out of it? You sound like Ken Harris," said Melissa. "My policeman friend," she added in response to Jack's look of enquiry.

"Well, you did ask for my advice." He gave a disarming

grin and patted her hand. "I'm sure Hassan will be very ap-
préciative of your help," he said in the emollient tone he had
used to such good effect when dealing with a tearful Rose
and an aggressive Dora.

Melissa felt her taut nerves start to relax. She drained her
glass and put it down. Jack was right, of course, but . . . "It's
so hard to picture Philippe crawling along that awful ledge,"
she said. "It seems completely out of character . . . he's so so-
phisticated, always looks so immaculate . . ." Perhaps after all
they were barking up the wrong tree. If Madame Gebrec had
her facts right, any number of people could have . . . oh God!
she thought, I'm shilly-shallying again.

"On the contrary, it would have been a doddle for him,"
Jack was saying dryly. "Speleology was his hobby as a young
man."

"And he gave Juliette his clothes to sponge and press that
very morning." Melissa put a hand to her mouth as she recalled the scene in the kitchen, the hiss of the hot iron on
damp cloth, the spurt of steam.

"You'd better make that phone call before Iris turns up,"
said Jack. "She'll be here any minute."

"You'll break it to her gently?"

He made a gesture of impatience. "You leave Iris to me.
Just get on with that call." There was a note of authority in
his voice that brought Melissa unquestioningly to her feet.

A bored-sounding gendarme informed her that Officer
Hassan was not available and suggested that she call tomorrow. When he seemed reluctant to take a message, she used
to good effect some of the *argot* she had learned during her
student days, upon which he grudgingly demanded what he
was supposed to say.

"Just ask him to call me at the Auberge de la Fontaine as
soon as possible," she said crisply. "Tell him it's urgent, extremely urgent, do you understand?"

When she returned to the terrace, she found Iris and Jack
watching the light fade over the Porte des Cévennes. They
stood close together, their shoulders almost touching. Iris had
changed into a Laura Ashley print dress; under the soft overhead lights her hair shone from brushing. She's come to

terms with things, thought Melissa joyfully, she knows her yen for Philippe is a dead duck and she's responding to Jack's admiration like a plant responds to sunshine and rain. It was the first truly happy moment in a long and stressful day.

"Jack's told me the news," said Iris. "Banana Split's got a job on his hands."

"You mean, organising the search? It shouldn't be too difficult, given the right equipment."

"Not that. Checking the prints if the golf-club's found. Thought you said half of Roziac knows about the cave."

"Oh, er, yes, I see what you mean." Melissa caught Jack's eye and when Iris turned back to admire the view she returned his wink. Full marks for diplomacy, she thought. It wouldn't lessen the eventual hurt if Bonard did turn out to be the murderer, but for this evening at least Iris could relax and be happy—and Jack would be there to give comfort when it was needed.

"I haven't actually spoken to Hassan yet," she told them. "He was questioning a suspect and couldn't be interrupted. He'll call back when he's free."

"I wonder if the suspect's Dora?" said Jack. The three of them exchanged guilty glances. The latest developments had pushed poor Dora's predicament to the back of everyone's mind.

"Perhaps we should have contacted the British Consul," said Jack, looking worried.

Iris cackled. "On a Friday afternoon? Got to be joking."

"We ought to do something to help. What do you think, Melissa?"

"If she's charged, she'll need a lawyer, of course, but my guess is that once Hassan hears what I've got to say, he'll realise he's made a mistake and let her go."

"Let's hope so."

"I'm starving," said Iris. "Let's have dinner."

They were sitting on the terrace with coffee and liqueurs when, without warning, Dora appeared. Her face was drawn, but she stood as erect as a guardsman with her chin tilted proudly upwards. For a moment they sat gaping in astonishment; then Jack leapt to his feet and offered his chair.

"No, thank you," she said stiffly. "The restaurant is about to close, but Monsieur Gauthier is getting me something to eat." She cut across the barrage of questions by saying curtly to Melissa, "Officer Hassan wishes to see you. He's in reception," before swinging round and striding back indoors without another word.

Madame Gauthier was on her usual perch behind the desk. She peered over her glasses at Melissa and made a stabbing movement with her pen towards the corner where Hassan was waiting, her scowl indicating that she held *"les Anglais"* entirely responsible for the upheaval in her well-ordered establishment.

The big gendarme looked tired and dispirited. It cost him an effort to get to his feet and the minute Melissa was seated he slumped back on his chair, his arms resting on his knees and his head bent. Everything about him drooped, including his moustache.

"I see you've released Mrs. Lavender," Melissa remarked.

He spread his hands and his shoulders climbed round his ears.

"What could I do? She refuses to change her story. My commandant is not pleased, but without evidence I am helpless."

"You received my message?"

"Yes. Have you something important to tell me?"

"Very important. I told your man it was urgent."

"Indeed?" It was clear from his air of surprise that her outburst on the telephone had not been entirely effective. "What have you learned, Madame?"

"You have no doubt heard of a secret cave which the Maquis used as a refuge during the Occupation?"

"I heard rumours when I was enquiring into the accident to Wolfgang Klein," said Hassan guardedly, "but I have spoken to no one who will confirm its existence." He shook his head dejectedly. "The people here, they do not like to talk to the police."

"According to Madame Gebrec, it lies under the belvedere at Les Châtaigniers."

"Indeed?" Interest flickered briefly in the mournful brown eyes, then died. "Excuse me, Madame, but I do not see how this helps my enquiries. It is surely not possible that Madame Lavender knows of this cave?"

"No, but many people in Roziac do . . . including Monsieur Bonard."

The change in Hassan's demeanour was instantaneous. He sat upright, gazing at Melissa like a dog with its eyes on a biscuit. "You are certain of this, Madame?"

"Quite certain." She repeated what she had learned from Madame Gebrec.

Hassan snatched his notebook from his pocket and scribbled furiously. "The weapon, it must be concealed in this cave! I shall take action immediately!" he declared, then slapped his forehead in exasperation. "Bah, I was forgetting, Bonard is away from home. I gave him permission to travel to Avignon on business."

"No doubt you know where to find him?"

"Naturally, but it will take time to arrange for his return to Roziac . . ." He glanced at his watch. "The search will have to wait until tomorrow morning."

It was on the tip of Melissa's tongue to inform him that an attempt to reach the cave in darkness would in any case be extremely hazardous, but she checked herself in time. He might insist on being shown the entrance and perhaps station an overnight guard. She hated the fact that it had become necessary, in the cause of justice, for the police to invade Fernand's beloved secret refuge and shrank from being openly associated with the operation. As it was, she felt like a traitor.

Hassan was on his feet. His depression had evaporated; he had the air of a prizefighter entering the ring and his smile outshone the dingy light bulb over their heads. "Once more, I thank you for your invaluable help, Madame."

At the door he almost collided with the Lovells, returning with Rose. He gave them a courteous salute and was rewarded with hostile glares.

"How much longer are you going to detain Mrs. Lavender?" demanded Eric with a trace of belligerence.

Hassan assumed the benign expression of a schoolmaster announcing an extra half-holiday. "Madame Lavender is already at liberty," he said, and hurried away before anyone could question him further.

Rose turned to Melissa. "Is it really true?"

"Quite true. You'll find her in the restaurant."

"Oh, thank God!" Rose hugged them in turn, her eyes brimming. "I must go and find her. It's all been so dreadful—I do so hope we can be friends again."

"I'm sure you can."

"And thank you all for being so kind." She was smiling through her tears, like a lost child whose mother has been found.

"So, what now?" asked Eric, as Rose darted off.

"I suppose the search for Alain's murderer goes on," said Melissa.

Passing through the restaurant on her way back to the terrace, Melissa saw Rose and Dora sitting at a table in the corner. They were sharing a bottle of wine but saying little, exchanging wary glances like two creatures of the same species meeting in the wild, each uncertain whether the other was friend or foe. She would have slipped past without interrupting, but Dora put out a hand.

"Could I ask a favour, please?" she said.

"Of course." Melissa noted with relief that colour was returning to her face and the stress lines had begun to smooth out.

"Would you be kind enough to drive me to Les Châtaigniers in the morning to pick up our car?"

Melissa's heart sank. The last thing she wanted was to be at Les Châtaigniers during the police search and possibly have to witness Fernand's distress, but she could hardly refuse such a reasonable request. "By all means," she heard herself saying. "What time?"

"The earlier the better. I . . . that is, we . . . want to set out for Antibes in good time." Dora flicked a glance at Rose as she made the hasty correction, as if acknowledging that from now on, more decisions would be made jointly.

"That suits me fine. Shall we say about eight-thirty, immediately after breakfast?" With any luck, they could be there and away before the police arrived. At least, it was going to be a pleasure to pass on to Iris and Jack the news that Dora and Rose had begun to mend their fences.

Twenty-two

LONG AFTER SHE AND IRIS HAD SAID goodnight, Melissa lay awake, too keyed up to sleep. On the face of it, the case was all but complete. Philippe Bonard had killed Alaine Gebrec with Dora's number nine iron, pushed the body over the cliff and concealed the murder weapon in the secret refuge. Tomorrow the police would recover it and Bonard would be detained while it was examined for finger-prints; later, he would be charged with murder. The sequence repeated itself in her mind in an endless loop.

In an effort to escape, she switched her thoughts towards her new novel and began composing the first chapter in her head—a habit of hers before she began the actual writing. It was not a happy decision.

The opening scene was a secret grotto where a group of hunted Camisards had taken shelter. There would be a graphic word picture of hollow-eyed, desperate men clad in the loose white shirts or *camises* from which their name de-rived, huddled in the light of a smoking lantern that cast weird shadows on the wall.

At some point in her uneasy imaginings she must have drifted into a fitful sleep. She was still in the grotto, but the men began melting away like ghosts. The flickering flame steadied and then burned more brightly; it seemed to escape from the lantern like a genie, moving with a power of its own as if searching for something or someone, coming to rest at last on the figure of a man who stood in a corner with his back towards her. As she watched, his *camise* became an artist's smock; slowly, he turned to face her, revealing the shattered features of Alain Gebrec. His eyes stared lifelessly through her, his mouth was twisted in a ghastly rictus. He raised a hand; instead of a paintbrush, the acorn-pull of a blind dangled from broken, bloodstained fingers.

Melissa's limbs had turned to stone and her throat was paralysed. Something gripped her by the shoulders and she had no power to struggle free. A familiar voice penetrated her brain, calling from a great distance. The voice grew louder; with a mighty effort she threw off the shackles of the dream and sat up in bed, gasping and trembling.

"That sounded nasty," remarked Iris, switching on her lamp. "Are you too hot?"

"No, it's not the heat." Melissa combed her hair from her face with a hand that shook. "It's this awful business of Alain's murder—I can't get it out of my mind."

There was a long silence before Iris said, "Philippe knows about that cave, doesn't he?"

"Who told you?"

"No one. Guessed. Why didn't you say?"

"Jack and I both thought it would upset you . . . and until it was known for sure . . ."

In the dim yellow light, Iris's eyes glittered more brightly than usual. "If Dora didn't do it, and Fernand and Erdle have alibis, it must have been Philippe, mustn't it?"

"It looks like it." Melissa clasped her knees and stared at the wall. "I never believed it was Fernand, but for a while I really thought it was either Dora or Dieter—only neither of them could have known about the cave. Of course, we shan't be certain until they find that golf-club and check it for finger-prints." She heaved a sigh. "Poor Fernand, it'll break his heart to have the fuzz in his beloved 'secret refuge.' He'll feel violated."

"He'll get over it."

"And you?" Melissa gave her friend an anxious glance. "I know you had a thing about Philippe."

"Don't worry about me. Been a nasty knock, but I'm all right. How about some herb tea?"

"Good idea. It'll help us both to sleep."

Iris boiled water in her portable heater and poured it over camomile tea-bags. Presently, just as Melissa felt herself drifting away, a small voice called her back. "What d'you think of Jack?"

"I think he's pretty good value," she replied drowsily.

"Me too."

Melissa smiled into the darkness. It wasn't all bad news.

Saturday morning saw the first signs of a change in the weather, with a sharp drop in temperature and a cool breeze chasing frayed patches of grey cloud across the mountains.

"I hope it's better than this in Antibes," remarked Dora, as she and Melissa set off for Les Châtaigniers. "Wind is such a nuisance when you're playing golf."

"I'm sure it must be," murmured Melissa, choking back an urge to giggle at the unintentional double entendre. "You didn't have any problems about getting away?"

"What kind of problems?" asked Dora sharply.

"Oh, er, I just wondered." It had not perhaps been the most tactful of remarks.

"If you mean, are my movements restricted, I had to give that overbearing gendarme our address in Antibes. I also let him know that our friend there is a lawyer and that I would be taking his advice on bringing a complaint for wrongful arrest."

There was a steely glint in Dora's eye that spelled possible trouble for the overenthusiastic Officer Hassan. It was quite clear that detention and interrogation had done nothing to blunt her cutting edge.

"Best of luck!" murmured Melissa.

When they reached Les Châtaigniers, the gates were open and a police van stood in the courtyard. Several young men were lolling against it, chatting and smoking. One, presumably the driver, was in uniform; the remainder wore jeans, sweat-shirts and stout boots. The side door of the van was open, revealing an array of ropes and climbing tackle.

"Whatever's going on?" asked Dora.

"Looks as if they're going to search the cliffs," said Melissa cautiously. She had no intention of telling Dora of the latest developments.

"If they find my missing iron, I shall demand that it be returned to me as soon as possible." Dora got out of the car and fished the keys of the Sierra from her handbag. "Thank you for the lift, Melissa."

"Don't mention it."

"I'll see you back at the *auberge* then."

"Yes, of course. Tell Iris I shan't be long, will you?"

Dora looked as if she was about to ask a question, but decided against it, got into her own car and drove off.

Melissa sat for several minutes resting her arms on her steering wheel, trying to decide what to do. It would be so simple just to drive away and put the whole wretched business behind her. If she stayed, there was little she could do to alter the course of events. Any minute now, Officer Hassan would arrive with Philippe Bonard under escort and the search would begin.

She could imagine all too clearly Fernand's agitation when he realised what was happening. He might do something desperate in a futile attempt to prevent the operation taking place. Perhaps, seeing the arrival of the team in the police van and guessing what it signified, he had already gone to the secret refuge with some wild notion of defending it. Hopelessly outnumbered, he would soon see that the cause was lost . . . and then what? The chilling memory of that dark line where the floor of the cave stopped short of the wall came rushing back; once again she heard the echo of his warning: "That way, it is death!"

With a groan, Melissa pressed her face against the wheel in an effort to obliterate the picture from her head. There was a tap on the windscreen and she looked up to see the young gendarme peering in at her. Hastily, she wound down the window.

"Are you all right, Madame?" he asked.

"Yes, thank you . . . I was thinking," she said in some confusion. "Are you waiting for Officer Hassan?"

"Yes, Madame. Do you wish to speak to him?"

"No . . . that is, what time will he be here?"

"I expect him at any minute."

"Thank you."

He saluted and moved away. Melissa made up her mind. If she had a word with Juliette, perhaps together they could think of a way to divert her brother's attention, possibly send him away on an errand that would prevent him from realising what was going on. It might avert another tragedy; it was worth a try. She got out of the car and hurried into the house.

Juliette was in the kitchen, standing at the sink with her back to the door. When Melissa entered she swung round, her look of alarm changing swiftly first to relief and then to anger.

"Ah, it is you, Madame! You see what we have to endure?" She flung her hands in the air. "Are we never to have peace in this house?"

"Juliette, where is Fernand?"

"In the orchard, gathering fruit. Why do you ask?"

"Oh, Juliette, the police are going to search his secret refuge!"

Juliette stiffened and her eyes seemed to glaze over; then she relaxed and gave a curious half-smile. "They cannot do that, Madame. They do not know where to find it."

"They soon will. Can you think of something we can do to keep it from Fernand? You know how it will upset him!"

Juliette did not appear to have heard the question. "Who will tell them?" she demanded.

"Monsieur Bonard. It's true!" Melissa insisted as Juliette dumbly shook her head. "The police believe that he killed Monsieur Gebrec and concealed the murder weapon in the secret refuge. He knows where it is . . . they will make him lead them there."

Juliette put a hand to her mouth. "Ah, no!" she whispered.

"Go up to the orchard! Keep Fernand there . . . make any excuse . . ." She broke off at the sound of another vehicle entering the courtyard. "That must be Officer Hassan. Hurry!"

Juliette did not appear to have heard. Her eyes were wild and she turned her head from side to side like a cornered animal.

"Hurry!" shouted Melissa. She tugged at Juliette's arm, but

with a convulsive movement the woman shook her off, whirled round and darted through the open door at the back of the kitchen. She ran along the gravel path behind the house to the gate leading into the forest, flung it open and headed for the belvedere.

"For God's sake, what does she think she's doing?" muttered Melissa through clenched jaws. Without hesitation she set off in pursuit, although she knew now that she was wasting her time. At any minute Hassan would follow with his prisoner and the team of climbers; probably Fernand had already spotted the police van and guessed what was going on. If she had any sense, she'd lie low in the kitchen until the coast was clear and then get the hell out of it. Yet she kept on running as if her body was moving of its own volition.

Juliette had an astonishing turn of speed. Now and again she stumbled on the rough ground, but nothing slowed her down. Her long skirt flapped round her legs; her hair escaped from the old-fashioned bun and straggled round her shoulders like a hank of grey wool. At the point where the path to the cave entrance branched off, she was almost out of sight.

Only then did it dawn on Melissa that she knew how to reach the cave. It was clear now what she must be planning to do: with her ingrained sense of loyalty to her master, she would try to find the weapon that he had used to strike down Gebrec before the police got there. If she succeeded, she would probably fling it over the edge of the chasm in the belief that it could not be recovered.

"And I told her where to look for it!" Melissa groaned. Now she was in all sorts of trouble; even Hassan's admiration and goodwill would be of scant use when he found out that she had interfered with the course of justice.

She glanced back down the path. There was no one in sight, but the chug of a diesel engine told her that the police van was approaching by the main track from the road, doubtless guided by Bonard. They would park in the clearing where she had first seen Fernand and walk the rest of the way. Perhaps there was still time to persuade Juliette to abandon her reckless plan.

By now the adrenaline was flowing so strongly that Melissa reached the edge of the cliff without experiencing a trace of the vertigo that had made her visit to the secret refuge such a terrifying experience. She dropped to her hands and knees and peered below the overhanging rock, but there was no sign of Juliette. She must already be in the cave.

"Juliette!" she shouted above the roar of the water that seethed and tumbled below. "Juliette, come back!"

There was no response. Melissa cupped her hands and called again, but her voice was tossed back by the blustery breeze. In desperation, barely giving a thought to what she was doing, she began to crawl forward. A hand gripped her ankle; feeling as foolish as a schoolgirl caught smoking behind the bike shed, she shuffled back, sat on her haunches and looked up at the furious countenance of Officer Hassan.

"Are you out of your mind, Madame?" he demanded. "How dare you interfere with a police operation?"

"That wasn't my intention," faltered Melissa. She was still panting from her run up the steep path and her throat felt as dry as dust. She pointed along the ledge. "Juliette Morlay has gone into the cave ... I was trying ..."

"Have the goodness to stand up and move aside!" he barked.

In the act of obeying, Melissa gave an involuntary glance along the ledge. "Look!" she croaked.

Hassan crouched, looked, and muttered an oath. Juliette had emerged from the cave and was standing on the flat stone slab by the entrance. She was gazing out across the river, her head flung back, her hair streaming in the breeze. Like some pagan goddess guarding her shrine with a sacred flame, she held Dora's golf-club aloft. The effect was both ludicrous and horrible.

Instinctively, Melissa froze, for fear of startling her into a fatal movement. No such possibility had occurred to Hassan.

"This is the police," he shouted. "You are handling vital evidence. Put that down at once and come here!"

Juliette turned towards the sound and Melissa shuddered at the expression of unholy triumph on her face. "It was I who struck him down!" she shouted exultantly. "I cut the rotting branch from the poisoned oak tree!" As if to demonstrate how she had delivered the fatal blow, she swung the club in a vicious arc. The momentum sent her lurching towards the edge of the cliff and she all but fell.

"Oh, my God, she'll go over!" muttered Hassan. He snatched out a handkerchief and put it to his mouth. His face had a greenish tinge and he seemed to be struggling not to throw up.

"May I try?" said Melissa. He nodded dumbly and moved aside. She edged forward a fraction. "Juliette!" she called. "Do you hear me?"

Juliette took no notice. There were sounds of a commotion; Fernand was shoving and elbowing his way through the waiting group, throwing off the hands that tried to hold him back. He rushed over to Melissa, his eyes full of fear and reproach.

"Madame! You were followed—we are betrayed!"

Hassan appeared about to explode. His eyes blazed, his cheeks blew out and his moustache quivered, but no sound came from his pursed lips. Melissa seized her chance.

"Fernand, these men mean us no harm," she said urgently. He looked puzzled. "Are they not the King's men?"

She grabbed his hand. "Listen to me. The wars have ended, the Camisards have won the battle for their freedom, but your sister is in danger. You must help her. See!" She pointed along the ledge and he dropped on all fours beside her.

"Juliette!" he murmured.

"She will not answer me. Can you persuade her to come back?"

Oblivious now to the presence of his supposed enemies, Fernand crawled forward under the great overhang of rock. "Pascale!" he called.

Peering past him, Melissa saw Juliette's expression change; for a moment she appeared puzzled and then a smile of delight spread over her face.

"Pascale, do you hear me?" repeated Fernand with an unfamiliar note of authority in his voice.

"Who calls?" Juliette's voice had become reedy and childlike, barely audible above the sound of the waters.

"This is your master, the Lord Villars."

"What is my lord's command?"

"His Majesty requires our presence at court. We must return to Paris at once. Come."

"Is there peace once more in the land?"

"There is peace. Lay down your weapon and come with me."

Obediently, Juliette placed the golf-club carefully on the ground, fell on all fours and began inching along the ledge towards her brother. She seemed half dazed, her movements uncertain. Seeing her erratic progress, Melissa closed her eyes and retreated, swallowing hard.

A short distance away stood Hassan, his officers, the group of climbers with their equipment and finally Philippe Bonard, erect and dignified between his guards. They were as still as statues; hardly a muscle moved, hardly a breath was drawn until at last Fernand brought Juliette to safety.

Hassan barked an order for the golf-club to be retrieved; the two guards released Bonard and moved forward to take charge of the new prisoner. They wavered when they saw the look on Fernand's face.

"Do not touch her!" he said fiercely. "I will take care of her."

The young officers glanced at Hassan for instructions. After a moment's hesitation he gave a brief nod and the little party, with brother and sister walking hand in hand in their midst, slowly descended the path back to the house.

Twenty-three

"WHAT KEPT YOU?" GRUMBLED IRIS. "Jack and I are starving. Wouldn't order till you turned up."

"That's nice of you both—sorry to be so long." Melissa scanned the menu. "I'll have melon and a steak *au poivre.*"

Jack poured out the wine. "The whole place is buzzing with rumours," he said. "Dora and Rose went off quite put out at missing all the gory details."

"And the Lovells," Iris reminded him.

"Ah yes," chuckled Jack. "All of them at pains to explain they didn't want to leave without saying goodbye to you."

Melissa frowned. "Anyone would think it was some sort of public entertainment."

"Only natural curiosity," said Iris. "Come on, Mel. Spill it."

Melissa contemplated her glass in silence, seeking the right words. Fresh in her mind was the anguish of Antoinette Gebrec as the reason for her son's murder sank in. Perhaps it would have been kinder for her not to know, to try instead to come to terms with the suicide theory and all its implications—although the real story would probably have come out sooner or later. How did the old French proverb express it? Truth, like oil, always comes to the surface. So be it.

"What it boils down to," she began after a long pause, "is that Juliette killed Alain in revenge for what her family had suffered under the Occupation."

Iris frowned. "Don't understand. What could Alain have had to do with that?"

"Juliette holds his father responsible for her brother being taken and tortured by the Gestapo."

"But you said his father was killed serving with the army."

"Madame Gebrec's husband was killed while fighting with the Free French forces," corrected Melissa. "Alain's father was Julius Eiche, who many people—including Juliette—believed to have been spying for the Gestapo." She turned to Jack. "The photos in the book are correctly labelled. I was so taken up with my theory that Erdle had something to do with Alain's death that I missed the obvious. The likeness wasn't to Erdle but to Gebrec."

"Of course . . . why didn't we spot that?" said Jack. "It wasn't a very good picture, of course."

"No, but Madame Gebrec showed me another. The resemblance was unmistakable. Erdle made the right connection immediately. That was what was behind all the aggro he was giving Alain. After the murder, he was naturally anxious to keep it all quiet in case his relationship to Pastor Erdle came out."

"Then *he* might have been suspected of a revenge killing?"

"Exactly."

"So Madame G confirmed that Eiche was Alain's father?" said Iris.

"Yes, but she hotly denies the accusations against him."

"What accusations?"

"Julius Eiche was a young doctor from Vienna who fled to France after the Anschluss—at least, that was his story, but later on it was suspected that he'd been planted by the Nazis as a spy. When the war broke out, he was working at a hospital in Nîmes; in 1943 Madame Gebrec went to work there as a nurse and they became lovers. The following year she had his child."

"How did he get mixed up with the Morlay family?"

"He'd become associated with a group of Protestant pastors who were helping refugees to hide from the Nazis. Often they arranged for them to be sheltered in remote mountain villages."

"Pretty risky for the locals," commented Iris.

"It was, but the people of the Cévennes had a lot of sympathy for them because of their own history of oppression and persecution."

"So what was Eiche's role in all this?" asked Jack.

"If any refugee needed medical help, they called on him. The story is that he took the opportunity of doing some intelligence-gathering for the Gestapo."

"Not like a doctor to go ratting on his patients," commented Iris.

"That's what Madame Gebrec maintains—she swears he never betrayed anyone—but local legend links him with a big operation by the Gestapo, during which hundreds of people were rounded up and shot. One of them was the Morlays' elder brother, Roland."

"That must have had a traumatic effect on Fernand," said Jack.

"It did." Melissa repeated the story that Juliette had so movingly told her.

Iris shook her head in mingled pity and disbelief. "Poor devil," she sighed. "Feel rotten now about calling him a nutter."

"There's no doubt that he's deeply disturbed, but his way of coping with the trauma is a return to childhood and the games about the Camisards," said Melissa. "Evidently it affected Juliette quite differently. She must have been nursing a corrosive hatred against Eiche ever since for the suffering he had caused both her brothers. I've noticed how protective she is towards Fernand—like a mother pelican with a chick."

"So, when Gebrec arrived at Les Châtaigniers, she transferred her hatred to him," said Jack thoughtfully. "How did she know who he was?"

"I imagine that at some time or other Eiche came to Roziac to attend a patient. She might even have met him."

"And identified Alain as his son all those years later?" Iris looked dubious. "Can't believe that."

"No, but once the war was over there would have been all sorts of stories in the press about people suspected of being war criminals. It wouldn't surprise me if Juliette has a collection of cuttings with pictures of Eiche that she's brooded over ever since, dreaming of revenge. And then, once she'd spotted the resemblance between him and Alain, she could easily have done a bit of detective work of her own. She and Madame Gebrec's friend belong to the same church and it wouldn't have been too difficult to find out something of her history. I'm pretty sure Juliette read that book as well—she saw me with it and recognised it straight away."

"So you think Alain's murder was premeditated?" said Jack.

"No, I think the actual killing was opportunist, although the old hatred must have been steadily coming to the boil as she saw the way he was bossing her brother around. Then there was that scene with the crowbar when Fernand appeared to be threatening Gebrec. He wasn't a violent man by nature, but he was obviously capable of anger—she might have been afraid that constantly being told how to do his job might one day send him over the edge."

"So when she spotted Gebrec heading for the belvedere, she grabbed one of Dora's golf-clubs from the open boot of the Sierra and went after him." Jack shook his head as if he still found it difficult to believe. "It's amazing no one saw her."

"I think that Dora very nearly did. Do you remember her saying that a little while after seeing Gebrec go through the gate into the forest, she went after him in the hope of intercepting him?"

"Thinking he was Erdle?"

"Right. My guess is that Juliette spotted her as she was returning from killing Gebrec, took fright and hid the golf-club in the cave, probably hoping to put it back in the car later on. The opportunity never arose but if it had, the verdict on Alain would almost certainly have been suicide."

"What happened to Eiche after the Gestapo raids?" asked Iris.

"That's a mystery. He disappeared a week or so beforehand, no one has ever found out how or why. That's how the stories about his being a spy started—everyone jumped to the conclusion that he'd done his dirty work and scarpered before he was rumbled."

"And he's never been heard of since?"

"Apparently not. Madame Gebrec insists he must have been either arrested and shot, or sent to a concentration camp and died there, but there's never been any confirmation."

For a while, they went on with their meal in silence. Melissa ate slowly, barely tasting the food, haunted by the memory of Antoinette Gebrec's impassioned cry, "It is not true, my Julius was a good man, not a traitor!" It would be a long time, too, before she would be able to forget Fernand's face as he watched the gendarmes taking his sister away.

"I wonder what was really on Alain's mind when he went storming off up to the belvedere?" mused Jack. He turned to Iris. "You've talked to Philippe since Juliette's arrest—hasn't he any idea at all?"

It was a question that Melissa herself had been longing to ask, but was reluctant to do so for fear of treading on delicate ground.

She need not have worried. Iris's voice was level and matter-of-fact as she replied, "Been thinking of that. There'd been a bit of a tiff, but that was nothing new."

"What about?" asked Jack.

"Philippe told him off for rowing with Fernand in front of the students and being rude to Mel over the book. Alain pleaded shock over Klein's death. Philippe said, no excuse for unprofessional behaviour. Things got heated and Alain went rushing out." Iris began fiddling with the cruet, her forehead puckered in a frown. "Philippe feels badly about it," she added sadly. "Thinks he's partly responsible for what happened."

"Oh no, there must have been more to it than that," insisted Jack. "He said something like, 'No one can help me.' Surely, if it had just been Klein's death, he'd have turned to Philippe for comfort . . . or to his mother, perhaps. By all accounts they had a good relationship . . . she accepted the fact that he was gay . . ."

After a further interval in the conversation, an idea came to

Melissa. She finished her steak and put down her knife and fork.

"I wonder if Erdle had anything to do with it?" she said.

The others looked at her in surprise. "How?" demanded Iris.

"Giving Alain such a hard time in front of us, about looking like a German and so on—that could have been the tip of the iceberg. Maybe he was being a lot more specific when there was no one else around—making cracks about his paternity, threatening to link him publicly with Julius Eiche."

"It could account for a lot," agreed Jack. "He must have been haunted by doubts about his father's past . . . and terrified of the effect on him and his mother if it all came out. On top of that, the man he loves gets killed . . . and then he finds Mel with the book that started all the trouble . . . it's no wonder he got so emotional and went charging off on his own."

"To the spot where Klein died. And Juliette followed him." Iris looked thoughtful. "Perhaps you were right in a way, Mel—maybe Erdle did contribute to Alain's death."

"Maybe," agreed Melissa. The thought gave her no comfort.

"What will happen to Juliette?" asked Jack as Brigitte removed their plates and went off to fetch the cheese.

"I don't know, but I hope she'll be treated with compassion once the court hears the full story. Maybe there'll be a plea of 'diminished responsibility' or whatever the French equivalent is."

"Didn't you ask Banana Split?" asked Iris.

"I'm not in very good odour with him at the moment." Melissa smiled for the first time that day. "His admiration for my books didn't prevent him giving me a bit of a roasting. Apart from muscling in on his act, I don't think he's forgiven me for being right about the motive for Alain's murder. Once he knew about the cave, he was convinced he was going to pin it on Philippe, but I felt all along it had something to do with the past."

"Philippe's going to pay for Juliette's defence," said Iris with a hint of pride.

"Really?" Melissa felt as if the skies had started to clear after a storm. "That's very generous of him."

"And he's going to make Fernand his estate manager."

"Better and better."

"There's one other thing that puzzles me," said Jack, helping himself to cheese. "Philippe told us that he heard Juliette shouting something about a poisoned oak tree. Any idea what she was on about?"

"I think so," said Melissa, remembering the tiny acorn with which Julius Eiche had signed his paintings. "Eiche's nickname among his friends and colleagues in France was *Le Chêne*."

"The oak? Was that because they thought he was strong and steadfast and all that?"

"No. That's what his name means in German."

"Why is it," said Melissa as she struggled to close a bulging suitcase, "that things always take up more space when you're packing to go home?"

"More things," grinned Iris, eyeing the books that Melissa had acquired during the week.

"I haven't bought as many as usual."

They finished their packing and went onto the balcony for a last look at the mountains by night. The rain that had fallen during the afternoon and evening had died out, leaving the moist air sweet with the scents of the forest. The peaks of the Porte des Cévennes stood like twin citadels in the moonlight.

"Lovely spot, but it can't beat the Cotswolds," said Iris.

"Glad to be going back?" Iris nodded. "Me too. I suppose," Melissa added carelessly, "you'll be seeing Jack after we get home?"

Iris smiled up at the sky. "Expect so."